Stan Barstow has published eight novels and three volumes of short stories. His dramatisation of his Vic Brown trilogy (*A Kind of Loving*, *The Watchers on the Shore* and *The Right True End*) was seen on the ITV Network in 1982. The Royal Television Society gave him its Writer's Award in 1975 for his dramatisations of his own *A Raging Calm*, *Joby* and Winifred Holtby's *South Riding*. Stan Barstow is an Honorary Master of Arts of The Open University. His books have been translated into ten languages. He is married, has two grown children, and lives in his native Yorkshire.

Also by Stan Barstow

JOBY
THE GLAD EYE and other stories
A KIND OF LOVING
THE WATCHERS ON THE SHORE
B-MOVIE
THE DESPERADOES
A RAGING CALM

and published by Black Swan

The Right True End

Stan Barstow

BLACK SWAN

THE RIGHT TRUE END
A BLACK SWAN BOOK 0 552 99187 2

Originally published in Great Britain by
Michael Joseph Ltd.

PRINTING HISTORY
Michael Joseph edition published 1976
Corgi edition published 1978
Corgi edition reissued 1982
Corgi edition reprinted 1982
Black Swan edition published 1986
Black Swan edition reprinted 1988

This book is set in 11/12 pt Mallard

Black Swan Books are published by
Transworld Publishers Ltd., 61-63 Uxbridge
Road, Ealing, London W5 5SA, in Australia
by Transworld Publishers (Aust.) Pty. Ltd.,
15-23 Helles Avenue, Moorebank, NSW 2170,
and in New Zealand by Transworld Publishers
(N.Z.) Ltd., Cnr. Moselle and Waipareira
Avenues, Henderson, Auckland.

Made and printed in Great Britain by the
Guernsey Press Co. Ltd., Guernsey, Channel Islands.

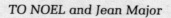

TO NOEL and Jean Major

'Whoever loves, if he do not propose
The right true end of love, he's the one that goes
To sea for nothing but to make him sick.'
                    John Donne:
                    Elegy 18 Love's Progress

Part One

1

'So what are you going to do?' Conroy asks me. Conroy, with his big head down in his shoulders, his square hand clamped round his pint pot, looks as though what he'd do is smash somebody. But he's not the tough, hot-tempered *hombre* I used to know when I first worked with him five, six years ago, up North. He's slower these days, quieter, and watchful; given to working things out instead of flying off the handle. Still capable, I reckon, of telling a boss to get stuffed, but less likely to get himself into a situation where he has to.

Anyway, it's a good question and it sends me quiet for a minute or two while I try to think of an answer.

It makes my flesh crawl when Conroy tells me he's sure he's rumbled this bloke who's been in the town collecting information about me and what I'm up to; the same creepy feeling I had behind the anger when Ingrid got those anonymous letters about Donna and me. Somebody poking his nose into my business and not for my benefit. Though the letters were pure malice and it's likely that there's nothing personal in it at all for this chap, who'll just be doing a job he's been paid to do.

But Ingrid . . .?

'Somebody must have put her up to it. She'd never have thought of a thing like that on her own.'

'I don't know about that,' Conroy says. 'You've hurt her feelings. She's got to look out for herself now. D'you think she's going to sit around waiting for you to make every move?'

'What moves would they be, Albert?'

So I've walked out on my missis, but I've lost the bird I left her for – no, the bird I left her *about*, because Donna had already left me, and you could say she was no more than the catalyst in a situation that had been just ready and waiting for one for years – and now I'm on my own. So what moves am I supposed to be making?

I shake my head. 'No, it's her mother all over. That old bitch never did like me. All this has just proved everything she ever thought about me.'

'True enough,' Conroy says, and I flash him a look, not knowing which why he means it: that he thinks I'm a swine, or it's not surprising that Ingrid's mother does.

This isn't a pub that Conroy and I use much and it's quiet now, in the early evening; so quiet that the barman's doing jobs somewhere in the back and we have to call him through for refills. But then a kid and a bird sitting on the far side run out of chat and get up to look at the juke-box. When I hear the money go in I reach for my glass and swallow the last inch of beer as a Beatles record pounds into the room.

'Let's go somewhere else, shall we? We can't talk with that racket.'

Conroy follows me out into the bright sunshine. The alley gives on to the High Street and we stroll along towards the theatre. Seeing it there, closed for internal alterations, only pushes further away, like a long-ago dream of happiness, last winter when it was all happening and the company used to get into the Mitre and I fell for Donna Pennyman and for a while it looked as though I'd found everything I'd ever yearned for in a woman.

Conroy nods across the road as we draw opposite that pub.

'The old place? Or would you rather walk a bit farther?'

I shrug. 'It's as good as anywhere.'

I know just where Conroy and I were standing the time I first saw Donna and Fleur and the rest of them; and the exact spot where Donna turned away from me to talk to a couple who'd been in the audience on the night I knew that something tremendous was opening inside me. I sit now in a corner as Conroy buys the drinks and let the ghosts haunt me. With Donna, I'm thinking, I could have faced the lot of them and whatever they might try to do to me. But without her what's all the trouble and disapproval going to get me, except a passport to loneliness?

'What do you reckon this bloke was after, then, Albert?'

'Evidence, I expect.'

'But I've already admitted to Ingrid that I'd been having it with somebody else.'

'Who heard you say it? You could always deny it now if you felt like it.'

'Well, what's he hoping he'll find down here?'

'Something – anything – that might help her case.'

'He won't see me with Donna, if that's what he wants. She's in Cornwall. And what did he think he'd get from you?'

'A lead. Who knows? Anyway, like I said, he guessed I'd rumbled him. But he'd know there was that risk, and I reckon he wouldn't chance giving himself away before he'd already spent a day or two keeping an eye on you.'

'You mean he's been following me about?'

'I'd say it's likely. Have you been up to anything you'd rather hide?'

'What have I got to hide? I went into town to see Fleur last week.'

'Oh, did you?'

'I never said anything to you because I thought ... well, I thought you fancied her at one time.'

'I haven't seen Fleur since the night they had the party for her at Donna's. When she left the Palace.'

'Well, I've been and taken her out a couple of times to find out what news she had about Donna.'

Which isn't the whole truth. Because when I first went to Fleur's, thinking that Donna was still sharing the flat with her, and she told me that Donna had gone home to Cornwall with Clive Carter's baby inside her, she made a move or two that suggested she wouldn't mind if

13

I went back again on a different footing. So why not? I thought later, when I'd finished reeling from the first shock of it all. I'd lost the girl I was mad about and left the wife I married because I had to. Fleur is one of those smashing bits of crumpet that nine out of ten men would like to lay hands on if they're being honest about it; and I was on my own, answerable to nobody, pissed-off with the world and everybody in it. It had to be good for what little ego I had left that I, the common or garden draughtsman from the northcountry backwoods, could probably make it with this stunning number who did TV commercials for bathsoap in a way that had the men viewers straining their eyes to see through the bubbles. But all that happened was a feel and a fondle that I somehow hadn't the heart to press through to a finish. And when she backed off without making the clinching move herself I thought maybe she's a teaser (which had crossed my mind before) or, giving her the benefit of the doubt, she'd too much pride to push it when she knew I'd still got Donna on my mind. Now, when I think of a glimpse of the inside of her thigh, the swing of her hips and the pneumatic loll of her breasts under the thin wool of her sweater, I can come on hard for her; but it's no different from the way I wanted Ingrid for a while before I married her, knowing full well I didn't love her but not able to leave her alone. No different, except that I know a thing or two now that I didn't know then. Though Fleur, as far as it's gone, is only number three in the astonishing lecherous career of Casanova Brown, who ran away from his wife to a life of debauchery with actresses in London – which is how I suppose they're all seeing it back in Cressley.

I don't tell Conroy all this, but he's giving me a man-of-the-world look over the top of his glass.

'As long as you didn't stay all night, with that bloke in the street, clocking you in and out, I suppose there's no harm done.'

I feel sick. 'Why should anybody else be dragged into it?'

'Because, laddy,' he says patiently, 'if Ingrid's decided she wants to divorce you she'll need some evidence that will satisfy first her solicitors and then a judge. You didn't think you could just shake hands and call it a day, did you?'

'Hardly that.'

'What had you in mind, then?'

'I dunno. Once I'd told Ingrid I was going, and walked out, I didn't think about it much. I thought she still wanted me back. She wrote to me not long ago and said so.'

'So now she's changed her mind.'

'She's been got at. I can see her mother behind this.'

'Whoever's behind it, if Ingrid wants to get cracking without waiting to sue you for desertion she'll need evidence she can use in court.'

'Oh, hell, what a mess.'

'Oh, aye. What about your sex-life with Ingrid?'

'What about it? Ingrid and I had a good sex-life.'

'You're sure you didn't make excessive demands? That you didn't have any little habits she put up with against her will?'

'I've told you – we had a good time and we both liked it.'

'Fine. So maybe it won't be all dug out and twisted in court for the public to tut-tut and slaver over.'

'If you're trying to scare the shit out of me you're doing well.'

'Aye. But it can be bloody disgusting, Vic. And if you don't end up loathing and detesting each other for the rest of your days it won't be the fault of the legal gents.'

I say, carefully, because it's something Conroy never talks about, 'Was your divorce like that?'

'It was bad enough.'

He goes quiet now. In a minute I tap his glass. 'C'mon, sup it off and I'll get us a refill.'

I could do to get a bit of a load on tonight, but Conroy has to be up extra early in the morning to start on a trip for the firm, and that holds us both back.

' "Dear Auntie Flo," ' Conroy begins as we walk back along the street, ' "I want you to advise me about my

15

husband, who is a sex maniac. He is at me at night and again in the morning. He's at me when I'm doing the cooking and the cleaning-up. He is at me all the time. You must help me. Please excuse the wobbly writing.'

I have to smile, but I don't find it all that funny in the circumstances, and I think he's a bit of a callous sod for making jokes at a time like this.

I kept Ingrid's letter to me. It said: 'Dear Vic, People say harsh things when they are angry and upset but now we have both had time to cool down and think things over I want you to know that I am willing to have another go at making our marriage work if you will.

'I don't believe you meant all the things you said. I know you were upset about that girl but when she's gone and you know now she was not worth it what's the point in ruining our futures over somebody like that?'

'We've had our ups and downs but we've had some good times as well. I suppose plenty of wives would say good riddance but I'm not like that, I don't see why we should break up everything over a thing like that if I'm ready to try to forgive and forget.'

In a day or two I wrote back: 'Dear Ingrid, Thanks for your letter. I'm sorry but you still don't understand. She was only part of the trouble, but knowing her showed me where we fell short and what the future was going to be like.

'I said to you that night that there was still time for both of us to make new lives, and I still think you deserve somebody better than me – or something better than I can give you.'

'It might be hard for you to take now but I hope you'll thank me for it in years to come.' That sounded a bit sanctimonious, so I added on: 'Or at least, you'll come to realize it was for the best.'

The morning after I've talked to Conroy I go down on to the factory floor (if you can call it that, because Joyce and Walstock's is no more at present than a long

16

prefabricated office building and a couple of workshop bays in a field at the edge of town) and find Bill Chisholm. He's one of the foremen, a bit of a shit if the truth be told, but quite human with me now since I found out that his lad Wally, who *is* a shit and no mistake, was the one who'd written the anonymous letters to Ingrid. What happened was that when I first came down here to Longford, after Jimmy Slade, Chisholm got the idea that nobody but Conroy's mates could get jobs in the drawing office and I'd taken the buffet he'd had ear-marked for their Wally. So Chisholm tried to show me up over a drawing I'd done; but it was Wally's marking-out of the steel that was wrong, and *he* was the one who ended up with the red face. Because of this – or because his mind was warped anyway – Wally, who'd seen me with Donna – but before there was anything between us – sent a couple of anonymous letters to Ingrid. When I found out who it was I gave Wally a thumping and his old man, dragging the tale out of him, gave him another. Wally left, along with his bird, Wendy Bamforth, who worked in Accounts, had access to my home address and had been daft enough to type the notes for him.

'Where's your Wally working now?' I ask Chisholm.

'A place in Deptford,' he says, giving me a wary look.

'Handy for travelling, is it?'

'Handy enough.'

'Is he still living at home?'

'Oh, yeh.'

There's a cropping machine thudding at the end of the bay and a general clatter of steel on steel. I don't want to bawl my business for all the shop to hear so I nod towards the door.

'Come on out in the yard a minute, will you?'

He follows me out, on the defensive as soon as I turn to face him in the open air.

'What do you want with him now? That's all over and done with, ain't it?'

'Has he said anything to you about a feller who says he knows me? Asks questions about me?'

17

'Oh, so that's it. He come home the other night and said a bloke in the pub had mentioned your name. Looked like a copper, Wally said.'

'What did Wally say to him?'

'Nothing. He drank off and scarpered. He got some idea in his head you'd sent him.'

'I've never seen him.'

'Then how do you know about him?'

'I've heard he's been about.'

And, Christ! he has been about. That daft bitch Ingrid must be spending it like water, paying for all that legwork.

Chisholm's getting the message. 'If I thought my lad had set all this up for you I'd bloody crucify the little –

'Well, he didn't help. But forget about it. It's a long story.'

And one of the oldest in the world.

There'll be some people, I suppose, who are tough enough, and clear-sighted enough, to stick out against the pressures: Circumstances, Society, the Family, the Way they've been Brought Up. We used to have some sayings among us when I was a lad up north. (As though, when it comes down to it, I've ever been anything else!) We used them to show what big men we were and that you kept your wits together where women were concerned, used them for one thing, and didn't let them get their hooks into you. But they were all piss and wind underneath, designed to hide for a while that we'd go the way our fathers had gone, in the end. One I remember was, 'A standing prick has no conscience', which I used to think was a scream. But it doesn't stand all the time, and I'd been guilty about Ingrid for long enough when the trap was sprung. Then along with the sick dismay was the feeling that there was only one thing to do. I just had no choice.

I've always wanted to marry you, Vic . . . And now it has to be this way. Forcing you into it. You'd never have asked me but for this, would you? I know you wouldn't . . .

– *I've asked you, haven't I? I've said we'll get married, haven't I?*

– *You've no need to if you don't want to. I shan't force you.*

– *You know damn well you won't turn me down, though.*

And after the first bust-up:

– *You all stood around pushing. There wasn't one of you said no don't do it if you don't want to.*

– *It wasn't a case of wanting to or not wanting to. You pushed yourself when you did what you did with Ingrid.*

My sister Chris said that. The one I'd always admired and looked up to turned out to be just like all the rest. Make the best of it. Accept your responsibilities.

So I did. For some time.

My landlady, Mrs. Witherspoon, has a letter waiting for me from the lunchtime post when I get back to my digs after work. I recognize the Old Lady's handwriting straight away and think, 'Oh, hell, here it comes!' because there's not been a cheep out of her so far since I hopped it, though I reckon I can guess well enough what she thinks from the way she turned her back sharpish the first time I walked out, when we were still living with Ingrid's mother and I just couldn't take any more. And now I really am at fault, with no chance of loading the blame on to Mrs. Rothwell's interfering ways.

But the letter, though it's all there between the lines in what she doesn't say, isn't about that.

'Dear Victor, Your father had a stroke at work on Monday and they took him to hospital. He is coming round a bit now though he is still rather poorly. Our Christine has been already and she thinks you ought to come and see him if you feel you want to. Mother.'

If I feel I want to! Our Chris thinks! What does *she* think? And the Old Feller himself? That because I've left my wife I can't have any human feelings?

Stamping about my room for a bit works some of it off; then I go downstairs to the phone and send a telegram,

19

saying I'll be there tomorrow. That's Friday, which means taking a day off work. And with Conroy away on business I can't tell him what I'm doing. So I wait in the morning till I know Mr. Franklyn, the boss, will have got in and ring him before I set off. He's a very reasonable chap and he makes no objection at all, though I have got a job on my drawing board that's wanted in a hurry.

'I hope you'll find him well on the way to recovery, Vic,' he tells me.

I say thanks, and then I'm on my way, on a train to Liverpool Street, then across London by Underground to King's Cross.

It's a journey I used to make every other Friday night, and one I hadn't intended to do again in a hurry. I don't *want* to go now. Oh, I'm worried about the Old Man and I'd like to know that he's going to be okay; but I didn't intend to stick my head inside that lions' den for a long, long time. Not until I'd got myself on such a firm footing that it wouldn't matter what they all thought or said.

I just miss one train, have to wait an hour for another, and what with changing to the local diesel at Wakefield, then taking a bus up out of Cressley town centre, it's the middle of the afternoon before I get there.

There's nobody in. I rap on the knocker and try the door again before going round the back. But there's no answer there either, and no sign of life when I stand on the top step and stretch over to look through the kitchen window. I sit on the step and light a fag. I can see the infirmary from here, on top of the hill, above the little park, and I wonder if I ought to go straight up there. But there's no knowing whether they've taken the Old Feller there or somewhere else. One of the neighbours should know, but I don't fancy facing any of them, having them eye me over, weighing me up, the wrong 'un who's turned up again because his father's badly. I feel very thin-skinned back here in this town.

So in a minute or two I wander back round to the front and lean on the wall, looking down the street. And then I see the square shape of her as she turns the corner by

the Prince of Wales and begins to come up the hill, very
steady, a shopping-bag in one hand. She looks either
tired out or bowed down by worry. It must have upset
her, first me scarpering like that, then this thing hitting
the Old Man.

I get up off the wall and walk down to meet her. She
doesn't appear to see me till I'm nearly on top of her.
Then her head comes up and she gives me a quick glanc-
ing look as I speak.

'Now then!' I reach to take the bag out of her hand.

'I can manage it.'

'C'mon, let's have it . . . How's me dad?'

'I waited in till after dinner for you, then I had to go
out.'

'That's all right. How is me dad?'

'As well as can be expected.'

'If you'd been on the phone I could have let you know
what time I'd be getting here.'

'The Coal Board wanted your father to have it put in
years ago but he allus reckoned he'd be at their beck and
call if he did. It's a bit late in the day now.'

At the house I follow her into the kitchen where she
takes the bag off me and puts it on the table, looking over
her shoulder in the general direction of my feet.

'You're not planning on stopping, then?'

'What? Oh! I've got a case outside.'

I bring it in off the back step as the Old Lady puts the
kettle on the gas and begins to empty the groceries out of
the bag. There's a long silence until she all at once looks
round again, as though she wonders if I'm still there.

'Well, what have you got to say for yourself, then?'

'What do you want me to say?'

'Nay, I don't know. It's come to summat, though, when
your mother can't step outside her own front door without hanging her head in shame.'

'You've got to live your own life.'

'Aye, an'a fine life you're making for yourself. We've
allus lived respectable, your dad and me. We've known
hard times but we've never owed anybody anything and

we could look people in the face. I thought we'd raised three fine upstanding bairns and shown 'em how to go on t'same way. But when you can go an' do a trick like that, leaving your wife for another woman, I –'

'There is no other woman. She's gone away.'

'An' a bonny sample she was, by all accounts.'

'All accounts? Whose accounts?'

'Ingrid's account. Your wife's account.'

'Oh, so Ingrid's been telling you all about it, has she?'

'Who else was there to tell us? We'd ha' known a lot if we'd waited for you, wouldn't we?'

'Well, maybe my account would've been a bit different from Ingrid's'

'Happen so. An' happen it all comes to the same thing in the end. I wonder you've t' cheek to show your face round here.'

'I wouldn't have if it hadn't been for me dad, don't you worry. I was going to wait a long time for the dust to settle before I showed me face again.'

'The dust never settles on a thing like that. People's memories are too long.'

'An' other folks' business is all they've got to think about. Well, I'm thinking about meself.'

'Oh, that's plain enough. There's not much sign of you thinking about anybody else. What you expect to gain by it all is summat I fail to see.'

'A new life, for me.'

'And what about your wife? What sort of life is there for her?'

'She'll find somebody else. She's young enough.'

'She was younger when you wed her.'

'She was having a baby when I wed her, an'all.'

'Was that all you married her for?'

'If you want a straight answer – yes.'

It's something I've never come right out with before. The Old Lady appears to think about it for a second.

'But you got on all right together, didn't you, as soon as you'd got out of her mother's way? And I'm sure she's a nice enough lass.'

22

'I've never said she wasn't.'

'Then what the devil do you want to go and do a trick like that for?'

'Because it's not enough for me. I want something else.'

'If you couldn't keep your vows you should never have wed her.'

'A fine time to tell me! God! that's the limit, that is. Who said that at the time? She was pregnant. What else do you do round here when you get a lass pregnant, but marry her?'

'You got her pregnant.'

'Aye, I did. But I've decided now 'at I'm not going to spend the rest of my life paying for it.'

Which brings us back to where we came in. It's hopeless to expect her to understand. However could she? I've done a wrong thing whichever way you look at it and it's something she'll never forget or forgive me for. Ingrid would have to be an idle, drunken, shrewish slut before the Old Lady could even get near crediting me with an excuse for what I've done. And she isn't that. She's an ordinary decent kid who does her best and it's not her fault that while I was fond enough of her part of the time, the rest of the time I felt like running screaming up the walls because she wasn't what I wanted, what Donna could have been to me, somebody who'd let me stretch and develop, keeping pace with me, or waiting on ahead while I did it. Somebody, I know at times like this, I've simply got to find. Oh! God, somebody I can *love*.

The Old Lady mashes the tea. I don't know if she usually has a cup about this time, whether she feels she needs one after pulling up that hill, or she's treating me like a visitor. Maybe she doesn't know what to say or do next and the ritual with the pot and kettle and cups helps to cover the awkwardness. Because she's got no time for me, that's sure, and if it weren't for the Old Feller I doubt if she'd have let me into the house.

– *She says she doesn't want to see you till you've patched it up with Ingrid again.*

– *She'll have to wait a long time, that's all.*

'If you're stopping,' she says after a while, 'I'll make your bed up.'

'It'll be too late to go back tonight, anyway.'

'You can go as soon as you're ready. Don't think there's anybody keeping you here.'

'Did our Chris stay over?'

'Yes. David brought her up in the car on Tuesday, then came back for her on Wednesday night.'

'Did they bring young Bobby with 'em?'

'Yes.'

'How are they all?'

'They're doing well. That Bobby's a ripstick.'

'You won't see so much of 'em nowadays.'

'She still likes to come home, does our Christine. And so does David. Leicester's not a million miles away.'

'She'd have something to say about it all, I reckon?'

'Oh, you can allus rely on a good word from our Christine. She's backed you up all your life. But if you think she sides with you in this you're mistaken. She thinks like everybody else, "at you ought to have a damn" good hiding an' your brains washed.'

An exaggeration, no doubt. But near enough to the truth. Ah, well, I stopped expecting too much from Chris some time ago. She might have a bit more give in her thinking than some, and be able to talk round a situation for a while, but she still finally homes on the same old target. I suppose she's like the Aunties who run the agony columns in women's magazines. What can you expect them to say but try harder and make the best of it?

'And what about our Jim?'

'Jim's on this special course abroad, in Paris. I didn't want to bring him back all that way, upsetting him, if your dad was going to be all right.'

'He is going to be all right, isn't he?'

'They say he's off the danger list now, but it'll be a while before they can tell if there'll be any lasting detriment.'

2

Just before seven that evening we're standing in the entrance hall of the infirmary, waiting for them to let visitors into the wards. I haven't been in here since I came to see Ingrid after she fell downstairs and lost the baby.

– *I wish Ingrid had never laid eyes on him.*

That's what Mrs. Rothwell said about me that night. Now, I suppose, she'll be saying the same again, with bells on, though for a while, after the bust-up when I first walked out, and then Chris and David got us the flat, it must have seemed promising to those looking on. Making the best of it. Except that I knew, if nobody else did, that my best wasn't nearly half good enough, that this couldn't be all, that some way or other – though I couldn't see how – there'd have to be a change, because, try as I might, I couldn't see forty-odd years of that as my life.

'They let 'em all in early last night,' the Old Lady's saying. 'I got here at five-to and they'd all gone in. I haven't seen this attendant before. He must be a particular one.' She clutches her bag with a bottle of Lucozade and clean pair of pyjamas and undervest of the Old Feller's in it and throws a baleful look at the little orderly standing at the bottom of the stairs.

But he's resting on what bit of authority he's got, and it's spot on the hour before he waves us on up. At the top of the stairs the crowd splits and goes different ways. I follow the Old Lady round a couple of corners and along a corridor with the open doors of a ward at the end, a big light airy room with windows down both sides and a big one in the end wall, giving a view right across the valley. Expectant faces turn as we go in with maybe a dozen others, but the Old Feller's resting back on his pillows and only his eyes swivel as we reach him.

I'm a bit shocked when I see him. His face is drawn up one side and he's got only one arm out of the sheets.

'Now then, Dad.' I go round to the far side of him and pull up a chair.

'Hello, lad.' He seems to have a bit of trouble in talking and his speech is blurred, as though he hasn't got his teeth in. He rolls his eyes my way. 'I didn't know you were coming.'

'You didn't think you'd keep me away, did you?'

'Nay, your mother said nowt.' He looks me over. 'It's a bit of a mess, in't it?'

'It is just now,' I say, realizing then that he could be just as likely meaning my situation as his own. 'How do you feel?'

'Better than I did. They say I'm mending nicely.'

'You've been lucky,' the Old Lady chips in. 'Only a month to go to retiring. And I've told you time an' time again you ought to slow down and take things easier.'

'Nay, it could have happened just t'same when I wa' bending over in t'garden.'

'All t'same, you'll happen learn a bit o'sense now.'

'Aye, this'll cramp your style for a bit, Dad.'

'Ah, well,' he says, his good hand smoothing the blanket, 'there's plenty worse off than me. You only need a day or two inside one o'these places to realize how much you've got to be grateful for.'

He starts to tell us about a chap who died yesterday and another, behind screens near the door, who they don't hold out much hope for. A nurse going by stops at the foot of the bed and looks at him.

'Would you like propping up a bit higher, Mr. Brown?'

'No, no, I'm all right. Here, this is my eldest son.'

'Oh, is it?' She looks at me, a pretty, dark haired lass with a good, buxom figure inside her uniform.

26

'Is he giving you any trouble?' I ask her.

'No, not just now. Another day or two and we might have to watch him, though.'

'A nice lass, that,' the Old Feller says as she goes on her way. 'Some of 'em's a bit moody but she's allus pleasant.'

'I expect they have a lot to put up with,' the Old Lady says.

'Oh, aye. You get some awkward customers to deal with. That one over yonder, with his leg strung up; he's a damned nuisance. Does nowt but grumble from morning till night. Aye, in t'middle o' t'night an' all, sometimes. He got on at one of 'em yesterday and called her all t'names under t'sun. In the end she went and fetched t'Sister to him. She didn't half give him a dressing-down. He's been a bit quieter since then.'

When the Old Lady thinks she recognizes a visitor at another bed she and the Old Feller launch into a long discussion, speculating about relatives and connections, going back as far as forty years to fill in the branches on the family tree until, as nearly always happens, they come to a point where they stick at a disagreement.

'Our Edna 'ull know. She knew 'em all.'

'Ask her, then. Just see if I'm not right.'

'One of 'em emigrated to Australia. I'm sure of it.'

'I just said so. Only, you've got hold of t'wrong brother. It wasn't Tommy, it was t'other one.'

'But I'll swear I've seen him inside t'last eighteen months.'

'I've told you. He came back. Married again and settled down here.'

At ten to eight I get up to go out and let them have a bit of private talk. Up till then the Old Feller's seemed to steer away from asking me about my affairs, and I'm grateful for it. But now, as I put the chair back, he suddenly says:

'Have you seen Ingrid?'

'I only got here this afternoon.'

27

'Are you going to see her?'

'Perhaps I will.'

'Ey, lad,' he says, 'this is no way o' carrying on,' and all at once there are tears in his eyes.

I suppose it's his condition that's softened him to that extent, but all the same I'm shaken and embarrassed to see him break down like this.

'Leave it be, Dad,' I tell him. 'Leave it alone. You just get better yourself and don't worry about us.'

I go down and have a smoke on the steps outside the main entrance until the bell rings and the visitors start to leave.

'Your father's very upset about you,' the Old Lady says as we walk down the road.

'Aye, I could see that.'

'Are you going to see Ingrid?'

'What for?'

'You told your dad you might.'

'There's no point in raking it all over again. It's best left alone.'

'That poor lass. She sobbed and better sobbed when she told us about it. She's heartbroken.'

'Mother, I'm not doing it for fun.'

'I never knew you could be so hard and selfish,' she says.

Backed at the house I say to her, 'You go on in. I'm going for a walk down the street.'

'A walk where to?'

'I feel like a drink.'

'You've taken that up an'all, have you?'

'Oh, for God's sake! I fancy a pint, that's all. If I have a couple I might sleep better.'

'If you had an easy conscience you might sleep better an' all.'

I turn to leave her, impatient.

'Here,' she says, 'wait till I've opened the door, then take this latchkey. If you're late I shan't be up.'

I walk down as far as the Prince of Wales. It's not a pub I've ever been in much; on the other hand, there's nearly bound to be some locals in there who'll know me. So I cross over the main road and make towards the town centre. Some way on, picking at random, I find a little place where the landlord serves me a lip-smacking pint that's like cream compared with some of the tepid swill I've drunk lately. But even another one and then a third don't give me any lift; they just sink me even further into brooding. I'm not being very practical, I think. There's still some of my gear at the flat (all I took was what I could pack into one case); I ought to see about getting rid of the lease of that place, arrange to sell the furniture, clear up my finances at the bank. I don't begrudge Ingrid her share, and I'm not going to argue who bought what and how much each of us put into the kitty. As it is, everything's been left as it was when I walked out and anybody could think that I'm deliberately holding off from burning my boats because all I need is the right terms offered for me to come back. Well, this is my home town and, standing here drinking among the familiar accents, it's Longford, with Donna gone, that seems the strange and far-away place I ought to try to forget. But I know it's the place I must go back to, because out there is where I've got to come to terms with myself, not here on square one.

It suddenly strikes me that now might be a good time to visit the flat and take stock while there's nobody about. I drink off; buy a packet of fags, and leave the pub to catch a bus. I'm lucky in getting a connection straight away and seven or eight minutes later finds me dropping off at the end of the road with a three-minute walk to the house. They built quite a few great stone mansions round here before the first world war, when the mill-owners and all the other rich men still lived in the town and could get servants to look after them. But now most of them have been turned into flats.

There's a light on in the flat that Chris and David had, but the ground-floor front is in darkness. I feel for my keys and let myself in.

All I can think of doing at first is wandering from room

to room, switching lights on in the dusk. It's not a big place – a living-room, bedroom, boxroom, bathroom and kitchen – and I used to think it was dear till I compared it with some rents down south; but it was all right for us. We were lucky to get it and it helped us over a bad hurdle. Now you might say it only postponed the real break. But at least I did try it on our own. I did try, even if wasn't good enough in the end.

Ingrid's clothes have all gone from the wardrobe and the drawers. I'll bet she hasn't spent a night here since I left. Back to her mother's bosom as soon as I'd gone. She was already staying with her during the week, while I was away, because Mrs. Rothwell was off it and waiting to go into hospital for an operation. I wonder what the old dragon's saying now she's got Ingrid back for keeps. 'Good riddance. You're better off without him. I always knew he wasn't good enough for you'? Something like that. A pound to a penny she's not telling her ways to tempt me back. And why should I resent anything that helps Ingrid reconcile herself to it?

My gramophone records stand, neat in a row, in the cupboard next to the radiogram. More than books, they mark the beginning of my climb out of ignorance; from taking things for granted to a state where I could start to compare, looking for terms of reference not just in my own little world but in a wider one outside it. Not that that means anything in itself: I read somewhere that there were death-camp bosses in Germany who could cry listening to Wagner and Beethoven. I look at a couple of Sibelius symphonies, but they're not for me tonight. Tchaikovsky and Berlioz neither. There seems to be nothing I can muster enough interest to put on; and then my hand falls on a brass band disc, with some old warhorses on it and a hymn or two, but a National Championship test piece as well that I once played for the Old Feller, who thought it was highbrow. But he always does tend to stick at *Gems from La Traviata*.

I put it on the turntable and start the motor. Its difficulties are ferocious. Starting in the middle-register instruments – tenor horns, baritones, euphoniums – there's a slow and quiet statement of a solemn theme which works up into a series of variations through the full range of the band, then eventually settles back into a restatement on solo euphonium, with cornets, trombones, basses, everybody, creeping in behind to close it. A crack band, this, playing like angels: the cream of the business, but still amateurs, and men with their roots in a long tradition of hard graft. Dry fellers, not given much to high-flown analysis of what they play, but turned into poets when the instruments are to their lips. It's the mixture of tough and tender in the sound of that solo euphonium which suddenly gets to me, bringing me near to tears as I think of the Old Feller and all his years of mining and banding, of where I went wrong with Ingrid, of how I lost Donna; of all the past, and the future I can't see, with marvellous things lying just out of reach, beautiful and heartbreaking, like this music.

Sitting on there after it's finished, I'm still so far away that even in the silence I don't hear the door open, and I've no idea that Ingrid's in the room with me till she speaks, starting me so that I swing round in my chair, my heart going like mad.

'What are you doing here?'

'Oh, hello. You made me jump.'

She moves over and stands by the mantelshelf.

'I thought it must be burglars when I saw the light on. Then I looked through the window.'

'I came up to see me dad.'

'He's going to be all right, isn't he?'

'They seem to think so. Have you seen him?'

'No, not yet. I've seen your mother, though. She told me.'

'Oh.'

'You're not thinking of sleeping here tonight, are you?'

'No, I'm staying at home.'

'I was going to say, the bed isn't aired.'

'You're at your mother's, I suppose?'

'Yes.'

31

'How's she getting on? Has she had her operation yet?'

'Yes. She came home a fortnight ago. She's picking up nicely.'

'That's all right, then.'

'As if you cared.'

'All right, then, I don't care.'

'I asked you what you were doing here.'

'I wanted to arrange to clear the rest of my stuff out. And it's time we gave the place up, unless you want to keep it on yourself.'

'I don't want it.'

'All right, then.'

'What about the furniture?'

'If there's anything you want you can have it. Otherwise I'll sell it and give you half the money.'

'You'll get next to nothing from a dealer.'

'Perhaps I can put it into some auction rooms.'

'Some of it's practically new. That three-piece has had hardly any wear at all. It's a crying shame to give it away.'

'You won't want to advertise it, sell it privately, will you?'

'I'm not showing people round, selling-up my own home.'

'No, I thought not. We shall just have to make the best of it.'

'You really are set on going through with it, then?'

I don't answer.

'I saw your girl friend on television the other night,' she says in a minute.

'I didn't see her. Why didn't I see her?'

'It's got nothing to do with me any more, what you see or don't see.'

How the hell did I come to miss her? I hardly ever see the telly in Longford but I should have remembered the couple of plays she recorded before she went away, and kept an eye out for them.

'Anyway, I couldn't see anything special about her.'

'As a matter of fact, she's a very talented actress.'

'You might think so.'

'Oh, come on, don't be so small-minded.'

'I've got a right to be small-minded about a woman who's taken my husband away from me.'

'No, you haven't. You can be bitter and resentful and you can hate her guts: but being small-minded is small-minded.'

'And you're above all that sort of thing, I suppose?'

'Anyway, she hasn't taken me away from you, has she?'

'Well, who's keeping you away? Is it that other one, Fleur Dunham?'

That's supposed to be the one that rocks me back on my heels.

'How do you know about Fleur?'

'Wouldn't you like to know!'

Like lasses in a playground. 'Boo-hoo! Wouldn't you like to know! New-sy!' My first reaction when she came in was to feel sorry for her. A bit paler, a bit thinner than when I saw her last, fidgety in the hands, but dignified enough with it. Now I feel I could hit the silly cow. Small-town, small-minded, dragging me back. – *What a row! Do you have to play it so loud? I don't know what you see in it.* And she never will; not if she lives to be a million. And yours truly's not stopping around on the off-chance.

'Who put you up to hiring that feller to snoop around after me, eh? Was it your mother's bright idea?'

'I don't know what you're talking about.'

'Oh, don't be so stupid.'

'Oh, no. I've been stupid for long enough. Now I'm looking after myself. If you must know. I've been to see a solicitor.'

'Great! And you ask me if *I'm* set on going through with it.'

'I asked you if you'd come back and you said no. So now I'm looking after my own interests. You'll be getting a maintenance order served on you any time now.'

'Oh, aye? And with you working, and living at your

mother's, how much do you think you'll get?'

'They have a way of working it out. They add the two incomes together, divided by three, then take away what the wife earns. What's left is the maintenance.'

She seems to know. I do a quick calculation. 'About a quid a week. You're going to court over a quid a week, are you?'

'It's better in my pocket than yours. and it'll be more than that if I don't go back to work.'

'How d'you mean, don't go back?'

'I've been off for weeks. I'm under treatment for my nerves.'

'What's wrong with your nerves?'

'I couldn't face people in the office. I used to burst out crying, if you must know.'

I feel half sorry for her and half irritated. I don't know how much of it's genuine, that's the trouble. I do know the state of mind she can get into with a bit of encouragement from her mother. Like that time after her miscarriage when she wouldn't let me touch her for months because she was still supposed to be poorly.

'You'll come out of it.'

'I might not fancy going back to work, though.'

'So you'll expect me to keep you while you sit at home knitting, with your bloody mother. That's not fair.'

'Don't you talk to me about what's fair. I'm getting all I'm due to, don't worry.'

'What about all you've got that you're not due to? Doesn't that count?'

'What d'you mean?'

'I mean that five hundred quid that Mr. Van Huyten left me. I said I'd give you half, but it's all mine if everybody had their own.'

'You shouldn't have put it into the joint account if you didn't want me to share.'

'I haven't said I don't want you to share. But I'll tell you what' – and though I can hardly believe it, it's only just dawned on me – 'I ought to have my head examined. You've still got that bank book. If you think I'm paying

34

for bloody detectives to spy on me out of my cut, you've got another think coming.'

'So what are you going to do about it?'

'I'll have that bank book, for a start.'

'You don't think I carry a thing like that about with me.'

'Where is it, then – under your mother's bloody mattress? Practically the last thing you said before I walked out was that you didn't want anything of mine.'

'I've changed my mind. I'm having everything I can get.'

I hold myself in, reaching out to switch off the radiogram, deliberately forcing myself to calm down.

'I didn't come here to row with you. If you want to meet me at the bank tomorrow we'll clear it all up. I reckon about three hundred and twenty-five quid apiece. If you don't think that's fair I don't know what you want.'

'I'm not going anywhere with you. The solicitor warned me that if I wanted a divorce I'd to steer clear of seeing you on my own. There's a thing called collusion, you know. He said I really shouldn't have said I've forgive you in my letter. That could be construed as condoning what you did.'

'Oh, bloody great. And where does flesh and blood come into all this?'

'You and I have finished with flesh and blood.'

'You'd better piss off out of here, then, because if anybody sees you they might think we've been having a poke for old time's sake, and that would never do.'

'There's no need to be crude.'

'No, you hate me and I'll hate you and everybody'll be happy.'

'What do you expect?'

My voice rises till I'm near to shouting. 'I expect a bit of bloody humanity. I don't want to get till I have to loathe and detest you for the rest of my life.'

'Well, I loathe and detest you, so why not?'

There are things I could say, but, again, I hold myself

in till my temper goes. Then a great tiredness falls over me.

'I shall go to the bank in the morning and take my share of the money. If you try to interfere with that I'll fight you for the full five hundred of Mr. Van Huyten's and see that you get nothing else. I mean it. I'll go to jail before I give you a penny-piece.'

She's quiet for the time it takes her to cross to the door.

'You've no intention at all of coming back, have you?'

'No, Ingrid. I've no intention at all.'

'I'm going to name her, you know,' she says then. 'I'm not hanging about tied to you for three years till I can sue for desertion. Adultery's quicker. And I'm goin to name her.'

I'm down at the bank as soon as it opens in the morning. I ask the clerk what the account stands at now and how much was in it a couple of months ago. Ingrid's blued nearly a hundred quid, though whether it all went on that gumshoe or not I can't tell. I tell the chap I want to draw three hundred and forty. It's a joint account, operated by either her signature or mine, which was fine in the days when we trusted each other, but part of it's on deposit so I have to go through the rigmarole of transferring enough into current to get at it. Then the laddo doesn't seem to want to give me all that in folding money so I let him make out a draft for their branch in Longford, in my name.

By the time we've negotiated all this a sizeable queue's piled up behind me and as I leave the counter a middle-aged woman whose face I seem to know speaks to me.

'Hello, Victor.'

'Good morning.'

'How are your father and mother?'

'Oh, fine,' I say without thinking, making to pass her.

'I don't seem to have seen either of them for such a long time.'

I think I really ought to tell her about the Old Feller, only I shall look daft now I've said they're both okay.

'How are you keeping, you and your wife?'

'Oh, we're both well.'

'Do give them all my regards, won't you?'

'Yes, I'll do that. Cheerio!'

I go out into the street, feeling a bit of an idiot. But that's one who hasn't heard about Ingrid and me, anyway. Because it seems to me that everybody else must have. It comes over me strongest later in the day when I've been up to see the Old Man again and then left the Old Lady, who has hardly a so-long for me; a feeling that everybody whose glance falls on me knows what a swine I am, and even the ones who don't look at me are oozing disapproval. The air seems to reek with it and standing on the station, looking at the people waiting for the same train, normal people living their nice normal lives, it strikes me that I'm turning into a kind of moral hypochondriac. Because, after all, Ingrid and I are not on our own, not by a long chalk. I was reading a newspaper piece that gave some facts about marriage and divorce. In a quarter of all first marriages the bride's under twenty. Fits. One in five is pregnant on the day. Fits again. The greatest danger period for divorce is when you've been married between four and eleven years. We just creep in. And the rate is biggest among those where the bride *was* under twenty. That's us. But being a statistic doesn't let you off living your own life, and knowing there are plenty more like you makes it no easier.

Ingrid's probably telling the truth about the nerves bit. When you're carrying a load like this, you and the world seem to get out of synch. People are short or surly, when they're not plain rude. You haven't got the right change for cigarette machines and when you get it the machine refuses to cough up the goods. Trains run just late enough to start you worrying about connections. You forget things, walking about in a waking dream. People speak to you and you don't hear them. You drop things for no apparent reason. Sudden noises make you

37

jump and when you're crossing the road it's as though every driver's out with the sole aim of crippling you.

One way or another, I'm whacked by the time I get to Longford, and my shirt's a wet rag. I go straight to the house. There's a light showing from Mrs. Witherspoon's quarters at the far end of the downstairs passage and I can hear her television set. A queer old bird, Mrs. Witherspoon, odd, faraway. Apart from coming out every now and again with some outlandish flight of her imagination among the tut-tuts about current events, she provides Conroy and me and the other two lodgers with breakfast and evening meal, then retires into a world of her own. I know she goes to some mission church on a Sunday morning, and she must go out to the shops, but I've never seen her on the street, and I get the impression that she wouldn't recognize any of us if we did run into her outside the house.

I try Conroy's door on the way up but he's out. In my own room I empty my case and dump it in the alcove, behind the curtain, then sit down with my feet on the bed. There's not space for much else in here. Two of you in and you've got a crowd. The light's fading outside and it's a hot night. In a while lightning flashes and there's a crack of thunder close by. Not long after that the rain starts coming down like stair rods. I switch on the bed-side lamp and draw the curtains. The room seems smaller than ever now. It comes upon me strong how sick I am of my own company. Will I ever, I wonder, have a really close relationship with a woman again? Will I ever have a home? I look round this cheerless cubby-hole that's all I've got now. Is this the kind of life that's in store for me from now on?

3

Get an interest. A hobby. Fishing, stamp-collecting, painting by numbers, bird-watching, join Conroy and Franklyn on the golf links. Learn the piano. Where's a piano? Well, the french horn, clarinet, fiddle, trombone; mouth-organ, jew's harp, tommy-talker, comb-and-bloody-toilet-paper . . . I could grow a moustache; take up smoking a pipe. Or return the whole caboodle to Stores and tell them, 'Here, I'm cheesed-off with this Vic Brown kit. Change it me for another.' And what would I get then except somebody else's secrets, worries, troubles? Is there anybody I'd like to swap places with?

Jimmy Slade's present sunny outlook, I wouldn't mind. He's marrying the girl whose family he's lodged with since he came down here. A mate of mine from the drawing office at Whittakers', he was glad to get away from his parents. Which just goes to show, because I never knew in the old days that he didn't get on with them. We've never seen very much of each other outside working hours here, what with Jimmy courting so strong, but the night before the wedding (which is to be a small economy-sized do with nobody from the office invited) Conroy and I take him out on the town. Martin, the fourth draughtsman in the office, joins us for a couple early on, polite as always, but not unbuttoning much, and we're not sorry when he makes his excuses and goes off to catch his train. Then we move on to another pub, the drinking rate stepping up as we get the taste; it's not long before Conroy and I are watching Jimmy pick his way between the tables to the bog with if not yet a thirty-bob stagger on him, a definite fifteen-bob list. Conroy looks at me.

'Happy as Larry.'

'Yeh!'

'Trotting quietly to the slaughter.'

'Oh, nay, Albert!'

'You think he'll be all right?'

'Most people make a go of it, don't they? And she's okay, isn't she?'

'Pamela? I suppose so. She's got a nice pleasant nature.'

'Well, then.' It's surprising what a soft spot I've still got for marriage.

'Aye . . . We can't judge everybody by ourselves.'

'A fat lot we've got.'

'Freedom.' I grunt. 'Speak for yourself,' Conroy says. 'I enjoy my life.'

'Do you really, Albert? Don't you ever fancy getting wed again?'

'Maybe I'm not the marrying kind.' He eyes me. 'You are, though, aren't you?'

'It wouldn't do for us all to be alike, would it?' I want to say that I get lonely. That I've always, in a way, been looking for the other half of myself. But I think it'll sound too soft to somebody as self-sufficient as he is.

'Have you heard anything else about your dad?'

'No. He'll be okay. You were right about that chap, by the way. Ingrid knew about Fleur.'

'Oh, you saw Ingrid, did you?'

'Yes.'

'Not very pleasant, was it?'

'You know us lot up there, Albert. We don't agree to differ, we crucify one another. Right's right and wrong's no man's right.'

'I don't think we're unique.'

'No? Well, I began by feeling sorry for her and ended wanting to screw her neck round. she says she's going to name Donna.'

'Ah!' He nods.

'Isn't it bloody ridiculous! Why the hell can't I just sign a form and say she's free?'

'It doesn't work like that.'

'No. So we have to have all this damage.'

'You've damaged her. Hasn't she a right to be hurt and bitter?'

'Come on, all I need is for you to disapprove and I've got the lot against me.'

'I'm not chucking stones, Vic. But I don't like to see you crashing about, smashing yourself and everybody else into little pieces.'

'So what do you think I ought to do?'

'Nay, I can't live your life for you.'

'No, come on, you've got your opinion. Let's have it.'

'Well ... what happened to you with Donna could have happened to anybody. It was bad luck. But she's gone now.'

'So I ought to call it a day and go back to Ingrid?'

'You could do a lot worse. I mean, you know?' – he shrugs and waves his hand – 'have a bit on the side when you get the chance, if you like. Thousands do it without rocking the boat.'

'Well, well, well! And I thought you were putting a moral arm-lock on me. It's the old nod and a wink, you mean. Fiddle the expense account, take a backhander when it's offered. Nothing serious, mind –'

'Don't put words into my mouth,' Conroy says. 'I was only trying –'

'All right, all right. Have you given the same advice to Jimmy?'

'It's early days for him.'

'And for me, Albert lad,' I say with feeling. 'And for me.'

Jimmy comes back through the door, eyes sparkling, face lit up like a shepherd's delight.

'We were just going to send the lifeboat out after you.'

'I was ready for that,' he says, beaming goodwill all over us. 'Are we having another round?'

'I think we ought to get something to eat,' Conroy says,

41

'or we'll be smashed before the evening's half over.'

To be smashed seems to me a condition devoutly to be wished for. Funny how knowing that you'll pay for it after doesn't seem to matter at the time.

There's a bit of a rumpus going on in the House of Commons over a Minister who's been mixing with a bird who's been mixing with a bod from the Russian Embassy. The old nod and a wink seem to have broken down there. I read about it in the paper over breakfast, with a throbbing head, no appetite, but a raging thirst for hot sweet tea. A temptation to use it to kid Conroy isn't strong enough to make me break into speech. Besides, he's probably nearly as bad as I am, though apart from his quietness it doesn't really show on him as he puts away his cornflakes and fishcakes, when I can hardly touch mine.

I remember we dropped Jimmy off to get his beauty sleep then took a bottle of Scotch back to Albert's room where we talked for a bit and then, somewhat to my surprise, Conroy started reading poetry aloud over a background of Bach's *St. Matthew Passion* turned down low on the record-player so that we wouldn't wake the rest of the house. I felt good for a while then, as though the quality of my feeling for Donna was enough for a kind of happiness in itself. But later, when I'd dropped off in the chair in front of Conroy and he had to rouse me and send me up to my bed, only the weight of the booze pressing me into sleep kept me from black desperation. It must have been sometime then that I decided I'd got to do something instead of hanging about letting things happen to me. But what?

It's Saturday morning and normally I'd have turned over for another couple of hours and slept the hangover off. But we're busy; Franklyn likes us to go in any Saturday morning we can, and I promised to work this week because of the time I had off last. Conroy comes out as I'm using the phone in the hall ('Ready when you are') and I hang up, all at once self-conscious about saying

Fleur's name in front of him. He's already going out through the door, as it happens, but anyway, I'd waited long enough to know there'd be no reply.

We're quiet for some time in the car until, passing a church, I say, 'I wonder how old Jimmy's feeling.'

'He didn't have the whisky.'

'He'd enough of a roll on with the ale. It's stupid when you think about it, going to the altar with a hangover.'

'I went to it pissed.'

'You did?'

'I had a row with her the night before. I was scared stiff she wouldn't turn up, and what little bit of sense I had left told me it'd probably be as well if she didn't. So I got at the bottle.'

'What was her name?' Conroy leaks his past in small occasional drops and you have to be careful the way you ask for more or he turns the tap off again.

'Vivien. She was a wilful, moody cat. Cold as ice one day, like fire the next. I caught her on the rebound. She married me to spite the other bloke as much as anything.'

'And how long did it last?'

'A year . . . It's not pleasant, being the one who's left, you know, Vic.' He's keeping his attention on what he's doing and he doesn't turn his head to look at me.

'Which is worse,' I ask him, 'that or being married to somebody who's always wanting something else?'

'I could never make my mind up about that.'

'Didn't you tell me once you had a chance to take her back?'

'I twisted that a bit for your benefit. I thought you might take the hint.'

'Sorry.'

'It's your life.'

'Aye, and it's a long time to be miserable.'

During the morning I try to ring Fleur from the office, again with no luck.

'Got any plans for the weekend?' Conroy asks me.

'I'm going up to town this afternoon.'

'Will you be seeing Fleur?'

43

'If I can catch her. Why don't you come with me? You can renew old acquaintance and we can have a meal and take in a show.'

'I don't think so,' he says. 'I promised Franklyn a thrashing at golf.'

For some reason I get the impression he's stalling. It's his choice; but all at once the thought of being in London on my own depresses me. Anything's better, though, than hanging about in Longford, and I do want to see Fleur, though I'm not clear what I want to say to her, even if I can find her, which I think now is unlikely, because she's probably gone away for the weekend.

But, surprisingly, when I try her from Liverpool Street she answers.

'Oh, what a pity! I wish I'd known you were coming up.'

'You're not all that easy to catch.'

'No. I'm on the dash now, actually. Another thirty seconds and you'd have missed me.'

'Are you tied up all day?'

'I'm afraid so, love. I do wish I'd known.' She really sounds as if she means it.

'Is there any time when you can spare half an hour to meet me for a chat?'

'Today? Umm . . .'

'It's pretty important to me, Fleur.'

'Look, I'll be back here at six, for about an hour. Could you come round then?'

'I'll be there,' I tell her.

Coming out of the station, I make my way along Bishopsgate, stopping at a pub for a pint and a sandwich, then cutting across to the Tower and the river. There's a sizeable queue of people filing past the beefeaters into the Tower to look at the execution block, the axe, the swords, armour and relics of England's glorious bloody past, and I go on to stand for a while looking at the water and Tower Bridge. Soon, then, I'm walking back to the Underground at Tower Hill and, not long after that, coming out to stand at the corner of Regent Street.

All roads in London lead to Piccadilly Circus when they

don't lead anywhere else. Here it's not mams and dads and
their kids looking for the past, but crowds drawn by a
bright and garish present: gangs of young 'uns rolling
about, arm in arm, laughing; people hurrying about their
business; other people standing and looking this way and
that as though stunned into a coma by the bustle, the flash-
ing coloured neon in mid-afternoon, the roar of the traffic
round Eros.

The evening papers are full of scandal. The Minister
who lied to the House of Commons has resigned. It seems
it's like they say: it doesn't matter what you do as long as
you don't get found out. Now the press is really digging the
dirt, raking up all kinds of names to add to the established
cast of Profumo, Christine Keeler and Stephen Ward. Just
who's been doing what with whom is hard to fathom,
though it's obvious there's been enough shagging around
to keep public interest on the boil and your man in the
street in a tizzy of righteous indignation about his so-
called betters' behaviour. Will Macmillan resign now?
Will the government fall?

'Bloody animals. They ought to be burnt, the lot of 'em,' a
bloke standing next to me says to his wife.

'C'mon, 'Erbert,' she says, 'the lights have changed.'

To red, for some. How many hearts are going pit-a-pat at
the thought of where the mud might land next? And what
are our little blemishes when there's all this going on?

'Donna Pennyman, the well-known stage and television
actress, has left her London flat and is staying for an
indefinite period at her parents' house in Cornwall. Yesterday, Miss Pennyman confirmed rumours that she is
expecting a child – her first – in the autumn, but refused
to name the father. Mr. Victor Brown, a close friend of
Miss Pennyman's, said in a statement to the Daily Sewer,
"Yes, it's true that I've left my wife, but I haven't seen Miss
Pennyman for a couple of months." Before her departure
for Cornwall, Miss Pennyman was seen around in fashion-
able television circles with Mr. Clive Carter, the TV
director, with whom, two years ago, she shared a flat for
several months.'

Crossing over to walk up Shaftesbury Avenue, I realize I'm feeling randy; a vague, generalized randiness that's centred on nobody in particular. (Oh, I want Donna, but there's more to that than the simple animal feeling that your privates are hanging out and painted red.) I turn into Soho and when the first magazine shop looms up, its lighted window papered from top to bottom, side to side, with tit, bum and come hither looks, I stop and stare in, torn between two poses for the sake of passers-by: one the gormless surprise of a chap who's never seen anything like it before, the other amused condescension at the blatant display; and ending, I suppose, at the simple truth that I'm yet another bloke enjoying a free eyeful. There's Cinerama on at the corner, which will be good clean fun for all the family, but I haven't time for that with having to see Fleur. I could kick myself for not going the whole hog with her while I had the chance. I have too much conscience for my own good. But if I didn't at the time – couldn't, I suppose – there's no use regretting it now. All the same, I'm wishing quite a lot that she wasn't otherwise engaged tonight.

I come on a strip club through the mixed smells of coffee and cooking and the tout gives me the spiel as my eyes slide sideways over the several square yards of photographed flesh framing him in the doorway.

'Continuous show,' he says. 'All live. Best looking girls in town. Latest Continental routines.'

Now what does the lying sod mean by that? 'How much?' I ask him.

'Membership and admission, a pound . . . Do you like coloured girls?' he goes on, when I don't bite, thumbing at a picture of a black lass with enormous knockers, and nipples like organ stops. He knows I can't meet his eyes and he's careful to look anywhere but directly at me as he gives with the patter.

Oh, what the hell! I think. I'm in the mood and it'll pass an hour.

'Where do I pay?'

'See the young lady, downstairs.'

The young lady turns out to be an anaemic-looking bottle-blonde, with dark in the roots of her hair, sitting in a cubby-hole at the turn of the steep narrow staircase. She puts her fag in a scruffy little bakelite ashtray, takes my quid, and points to an open register with a long red nail on a nicotine-stained finger, all the while, like the tout on the door, never looking directly at me. With the tout it'll be deliberate policy, but I reckon she just couldn't care less; she'll see 'em come and she'll see 'em go, and the only thing that matters is what they have in common – a liking for looking at bare flesh and ready money in their hands. I hesitate just long enough for her to realize I'm not signing my real name, then write, 'Vernon Broadbent, 36 Heseltine Rd, Huddersfield.', and go on down, hoping that if there is such a guy at such an address my making free with his name won't rise up to embarrass him sometime in the future.

The cellar's tiny and hot and dark. I stand for a couple of seconds accustoming my eyes to it then move to a chair at the end of a row. You don't look round much in these places – or you don't if you're as self-conscious as I am – but I reckon more than thirty in here would class it with the Black Hole of Calcutta. The blokes on the front row could reach on to the little stage and touch the performers. I wonder what precautions the management take against some bod breaking out in a muck sweat and running amok. A couple of bruisers in the back, probably. You feel uneasy here, on the fringes of God knows what, with one false step between you and a short slide out of all the light and warmth and goodness you've ever known. Perhaps it's this that stops me feeling any excitement over the birds on the stage; or maybe it's because, despite it, the show itself is so seedy and dull. The woman up there when I come in is doing a routine with an imitation snake, a stuffed object like the draught excluder Ingrid's mother used to roll behind their front-room door, only three times as long. She sways from side to side, knockers swinging, pulling this thing up between her legs and across her chest, holding her head away and giving it frightened looks, though of course it's not putting a dicky bird into the act itself. Then she manages to get it coiled round her and the lights go out as she sinks to the stage and surrenders to its loathsome embrace.

There are two of them next, in a mistress-and-maid act, involving a bit of tickling-up with a feather duster and ending with them both stripped off and squaring up for what looks like a lesbian session, only of course, we don't see that. If this is what they're importing from the Continent, I think, it's time they sent it back. Eventually the coloured bird comes on and she's a distinct improvement. She does a straight strip with nice style, and somebody's shown a bit of imagination in picking her underwear. When she uncovers she makes a great play of running her hands up over her ribs and lifting her big boobs and holding them as though she's offering them to the audience. But when you look at her eyes they're blank. I begin to wonder what you'd see there if she let her thoughts show, and when I realize that I don't want any woman to think about me what I think she's thinking about all of us, I decide I've had enough.

It won't do, I tell myself, out on the street again. I could drift now, down, down, down; paying for a bit when I can't get it free, looking at pictures and wanking when I can't get either. All this sex for sale around me; all that frustration bottled up inside the customers. Where's the genuine warmth in somebody's eyes, the touch of a loving hand?

I go through to Charing Cross Road and wander along looking into the windows of the bookshops. When I come to Foyle's I go in, walking about for a bit among the shiny piles of new books on the ground floor, then going right to the top of the building to browse my way down through the various specialized departments until it's time to go and see Fleur. And then an annoying thing happens. I lose all real sense of time and it's not till they start closing down round me that I realize my watch has stopped somewhere along the way and started again.

I'm already late. My first thought is to get a taxi, but it's come on to rain while I've been inside and they're all trundling past, busy. So I take a gander at the Underground map in the back of my diary to see what's the best way of getting to there from here, and run for the station.

It's half-past six by the time I'm standing on Fleur's step, in the pouring rain, my hair soaked already in the short walk to the house. I press the middle bell, feeling hot, flustered and foolish. When, eventually, she comes down and opens the door, I start to apologize.

'I'm sorry, Fleur. My stupid watch stopped and started again.'

'I thought you weren't coming.'

'You would. Am I too late?'

'No, no. Come up. I've just got out of the bath.'

She's in a long robe. Her thick glossy red hair is pinned up loosely and I see damp tendrils of it escaping at the back as I go upstairs behind her. I think I should have kissed her hello as soon as I got in – it's nice to keep these little intimacies going – but that moment's passed and when she turns to face me again on the landing she's brisk and practical.

'You're wet through. Take your coat off and dry your hair in the bathroom. I must go and get dressed.'

I towel my hair and comb it in the steamy, scented atmosphere of the bathroom. When I come out she calls to me.

'Can you find yourself a drink?'

'I'm okay for a minute.' I go and lean against the wall by the open door of the bedroom, hearing the rustle and swish as she moves about, dressing. 'I'm sorry I was late,' I say again. 'Daft thing to happen.'

'That's all right. Only I've got somebody calling for me at seven. Was it something special you wanted to see me about?'

'The same old subject.' As if she didn't know.

'I see. Any developments?'

'I hoped you might be able to tell me that. Have you heard from her lately?'

'I had a letter at the beginning of the week.'

'I see . . .'

'There's some whisky in the living-room. I shan't be long now. I'm just putting my face on.'

Dismissed, I go and find the Scotch and pour myself a dollop. What news has she got that makes her stall? I walk up and down with the glass in my hand until Fleur comes in. Then I just have to stand and gawp at her in admiration. The scooped-out neck of her long dress shows the cleft of her breasts and a heavy, musky scent comes up out of the warm valleys of her body. What a smasher she is; a real beaut. Too, too far out of my league. And Conroy's as well. Which, I think now, is a fact Albert must have faced and accepted some while ago. All the same, she does like me more than she does him, because she told me so once; and a bit more single-mindedness on my part would have got me between the sheets through there. I'm sure of it. But that was then, and standing here looking at her now I feel all big boots, shrunken sleeves and clumsy red hands. A peasant looking at a princess.

'You look good enough to eat,' is all I can think of to say.

'Do I?'

'Going somewhere posh?'

'A dinner party. But I'm hoping it might lead to some more work.'

'Are you doing all right?'

'I can't complain.'

'Shall I pour you a drink?'

'Just a tiny one, please.'

'Did Donna have anything in particular to say?'

'She's quite definitely pregnant.'

'Ah!' I'd come to accept that but it's still a bit of a jolt to have it confirmed.

'Is Carter down there?'

'She didn't say.'

'Do you ever see him?'

'No, we don't move in the same circles.'

I hand her the glass, 'All I want to know, really, is does he know about the kid and are they getting together again.'

'That I can't tell you. Why don't you let it go, love?'

'I've got to get myself sorted out.'

'Is it really all over between you and your wife?'

'Yes, all finished. Bar a bit of shouting.'

'You're an attractive man, Vic. You'll find somebody else. If that's what you want. You're not much of a loner, are you?'

'I'd like her address, Fleur.'

'Oh, I'm not sure I –'

'You can't deny me that.'

'I'm not sure she'd want me to give it to you.'

'I can't leave it like this, Fleur. It's unfinished business.'

'But surely if she'd wanted you to know what she was doing and where she was she'd have written to you when she left.'

'Pregnant with another bloke's baby? How do you explain a thing like that?'

'You want to make her, though, don't you?'

'What?'

'Explain. You want her to justify herself to you.'

'I don't know what I want, Fleur. Or what she wants. I can't just close the book on it. Not like this.'

'I think you're being very foolish to yourself.'

'Maybe I'm built that way.'

'All the same, after the way she treated you . . .'

'What way? Don't you like Donna? I thought you were mates.'

She shrugs. A thought comes. 'If I didn't know you better I'd think you were jealous.' I blush for my stupidity as she comes round from putting her glass down to face me.

'Would you, indeed?'

'I'm sorry. That was a daft thing to say. What have I got that you could be interested in?'

The hoity-toity look slips off her face. 'Oh, you'd be surprised.'

She *does* fancy me, I think, astonished again, because though I've had hints of it before I'm always stunned by every fresh sight of her. She fancies me in a way I've always thought only men could fancy women, in straight-forward lust. One part of me says it can't be as simple as that, and another tells me it's got to because what else could be possible?'

'Look at you, then look at me,' I say to her. 'If you think I don't fancy hopping into bed with you you're dead wrong. But you're out of my class.'

'You could have let me be the judge of that.'

'Oh, I reckon five thousand a year would work wonders on my self-confidence, but I'm just a dogsbody draughtsman, love. I hardly earn a quarter of that.'

'Who's talking about permanent arrangements?'

'You mean the occasional one-night stand?'

That upsets her enough to fetch the colour. 'I wouldn't have put it quite like that.'

'No. And I'm sorry again.' I really am. Here I'm being offered a consolation prize that any number of men would grab my hand off for and all I can do is go on pining for the thing I can't have.

'I still don't understand why me. You can take your pick.'

'Oh, stop running yourself down. All the things you're saying apply to you with Donna as well, don't they?'

'Her pastures aren't as lush as the ones you're grazing on.'

'She comes from a better background than I do.'

'Mebbe so. And you know, we really had something going together for the short time it lasted. We really did.'

'I shouldn't count on getting it back. You'll just make yourself more miserable.'

'We'll see. Give us the address, Fleur.'

The doorbell rings.

'That will be for me. Would you like to go down and let him in?'

'If you'll give me the address I'll do that and then scarper.'

She gets her handbag, taking out the letter and a ballpoint. She copies the address on to a slip of paper.

'Thanks. Have a nice time.' I pocket the piece of paper and step towards her, putting my hands on her shoulders. 'You won't miss me for a minute after I leave here. But thanks all the same. I really mean that.' As I lean to kiss her cheek that warm scent hits me again and my imagination flashes up umpteen voluptuous pictures to the half-second. 'God, it really is a shame, Fleur. And I must be out of my mind.'

'I think I must be out of mine, to get myself into a situation where a man can talk to me like that.'

I have to laugh at the wry voice. 'Especially a fifty-bob peasant like me, eh?'

I look at her, grinning, until her mouth starts to twitch and she smiles as well.

'That's better. That's more like it.'

'Go on,' she says, 'clear off, and let my man in.'

I retrieve my raincoat from the bathroom and go down stairs as the bell rings for the third time. I let him in, a bloke in a pink shirt and a handstitched thigh-length suede top-coat. 'For Fleur Dunham? She says will you go up.' A foreigner, I think, from the colour of his skin and the weight of his after-shave. 'Two sweet-smelling people together . . .' I sing under my breath as I go out again into the rain. Oh, but I am a bloody fool.

4

One night in the next week, at a bit of a loose end, I drop into the Odeon in Longford and see a picture called *The L-Shaped Room*. When I get home I find Conroy downstairs watching television, not in Mrs. Witherspoon's kitchen, but in the dingy little hole with a bob-in-the-slot electric fire and couple of wooden-armed easy chairs she calls the Guests' Lounge. He waves an open pint bottle of light ale at me and I go next door to the dining-room for a glass, pour myself a drink and sit down with him.

It's some sort of play he's watching and I don't disturb him by talking, but sprawl in the chair, half looking as I brood about the picture I've seen, and wondering at one daft moment what I'll do if Donna suddenly pops up on the screen.

When it's over Conroy gets up and switches off the set then looks round at me and says something.

` 'What?'

'I said don't pick your nose. Ma Witherspoon's swept up in here.'

'Ah! Have you got a record of Brahms' D Minor Piano Concerto?'

'No, why?'

'It's the theme music in a picture I've just seen.'

'Good, was it? The picture, I mean?'

As a matter of fact, it was all a bit too near home for it not to have upset me. It's about this bird who's pregnant by a bloke she doesn't want to marry. When she holes up out of the way, in the L-shaped room, she gets fallen in love with by a young, unsuccessful writer bod who, after a bit of ranting when he first finds out, seems to come round to being able to overlook that she's carrying somebody else's kid. Then, of course, it all turns out sad in the end.

'Why?' asks Conroy, when I've given him a run-down of the story.

'Oh,' I shrug, 'he just slopes off. Can't cope with it at the finish.'

'Can't blame him, I suppose.'

'Well, if he really wanted her . . . And it wasn't as if she'd copped for this other bloke's kid while she was already thick with him.'

'With who?'

'This writer bod – Tony.'

'Oh! Well, I suppose that does make a bit of difference.'

''Course it does. One's a past mistake. The other's a straight kick in the teeth.'

'Supposed to be forgiven for your past mistakes, are you?'

'It'd be a damn' sorry world if a lot of us weren't. Anyway, like you say, there is a difference.'

'Yes. And very few things in this life come perfect and gift-wrapped. You've got to decide what you want, then get off your arse and go and find if it's available.'

Which could be one way of telling me I'm getting too wet to be fit company, and it's about time I either put up or shut up.

But what am I going to say to her now that I've got her address? Is there anything she wants to hear from me? I get out the letter she wrote to me after she'd left Longford for London. 'If I say that I don't want you to leave your wife for me you'll think that I never had any real feeling for you, which isn't true. It would never work for us . . . If you decide to come and see me here I'll be glad. If you don't I'll miss you terribly, but understand.' I never answered that and, of course, it was written

55

before she got pregnant and ran for cover without another word. Does she know that I went to Fleur's that time to look for her? That I know about the baby? *It would never work for us.* But she still wanted to see me, even though she was seeing Carter as well, and I didn't go till it was too late. So if there's to be a move it's got to come from me.

I have two or three goes before I manage anything I'm at all satisfied with, and then I've got it pruned to the bare essentials: 'Dear Donna, I got your address from Fleur and I practically had to prise it out of her, so don't blame her if you didn't want me to have it. I left Ingrid some time ago. It wasn't your fault. Knowing you just brought to a head what had been festering underneath for a long time. I'm afraid she's very angry and bitter, though. She went so far as to set a private detective on to watch me and now she says she's going to name you. I don't know if she means it or not but I thought you ought to know. I'm sorry about it. I expect you've got enough on your plate without that. (I found out who wrote those anonymous letters, by the way. I'll tell you all about it some time.) The Palace is closed for internal alterations. All very sad when you remember last winter. Fleur seems well, and as beautiful as ever. Don't you get up to London these days? I'd love to know how you are. Will you write to me? Love, Vic.'

Posted, it becomes something done. Just what, I can't tell. But the thought of her opening and reading it brings some of the old excitement to churn my stomach and sharpens my memories of our time together. She never pushed, I remember; always leaving the moves to me. Now I wonder if that was less consideration for my situation than a knack of living in the present, and once I was out of her sight I dropped out of her mind as well. How special to her were all those special things between us?

In the meantime. I have to go up north again to sort out my affairs. 'Breaking up your home,' the Old Lady calls it when, after a lot of hum-ing and ha-ing she agrees to take some of the furniture from the flat into her house. These are moves which say no turning back, and that's what she doesn't like. She'd have preferred everything to hang fire against the day when I came to my senses and Ingrid and I got together again. With the flat gone she knows that'll be all the harder.

I've had a brainwave and remembered an old mate of mine, Willy Lomas, who has a little plumbing business and runs an old Morris van. Like a sad clown to look at, Willy; white-faced, dark hair slicked straight back, mournful in his speech. Married now. I had an idea in the old days, when we used to look the talent over at the Gala Rooms on Saturday nights, that Willy would end up saddled with some great mountain of a woman who'd lay the law down to him for the rest of his natural.But the wife he's got is thin and dark, nearly like a sister to look at, with an odd and striking prettiness when the light catches her face in a certain way. Willy asks no questions till we've walked round the corner to the boozer.

'I heard you'd left the district.'

'I have. I'm working in Longford, in Essex.'

'Aye. You're not wanting me to shift your stuff all the way down there, are you?' His little joke.

'No. Some to my mother's, some to Ingrid's mother's, depending on what she wants.'

'Ah!'

'We've spilt up.'

'I didn't know that. I'm sorry to hear it.'

'It's my doing.'

'Somebody else, is there?'

'Not exactly. It's hard to explain.'

'Just want to be your own boss again, is that it?'

'I do as far as Ingrid's concerned.'

Willy empties his glass. 'Get it off, then.'

'Steady on!'

'What's up? Don't you like it?'

''Course I like it. And I like to taste it as it goes down.'

Willy, I'd forgotten, sups ale better than anybody I've ever known, putting it away as though he's got hollow legs, and never turning a hair. Very fond of the pictures, too, at one time. He saw just about everything that came round. Now, I reckon, he'll be like most other people, putting his feet up on a night and making do with what's on the box: *Bonanza, Dr Kildare, Bootsie and Snudge*, and all that. I wonder if he and his missis saw Donna. All those millions, probably, who did see her, while I'm craving for a sight of her and missed her. It's odd, when I think back, how Willy's been around at crucial times in the story of Ingrid and me. He was in the pub by the Gala Rooms the Boxing Day Chris got married and I made a first definite move by going to look for Ingrid. And later, when everything had changed and I didn't want her in that way any longer, but knew she was still available, it was Willy I went to because I was too embarrassed to go into a shop and ask for french letters. If Willy had happened to have one on him that night could it have turned out that I might never have put Ingrid up the stick, never got myself into the corner where I had to marry her; that all this grief and woe would have been avoided? It hardly bears thinking about. I've always looked at it as some bigger, deeper matter of cause and effect – crime and punishment, sometimes, even – as though it was somehow inevitable that I had to pay for messing about with her like I did; that I only got what was coming to me, though there were thousands more who got away with it. But such a litle practical thing might have changed it all. And now Willy's in on the end, at the dissolution of the happy home.

I'm quiet for so long thinking all this that Willy finally says, 'You're not very talkative.'

'No. I was just thinking.'

'Oh?'

'It's funny how things turn out.'

'Ah!'

'How are you doing, anyway?'

'Oh, keeping my head above water.'

'Above Tetley's bitter, you mean.'

'Oh, no. I only go out drinking once a week now. I can't afford any more because I like a lot.'

'Isn't business all that good?'

'It's okay, but we've got to take it easy till we get built up a bit more. There's things I want. A better house for Margaret, some premises and a yard. It's early days yet, and I've seen too many blokes come a cropper through getting big ideas too soon.'

'We didn't have a care in the old days, did we?'

'Course we did. We were allus looking for summat, weren't we? Down the Gala Rooms, Saturday night, weighing the crumpet up, disappointed nine times out of ten.'

'Oh, you're admitting it now, then?'

'What?'

'You allus used to reckon you were fighting it off.'

'I had me share,' says Willy, a touch of the old bullshit merchant showing through. 'But you can't carry on like that all your life. Besides, it's all changing now. There's a different generation coming up. Pop groups, long hair. They make me feel like an old man.'

'Aye, me an' all.'

'Anyway, I'm all right now. Like I say, if I can build up a nice little business, get a decent semi and a car; a couple of kids in a year or two, that's all I want.'

'You've got it all worked out.'

'Barring accidents.'

'Yeh, barring them ... I'm working with Albert Conroy and Jimmy Slade again. D'you remember them?'

'No. I didn't know any of your mates at Whittakers. I was just a City and Guilds type, black hands and overalls.'

'I didn't know you cared.'

'Oh, aye. I come from a rough family, Vic. Youngest of five, me mother a slut, me father never working unless he was forced. I've a brother who's done time, and a sister whose kids have been in juvenile court because she's separated from her husband and likes owt in a bottle, specially if it's summat in trousers 'at buys it for her. But me, I've got a good wife and I'm going to end up with summat solid behind me.'

'You'll end up richer than any of us.'

'That's as maybe. I don't need a lot to make me happy and I know how to look after what I have got.'

'I'm not exactly crying for the moon meself, kid. Only I want what I get to be the right thing for me, because the wrong thing's pure bloody murder.'

Which is all riddles to Willy because he doesn't know the full tale. And there's not much he could say if he did, so I don't try to tell him. But just keeping pace with him as he sinks pints to a steady rhythm, with no noticeable effect, is enough to get me slightly sloshed and bring to the top all the wanting her that I usually manage to keep down to a manageable background ache, and I wish – I wish, I wish, I wish – she was here with us, perched up on her bar stool, sipping her Scotch and dry ginger and lighting her cigarettes the way I remember, a little frown between her eyes as Willy and I lay on the Yorkshire thick for her benefit, the grin eventually breaking through as she realizes she's being gently sent-up.

When Willy asks me back round to his place for a bit of supper I'm tempted to say no, being not much in the mood for happy families. But then I think of the alterna-tive waiting at home and change my mind. His house is a one up and one down in Kitchener Street, an area that looks from the rows of empties to be ready for demoli-tion.

'Looks as though they'll be turfing you out afore long, Willy.'

'Aye, they're all for the bulldozer.'

'I've just let a flat go that I might have got you.'

'Naw. The rent here lets us save a bit. By the time they get round to pulling this down, in another twelve months, I'll have the deposit for our own place.'

Cosy enough, though, even if you have to go across the yard to splash your boots, and lug the zinc bath up out of the cellar to have a good soak. And clean as a new pin, like Willy's missis, who moves about between sink cor-ner and table, saying little, her long legs in sheer nylons, feet tucked into slippers with pink nylon fur on them, as she boils the kettle, warms plates and butters bread before sharing out the fish and chips we've brought in. 'Bill', she calls Willy, in her calm, quiet voice. Well, that's between them, and he doesn't seem to expect me to change old habits at this stage. I'm just pleased to see the old sod so happily settled. Here I am, I tell myself, having lately broken up my own marriage and enjoying myself in theirs. The trouble is, I'm a sucker for the institution. Oh, I am, I really am.

Willy watches as I fall on the fish and chips and wolf them down.

'You look to be enjoying them.'

'Best fish and chips I've tasted in months.'

'Aye, it's a good shop.'

'Fish and chip shops are a bit thin on the ground down Longford way,' I tell him. 'And good ones are scarcer still. Rock salmon and batter like Yorkshire pudding, Ugh!'

Willy's wife laughs.

'You should go into business,' Willy says. 'You'd make a fortune.'

'Nay, Willy, it's the same as their ale, lad. They seem to like it that way.'

'What about this little job, then?' he asks after a while. 'How long are you stopping at home?'

'Till Sunday.'

'We can mebbe get it done Sunday morning then. Will that suit you?'

'There's no great hurry if it's inconvenient. I thought you could p'raps do it in your own time.'

'Sunday's the best day. And I shall need a hand with the lifting.'

'Aye, right enough.'

I wonder now what made me think I could get round it without facing Ingrid's mother.

'Who wants to speak to her?' she asks, in her 'this is the Rothwell residence, her ladyship is resting' voice, though I'm damned sure she knows who's talking to her.

61

'It's Vic.'

'Oh' – a short pause for effect – 'I'll see if she's available.'

I feel for some more coppers during a wait that starts my fingers tapping on the coin box. Then there are voices just within range of their receiver: 'Mumble, mumble . . . have to talk to him.' 'Just as you like . . ., mumble . . .'

She comes on. 'Hello?'

'Ingrid, it's Vic. About all the stuff in the flat . . .'

'Yes?'

'I've found a bloke who'll shift it for us, only he'll have to do it tomorrow morning.' No answer. 'Are you there?'

'It's a bit short notice, isn't it?'

'If we can get it done with I can let the landlord have the keys. I'm paying rent while ever there's furniture in.'

'But I don't know what I want, what there's room for here.'

'Me mother's got a room I can shove what you leave in. I just don't want you to think you're not getting your fair share. So long as I get my radiogram and records you can have the lot for me.' No answer again. 'What do you say?'

'It's all in a rush, like everything you do.'

'Look, we've been into all that. Let's be practical. If you and your –' I'm beaten by the pips and shout 'Hang on' into a phone that's still dead when I've pushed in another two pennies. Button B gives me nothing back so, swearing, I find a bob and start afresh.

'Hello?' The old dragon again.

'We got cut off.'

'Ingrid's gone up to her room.'

In tears, I suppose. 'We hadn't finished.'

'I don't want to fetch her to the phone. She's upset.'

'I'm sorry.'

'Don't say things you don't mean.'

'I'm sorry she's too upset to talk. I've got to get this sorted out this weekend because it's likely I shan't be coming up again for a while.'

62

'There's nothing to bring you, I suppose.'

'Well, I certainly don't want to be spending all that money on fares and trailing all this way just to sort out a couple of roomfuls of furniture.'

'You'd better say what you want her to do, then.'

Grudging, but better. 'If she'll go round to the flat and make a list of what she wants I'll call and collect it before we start in the morning.'

'You mean you'll come here?'

'I shall have to anyway, to help this chap with the lifting.'

'You're not employing a firm, then?'

'It's too complicated. They'd probably want a couple of weeks' notice, and then do it when I'm not here.'

'If you'd got to do it it would have been more considerate to have done it after dark, instead of on a Sunday morning, with all the neighbours in their gardens to see what's going on.'

'It'd give 'em more to talk about if we pottered about at going up to midnight, like a moonlight flit.'

'Oh, well, you'll get your own way, I suppose, as usual.'

'I'm only trying to do what's best for everybody.'

'After having done what you think is best for yourself.'

Oh, not all that. Not on the phone.

'Look, I shall have to go. I've no more change. Will you tell her to go round and make a list?'

But I'm talking to myself. The line's dead. She's quietly hung-up on me.

My own mother's not spreading much sweetness and light, either.

'Well,' she says when I get in from the callbox, 'have you made your mind up what you're going to do?'

'I'm going to take a bloody great bomb and go round there and blow the lot to smithereens.'

'Talk like that won't get you anywhere.'

'It helps to relieve my feelings.'

Well, I say so, but all it does really is encourage them. Take it easy, I tell myself. Get this one last job done and it's the end of the road for you and Ma Rothwell. You won't have to lay eyes on her or listen to her yapping ever again.

'Where's the morning paper?' I ask the Old Lady as she potters in and out of the kitchen, laying the table and making the dinner.

'Your father has it.'

'And where's he?'

'Sitting out, at the back.'

I go and find him, in a chair at the foot of the back steps, with a rug over his knees.

'Dad.'

'Hello, lad.'

'How are you this morning?'

'Oh, fair to middling.'

'Have you finished with the paper?'

'Aye, take it. There's nowt in it but muck and scandal.'

I lift the paper off his knee and glance at the headlines. We're quiet for a minute, the warm sun on us.

'This chap Ward. He's got this practice as a . . . what is it?'

'Physiotherapist.'

'Aye. An' he can draw a good likeness. What's he want to be livin' off loose women for?'

'Looks as if they're going to do him for it.'

'His posh mates'll be a lot of good to him now. Anyway, it strikes me they're mostly tarred wi' t'same brush. An' them's your so-called betters.'

'He's mebbe carrying the can back for the lot of 'em.'

'I dare say. If he's the only one they can pin owt on it's hard lines for him. On the other hand, if he'd lived a decent life he wouldn't be in trouble now.'

'I don't see what he's supposed to have done that's so bad.'

'Don't you? Well, I'm not all that old, but it wasn't much afore my time 'at they were buying an' selling young lasses barely in their 'teens.'

'These lasses are loving every minute of it. Yesterday they were nobody, now they're famous.'

'The law's the law. That law wa' passed for a good purpose and if yon' Ward's broken it he'll have to pay. An' don't tell me to wait an' see if he's guilty. They're setting their stall out. They've been made to look silly. Ministers sleeping with women 'at's sleepin' wi' Russians. State secrets for bedroom talk. Lying to the House o' Commons. When folk like that are shown up they look round for somebody they can make pay. If he'd been satisfied to use the gifts God gave him, 'stead o' providing women for his society friends, they'd have had to find somebody else to make an example of, or do wi'out . . .' He stops and coughs. 'An' it's a stupid feller 'at can't profit from somebody else's example.'

I've a strong feeling that's one for me, but I can't resist asking, 'What d'you mean?'

'I mean 'at there's only one way to live your life, and that's so's nobody can point the finger at you; whether it's a bobby or your next-door neighbour.'

'Oh, come on, Dad, you've lived long enough to know it's not always as easy as that.'

'Who said owt about it being easy?' A pause. Another cough. 'Still, I reckon you've more experience in these matters than I have.'

It's a snide crack, more the Old Lady's style than his. You could always rely on his common sense to balance the Old Lady's sermonizing, and I wonder, while my reaction swings between sad and mad, whether it's the shock of the stroke that's turned him sanctimonious.

'I'm getting a couple of whores next week,' I tell him.

'Nay, lad, there's no need for talk like that.'

'Isn't there? I thought there was.'

'I just want to know if you think she's worth it, this woman you've thrown Ingrid over for.'

'What do you know about her?'

'Only what your mother's told me. What Ingrid told her.'

'Aye, well . . .'

'If it's not the truth, you'd better tell me what is.'

'I didn't throw Ingrid over because of her. I haven't *got* her.'

65

'You're well shut, from all I hear.'

'That's as maybe.'

'I can't fathom what you do want. I can't make you out at all.'

'I'll tell you what I want, and it might surprise you. I want a clean and decent life.'

'Then what the hangman –'

'I made some promises when I married Ingrid. And I'm getting out now, before I break 'em again.'

'You seem sure you will break 'em.'

'I am sure. As sure as God made little apples.'

The Old Lady calls as she passes the doorway. 'You'd better be coming in, you two. Dinner's ready.'

The Old Feller's got his eyes fixed, brooding, on the garden. 'That grass needs cutting.'

'I'll do it this afternoon.' I take the rug from round his legs and fold it, watching as he puts his hands on the chair arms to pull himself up, then relaxes back again. 'Can you manage the steps?'

He says something, low but hard, that I don't catch.

'You what?'

'Settled,' he says. 'I want to see things settled.' I stand there holding the folded rug, warm from the sun, and wait for him to go on. 'A business like this –' he waves his hand at himself ' – it shakes you. You know you're not a spring chicken any longer, but you somehow never expect owt so . . . so drastic. You start to tidy up. In your mind, I mean. Make a sort of balance-sheet.'

'If you take it easy for a while you'll soon be your old self again.'

'Nay, lad, don't start humouring me. I'm bloody done for. I might live another ten year, but I'm still knackered. And I want to see things *right*. Your mother an' me, we started our family a bit late – least, I did, 'cos I'm older than her – an I allus knew I might not see a litter o' grand-bairns laiking round me knee. But I thought things were set on t'right course. Our Christine seems happy wi' David; our Jim's studying hard for his own choice o' future; an' you looked content enough after a shaky start. But now ...'

'I'm sorry, Dad. I really am.'

'But are you going to spend all your life pining for summat you'll never find?'

'I don't know. But I never will know if I never try.'

'Did somebody let you *down*? Was there some other advice one of us could have given you?'

'Dad,' I say to him, 'I went into that Register Office with Ingrid with me heart in me boots. If just one of you that I care about – you, or me mam, or our Christine – had said even then, "Look, if this is not what you really want, there's no need for it," I'd have turned round and walked out and left her.'

He nods and breathes out 'Ah!' on a little sigh.

'Did you hear me, you two men?' the Old Lady says from the doorway. 'Your dinner's on the table.'

The Old Feller clamps his hands round the arms of the chair and pulls himself up. I give him a lift under one elbow.

'Aye, well,' he says when he's on his feet, 'it's a shame . . . But as long as we know . . .'

5

Ma Rothwell, if you ask me, is a woman in a bit of a quandary. She never did care much for me. I certainly wasn't her choice for her little girl, and I reckon she'd have seen that any kind of normal courtship, even, would have suffered heavy weather. But the fact that *I* don't want *Ingrid*, that I'm the one who's done the walking out, sticks in her craw. She might be thinking privately that it's all for the best and that Ingrid, at her age and without any kids hanging round her neck, has still got plenty of time to find somebody more her own class; but her pride's been got at, she can see that Ingrid's miserable, and she just can't help re-casting me as Chief Swine, a part she's had no bother at all seeing me in since Ingrid first told her I'd put a bun in her oven; since I talked back and even sometimes argued with her, when anybody brought up decent would have recognized the commonsense in what she was saying; since I got so stinking drunk I was sick over the back of her settee; since Ingrid fell downstairs and lost the baby (somehow as much my fault as if I'd stood behind her and pushed); since I walked out the first time and then took Ingrid away from home to live in the flat that Chris and David got for us. Oh, but we've had some fun and games at 26, Park Drive.

Tell the truth, I've always been a bit timid of her, except when I've had a few jars under my belt, or been so mad I couldn't help speaking my piece, like she always spoke hers. And as I'm stone-cold sober just now, and in the wrong, I wish as I ring the front-door bell that it was all over, and wonder what I'm going to have to put up with before we finish the job and get clear.

She answers the door herself and looks past me with those narrow, cold blue eyes to where Willy's sitting in the van at the gate. I look her over and think she seems even more prominent in tit and bum than ever, and remembering her operation it occurs to me that she's put on weight like a neutered cat. Why doesn't she get married again herself? I wonder. She'd make a nice bouncing bedful for some middle-aged bloke who likes plenty to get hold of and could put up with her other ways. And if that sounds as if I've got a secret fancy for her myself, all I'm saying is, there's no accounting for tastes. Flip-flop, she'll go as she falls out of her corsets. She's a vulgar woman who doesn't know she is, and I'm suddenly ready to bet she'll giggle while she's taking it.

A sniff as she draws herself up is all I get for either me or the van, before she turns and walks away down the hall, leaving me standing by the open doorway, wondering if I ought to go in. Sure enough, the neighbours are out in the fine morning; one mowing his lawn, a couple washing their cars. A feller dousing a Morris Oxford in the next drive, where the Oliphants used to live, looks up at me and nods.

''Morning.'

''Morning,' I give him back,

'Grand day.'

'It is.'

I wonder if he knows who I am and think that I can't stand here like an encyclopaedia salesman much longer. I venture a step or two over the threshold, hanging about in the hall until Ingrid turns the landing and comes down the stairs.

'Oh!'

'Hello.'

'Where's Mother?'

'Kitchen, I think.'

She goes away from me. She's wearing stretch slacks, held with elastic under her instep, and a sweater, all of which show that if she might eventually run to fat like her mother she's still a long way to go. Funny to think I've forfeited my right to lay hands on her like I used to. More upsetting to know I still want to. It's been a long time and she could always turn me on that way. Till it was over.

I go to the door, feeling a right spare part, and give Willy a wave. He nods back, sitting there patient and thinking his thoughts, which he's so far kept to himself. In a minute I feel Ingrid at my side. She looks out at the van.

'Is that it? You'll do a little in a long time in that.'

'Well, it's not Pickford's but we shall manage. Have you made that list?'

'No. I didn't have time to go round. I'll come with you and tell you what I want.'

She goes out, careful not to brush against me as she passes. Is she angling after my company? Or hoping that by having the share-out face to face she'll make it so painful I'll soften and change my mind? Well, if she wants to twist the knife it's up to her. But I hope to God there'll be no tears.

The first problem is where to sit her in the van. I can't take her on my knee, like I would have at one time; so I open the passenger door and motion her in.

'I'll get in the back, Willy. Ingrid'll show you the way.'

I perch on the wheel-arch and brace myself with my legs as Willy grinds through the streets, his engine sounding more than ever like it's firing on only three cylinders. There's a stink of petrol as well and I put out the fag I've lit, not from fear of fire but because that and the fumes together are getting at my breakfast. The van's open right through and I can see Ingrid sitting there, looking straight ahead and saying nothing more than's necessary to point Willy round the right corners. I don't think they've ever met before, and I didn't introduce them. But what the hell! As far as she's concerned Willy's on my side, somebody I've no doubt poured my tale of woe out to, with no special effort to give her a good word.

'All right, Vic?' Willy asks me once as I pick myself up after he's taken a corner a bit sharpish, on a late direction.

'I'll manage,' I tell him.

Ingrid never turns her head. I once rode on a bus with her like this, looking at the back of her head, loose inside with wanting her, wondering how I could get talking to her and let her know I was living in the same world. 'You don't think I'm common?' she asked me later, the first time I dared to put a trembling hand up her skirt. No, love, not in that way. Just common in her mind, in the way she never searches for anything herself but just sits back and lets it all wash over her. Predictable's the word for the way she takes to the latest pop hit, the latest television catch-phrase, the latest block-buster film, just as easily letting them all go when the replacements come along. 'Oh, I can't take that,' she'll say about anything with any real individual flavour, 'it's weird.' But I think 'ancient' is her favourite knocking word, and anything that wasn't new yesterday comes under the heading.

Okay, okay; as long as it doesn't stunt *my* growth.

I get Willy to back the van into the drive, making it easier both to load and to get out into the street again.

I've heard of separated couples squabbling their way item by item through an inventory, in a solicitor's office, and I reckon any solicitor of mine would have gone hairless at what happens here this morning. As it is, I try to imagine Willy reporting back to his missis. 'She took the lot, love. Cleaned him out of every damn' thing except his radiogram and records. It seems he'd told her in a weak moment that she could, as long as they got the place emptied, and she took him at his word. He just stood there, looking as if he didn't know whether it was Ash Wednesday or Pancake Tuesday, and let her get away with it.'

Well, I do ask her where the hell she's going to put it all.

'We've cleared the spare bedroom. The bedroom suite and the bed can go in there. The fireside chairs in

71

Mother's dining-room are ready for replacing, so the three-piece'll come in for there. And I might have a customer for the dining-suite. I think I know somebody who's looking for one.'

Willy slips out of the room as I catch my breath. But if he's expecting an explosion, it doesn't come. I'm just too tired of it all to bother.

'You've changed your tune, haven't you?'

'I'm only going by what you said. You did say on the telephone that I could have it all, didn't you?'

'That's what I said.'

'Well, then . . .'

'I never thought I was paying two year's hire-purchase to make your mother a present of the three-piece.'

'I helped to pay for it, didn't I? And that's my home again now, so I may as well have the use of it. Some people would think you owe me that much.'

'You'll be able to tell 'em how generous I was, then. Let's get it shifted.'

'As a deserted wife I've every right to live here and use it all, so I don't see what the difference is.'

She makes it sound as if I've left her destitute with six kids in some leaky old cottage on the moors. Please enter status: 'Deserted wife.' 'Have you met my daughter, Ingrid? She's a deserted wife.' 'There goes Vic Brown, the well-known deserting husband.'

So . . . that's the way it this morning. It's as though she's had some advice: play it cool, give him no satisfaction. There are no tears, no feeling at all, in fact, except this cold distance she keeps. Is it something she's putting on, that costs her a big effort to carry? Or is it what she's finally come to after sitting down and telling herself that there's no way to make me come back? Four years of marriage laid waste behind her. Eighteen months of a kind of courtship, frustrating and hopeless for her, before that. Five and a half years with maybe hardly any time when she could honestly believe that I wouldn't rather be somewhere else. And if there were times what is there about them now that she can keep and say that it wasn't all for nothing? Because aren't they the bitterest memories, nothing more than evidence that then was when she was kidding herself most of all? She hates me for what I'm doing to her, when what she should be hating me for is ever trying to do right by her in the first place; because that's when I did her the biggest wrong.

But mistakes shouldn't be made to last forever, and one day she'll get over it. I know she will.

Willy's van being the size it is, and our furniture mostly shapes that won't tuck tidily in together, it takes us half a dozen trips to the Rothwells'. Ingrid goes back with us on the first journey and waits the other end to show us where to put everything. Of her mother there's no sign until we've carried in the last item, the living-room carpet, and dumped it in a roll in the hall. Then she comes out of the kitchen with her mouth pursed up as she nibbles something.

'That's the lot, then.'

I'm standing there wondering where Ingrid's got to, how I ought to say so-long to her, and generally feeling like a tradesman hanging back for a tip, when Ma Rothwell casually reaches out with the toe of her shoe and flips down the edge of the carpet, looking at it and then throwing a half glance through the open door of her front room. I've always been fond of that carpet. A square of peacock-blue Wilton with a little yellow fleck, it is. I remember the sleepless night buying it gave me, when I lay awake with the collywobbles, knowing we were flat stony broke till the next pay-day. Seeing Ingrid's mother in that minute, for all the world as if she's at a sale and knowing it's a bargain but will it match her curtains, something rears up in me, some last urge to have a spat at her old power to make me wish I'd never been born.

'I've changed my mind,' I hear myself say in a loud voice.

'What?'

Her head comes up and she looks straight at me for the

first time today. Ingrid, now on the stairs, freezes a step down from the landing like a character in a play who can't move till the next line's said.

'About the carpet,' I say as I realize what they both could be thinking. 'I want it meself.'

Ma Rothwell shrugs. 'That's between you and Ingrid.'

And that's how the good-byes I've been bothered about saying are left unsaid, when I grab one end of the carpet and walk out without a look back, bumping it down the steps behind me and trailing it along the path to the gate where Willy, seeing what I'm up to, comes round the front of the van and gives me a lift.

'Fuck her,' I say as we stow the carpet into the van. Willy grins.

'Where to now, then?'

'They're open. Fancy an odd one before we make the last trip to my place?'

In the pub I try to give him a couple of quid for his trouble, but he pushes it away.

'Forget it.'

'You're out of pocket with the petrol, man.'

'Say it's for old time's sake.'

I buy the ale.

'What's your mother-in-law like, Willy?' I ask him.

'Six feet under, kid.'

In a second we're laughing together and just for a while none of it seems to matter.

For a while. Because if the mood could last, which it can't, what the Old Lady says when she sees what we bring is guaranteed to turn it off.

'Is that all she's left you with?'

'It's all I wanted.'

'What's she going to do with rest of it?'

'She can do what she likes.'

'You're entitled to more than that, you know, even if you are in the wrong.'

'What I'm entitled to and what I want are two different things.'

'What you want and what you get are different, an' all.'

74

With which shaft of bleak homespun wisdom she ambles off into the kitchen.

I go upstairs to pack my bag, and plug in the radiogram, which Willy and I carried up to my old bedroom. The *Siegfried Idyll* is top of the pile of records and I put that on the turntable. Wagner composed it to celebrate the birth of his son and got a group of musicians together to play it on the stairs as a surprise for his wife, Cosima, who was Liszt's daughter. You might say he never would have written it if he hadn't pinched Cosima from Hans von Bülow, who was a mate of his and a champion of his work. But von Bülow must have been a special kind of feller because he didn't let such a rotten trick interfere with his dedication to music, and he went on conducting Wagner for the rest of his life.

I wonder as I'm shoving my kit into my case how many people all over the world are listening to this same music just this minute. I wonder if it will ever be heard again in that flat we've just emptied.

People sometimes say about present troubles 'Oh, it'll be all the same in a hundred years' time.' Well, Wagner's not around to worry, but his music is. I've got nothing like that to leave behind, and as for a hundred years, I'm more concerned with wondering what might be happening in, say, five, or ten. Perhaps if I could see so far ahead I shouldn't want to know.

Part Two

6

1963 was a year many people remember as being full of incident; a turning point in many people's lives; the end of life for some others. Stephen Ward brought his can-carrying to a stop by taking an overdose of drugs which killed him on 3 August. John F. Kennedy, President of the United States, after visiting West Berlin in June and rallying the populace with his proclamation of 'Ich bin ein Berliner', made a less obviously hazardous trip to Dallas, Texas, in November and was assassinated there on the 22nd, apparently by a disgruntled nut-case called Lee Harvey Oswald, who in his turn was shot dead while in police custody by a nightclub owner, Jack Ruby. A gang of men took two and a half million pounds off a mail train in Buckinghamshire in August. They carried out the robbery, according to some newspapers, with 'all the precision of a military operation', a phrase which amuses a number of ex-soldiers I've met, who claim that every military operation they were involved in had more the characteristics of a cock-up. I suppose it depends where you're standing at the time. Another name was entered into the annals of treachery (or ideological com-mitment, again depending where you're looking from) when Kim Philby, long-time secret agent for our side, disappeared in the Lebanon and re-emerged in Moscow, where he took Soviet citizenship in July, turning out to have been on their side all along, the mind of the average man grappling vainly with the problem of beginning to fathom a temperament that could allow someone to live a double (if not triple) life for so many years. While

Professor Buchanan was preparing his report on Traffic in Towns, Dr. Beeching was dismantling over a hundred years of railway supremacy by closing 'uneconomic' lines. It was rumoured that Elizabeth Taylor and Richard Burton would marry and, in December, Mrs. Burton got a divorce in Mexico. The first British oral contraceptive became available on prescription in June. Young people, through their music, their fashions, their spending-power began, with huge encouragement from the caterers of commerce, to shape their own life-style, a way of living in the present rather than looking back to the past of childhood or forward to the future of the adult world. The western countries began to move away from hypocrisy and into an age of candour and so-called permissiveness, an age that would eventually allow – nay encourage – an actress call Donna Pennyman to admit openly in a newspaper interview that although she had never married she was the mother of a nine-year-old boy who doted on her and was doted on in his turn.

I read the piece about Donna in a copy of that morning's *Guardian* which I've picked up at Rome Airport before taking the afternoon flight to London. On the opposite page is a goodish review of a play she's opened in in the West End and, with the interview, a picture of her that I think is very unflattering, unless she's changed a good deal, which I'm ready to accept could have happened since I've seen her only once – on the television screen – in ten years, and that in a recording of a play she'd done while I still knew her.

The heading to the interview is stretching it a bit even by the standards of *Guardian* punning. It says 'Pennyman Donna-llow', which is a reference to her not having let her acting interfere with her son's upbringing. She has, in fact, sacrificed several years of her career to stay close to him at her parents' home in Cornwall, and is only now making a return to the West End in what she hopes will be the luxury of a long run. She's apparently worked just enough for her face not to be forgotten altogether and the interviewer thinks that the lapse of years has brought her to 'a new and compelling maturity'.

I've changed myself, more than a bit. I'm no longer a twenty-six quid a week draughtsman but a six thousand a year design and development engineer who has just been out to Australia for six weeks, at the firm's expense, to supervise the installation of a dust extraction and ventilation system in a tannery and shoe-making factory outside Melbourne. 1963 was the turning-point for me, the time when I realized it was no longer possible for me to coast along, taking things as they came, as – leaving aside the upheaval of parting from my wife – I had done before. I never heard from Donna. What, when it came right down to it, was there for her to say? I mooned about, pretty hopelessly, for a couple of months, my work getting more and more slip-shod, until first Conroy and then Franklyn had to speak to me about it. It seemed to me then that the choice was between climbing and sinking. Any ambition in my trade that I might have cherished when I first went, bright-eyed and bushy-tailed, into the drawing office at Dawson Whittakers' had been diverted by the false promise of the interlude in Mr. Van Huyten's music shop, and Conroy's offer of a job with Joyce and Walstock I'd seen less as a step up than an an escape route from having to return to Whittakers' and an antidote to my restlessness in my marriage, which Mr. Van Huyten's death and my sudden loss of prospects there had seemed to make me more acutely aware of. The decisions that the past five years or so had seemed so full of were – apart again from my leaving Ingrid – not really decisions at all, in the sense of their arising from a rational assessment of my situation, but either, as in the case of my marriage to Ingrid, a consequence of error, or else opportunities which seemed to arrive according to some pre-ordained plan.

But it took a sickening tragedy really to bring me round. Driving home in the dark one Saturday night after a day at the coast, Jimmy Slade ran into the back of a lorry parked, broken-down and without lights, round a blind bend. Jimmy's parents-in-law, sitting in the back, got off with minor injuries, but Jimmy and his wife, Pamela, were dead before they reached hospital. They'd been married three months.

The senselessness of it stunned us all. But since I couldn't bring them back I asked myself what, to be self-centred, did it mean for me? It meant that I was alive and Jimmy was dead. Jimmy had died happy and I was alive and miserable. I'm not going to pretend to anything as nauseatingly sentimental and phoney as deciding I owed it to him to make something of myself; but what it did mean, it seemed to me, was that if life was all any of us had got, and that it time and again appeared senseless to the point of lunacy, then the only choice was to get out or take it by the short hairs and make it sing something at least resembling our tune.

I even read a book or two on positive thinking. And I took the drastic and positive step of enrolling for a degree course in mechancial engineering at a London Polytechnic with the idea of having a clear and useful purpose to occupy most of my spare time.

I'll try neither to minimize nor exaggerate the effort of the next three years. I'd always been pretty good at my job – any complaints were on the grounds of temporary slackness or inertia, not ability – but I knew then that I'd never really stretched myself and there was more than one occasion when I felt like turning my face to the wall.

Franklyn, after watching the seriousness of my intention over about twelve months, called me into his office.

'I admire what you're doing, Vic,' he told me, 'but you do realize that we've no scope in this set-up for a man with the qualifications you're aiming to get. We've got neither the job nor the money that goes with it.'

'I know that,' I said. 'I've thought that a change would do me good, anyway. When the right time comes.'

'I shall hate to lose you. After that month or two's

82

lapse – which was easily understandable with your domestic troubles – you really buckled down to it.' He shrugged. 'But I've never believed in holding a good man back.'

His confidence in me, which lay in his implication that I both could and would succeed, came at a crucial time, when the end of it seemed still so far away and my confidence in myself was at a lowish ebb.

My divorce from Ingrid became final a few months after I got my degree. Or, to be accurate, her divorce from me, since she brought the suit. The quickest way out in those days, before the doctrine of irretrievable breakdown, was to prove adultery, and the best way to prove that was to name names. But though Ingrid had threatened to name Donna she must have relented, because she let the required time elapse and then sued on the grounds of desertion. As I wasn't defending, there was no obstacle except the seemingly interminable time needed by solicitors to marshal a few crucial facts and the court to assess them and give judgment.

I'd been lonely, of course; but as my sexual confidence increased with my improvement in position and income I found the company and comfort of enough emancipated young women willing to hurry to my place with their diaphragms and jelly or folders of calendared pills in their handbags to stave off the worst pangs. They visited for a time and then they left. For although there were a couple of whom I became fond enough to be tempted into thoughts of a permanent relationship, always there was some reserve, some knowledge of possibilities beyond those immediately available that drew me back from the brink.

We're flying over the Alps now, in clear weather, and I fold the newspaper, unable to deny the tremble of old excitement that reading about Donna has resurrected in me, and look out at the panorama of jagged snow-topped peaks sailing by beneath us, with silver-glinting streams and torrents, and the houses of villages huddled together high on seemingly inaccessible ledges. Then I lose it as

83

the young chap sitting between me and the window leans forward as though trying to see what's directly below and thoughtlessly (or ill-manneredly, but I give him the benefit of the doubt) blocks my view. Before deciding whether or not to prod him I turn my head to see what's visible through the window on the other side, just as the empty seat across the aisle from mine is re-occupied by a bloke who's been down to the back of the cabin. Something in his profile and the set of his head tug at my memory. I'm sure I've seen him somewhere before. He's no more interested in what's outside than if we were flying over Wolverhampton and I look at him as he thumbs his way through an Italian picture-magazine which he's got from the stewardess. When he suddenly turns his face towards me I flick my gaze past him to the view of sky beyond the window. But the expression in his eyes has all at once placed him for me. I know who he must be.

He's not as good-looking as I remember his being. There's a puffiness about the cheekbones, and the way he's grown his hair to shoulder-length in an effort to keep up with the style of younger men only gives an impression of seediness, complemented as it is by a wispy gingerish excuse for a beard. But the pale, almost cream-coloured jacket he's wearing, made of some kind of very soft thin animal skin, has come from no fifty-bob tailors'.

'Excuse me,' I say. 'Aren't you Clive Carter?'

His slightly bulging blue eyes come round and look me over for what must be three clear seconds before he answers. 'Yes.'

'We met once, ten years ago, at a party in Donna Pennyman's flat in Longford. You were with Wilf Cotton, the writer.'

'Oh, yes?'

He must surely remember that, if not me.

'Vic Brown,' I tell him.

He nods. 'Yes.' But I can tell he hasn't got me, which I think is a bit odd, since I'm sure he twigged at the time

84

that Donna and I were something other than just good friends, and in fact I came near to doing him an injury because of the high-handed, not to say brutal, way he was behaving towards her.

'Have you been far?'

'Only to Rome.'

'Business?'

'I thought there might be a chance of setting up a feature film.' He says it reluctantly, as though bored out of his mind at the prospect of discussing a profession which laymen see only from the glamorous end.

'No go?'

He clears his throat and sniffs before apparently deciding that he may as well satisfy my curiosity.

'I'm not hopeful. The big money's gone. Even the days of Spaghetti Westerns and filming the Bible seem to be over. Soft porn's what they're into now and they've got their own talent for that.'

When he doesn't ask me, I say, 'I've been on a trip to Australia for my company,' and immediately think, What are you trying to do, you twit, impress the bastard? (Oh, Donna, how could you ever love both him and me? But did you ever love me as I loved you?)

'Oh?' he says. 'What did you make of it?'

'I liked Melbourne, where I was most of the time. It's clean and white, laid out like an American city, in a grid pattern, though the buildings aren't so tall and there's still a strong British feeling about the people. Not as racy and brash as Sydney.'

He nods. 'I've never fancied it much myself. Too far out of the mainstream.'

'Oh, I'm not saying I'd want to live there. Britain's still good enough for me.'

'They say their TV's a bit ropey.'

'About six channels and nothing to shout about on any of them.'

'Quite.'

He turns back to his magazine. End of conversation.

'A bit of a coincidence, really,' I say. 'I was just reading a piece about Donna in the *Guardian* before I recognized you.'

He looks at my paper, his eyes narrowing. 'May I see?'

I pass it over and wait a minute while he scans the article. I don't really know how to get to know what I want to know now, so I ask him, as if in all innocence:

'Do you see much of her these days?'

He answers me without looking up from the paper. 'I haven't seen her in years.'

And what about the kid, you cold sod? I'm thinking. Don't you ever see *him*? Don't you even send the maintenance cheque at the end of the month?

He reads quickly and grunts, 'Huh!' as he nears the end.

' "A new and compelling maturity" . . . I suppose that means she's lost her looks and will have to rely now on character parts.'

Well, maybe, I think – to put the construction a bloke like you would put on it.

His gaze lingers for a moment on Donna's picture before he passes back the paper. Time's improved his personality no more than it has his looks, or my liking for him. But though now doesn't seem the right moment to prod conversation further there are things I'm interested in knowing which only he can tell me, and I think as we begin the landing approach and the stewardess appears with her tray of boiled sweets that I might ask him to share a taxi and see what transpires from that.

By the time I've waited for my luggage, though, and checked with customs a few souvenirs that I think take me over the duty-free limit, I've lost him and it's not until I'm out of the building that I spot him again, as he gets into the back of a cab and shuts the door. I don't know who's picking up his expense account but some lurking trace of Yorkshire thrift prevents me from spending another several pounds of the firm's money on a taxi to convey me in solitary state all the way from Heathrow to town, and I board the BEA bus, to ride cheaply as far as the Cromwell Road Terminal, and take a cab from there to home.

I've dried myself after a shower and put on pyjamas and dressing-gown when I hear a key slide into the lock and the outer door open. It can only be either my cleaning lady or Miriam, and my cleaning lady comes in the morning, twice a week, never in the late afternoon. I've debated with myself often the wisdom of giving Miriam free access to the flat. She is, I have to confess, married – the only married woman I've ever had an affair with – and since she isn't always sure when she can get away from home, and I'm not always available on the phone, it was practical to let her have a key so that she could come in and wait for me. At least, she persuaded me so.

'Hi!' she says from the living room doorway. 'So the travelling man's returned safely.'

'All in one piece,' I say. 'About half an hour ago.'

I'm not altogether sure how happy I am to see her so soon. Later, yes, when my metabolism has adjusted itself to British Summer Time; but what I want now, more than anything, is a good long snooze.

Miriam moves in on me and offers her mouth, her lips opening almost immediately on contact and her tongue probing for mine. What tenderness there is in her always passes quickly over into lust and I'm aware that I'm slow on response. She drops one hand from my shoulder and into the open front of my pyjama trousers. I can never altogether resist that.

'A fellow down there seems more pleased to see me.'

'Treacherous little bugger.'

'Oh, I wouldn't have said little.'

'He thinks he should have had a topless barmaid in Wanchai.'

'Wanchai?'

'Hong Kong.'

'Oh, does he?'

'He's very undiscriminating.'

'Unlike his owner.'

'Well, rather more so, anyway.'

'Mmm . . .' She moves away from me and goes for a cigarette from the packet on the table. 'Was it a good trip?'

'Good for interest, good for business.'

'I missed you, you know. I even got the jitters a couple of times, thinking of you flying all that way.'

Love, when you spend as many hours as that in aeroplanes you forget any fear of flying. It becomes a way of life.'

'But the longer you spend in them the more at risk you are.'

'You've flown yourself, many a time. Were you really scared for me?'

'It's probably because I was totally out of touch, not knowing just where you were and what you were doing.'

'How did you know I was arriving home today?'

'You forget I've got sources of information in the corridors of power.'

No, I don't forget that.

'Anyway,' she says, 'I don't suppose you missed me for a minute, what with all those new faces and places, not to mention topless barmaids in Wanchai.'

I laugh. 'Who do you think I thought of when I lay in my lonely bed, feeling randy?'

'Are they attractive? The topless barmaids, I mean?'

'Some of them. They wear long black evening gowns that cover everything except their arms, shoulders and breasts; and they have little felt flowers over their nipples.'

I recall one girl in the bar I was in idly and totally unselfconsciously adjusting the lie of her right breast in the scooped-out neck of her frock, and giving me a cool, impersonal stare as she caught me watching.

'And did none of them offer to go to bed with you?'

'I didn't give them the chance. I just had a couple of drinks there out of curiosity.'

As a matter of fact I found the girls waiting-on in the

cocktail bar of the Hong Kong Hilton more fetching: pocket Venuses, their cheomsongs, apart from a slit to the thigh on one side, covering them from neck to toe and encasing hips and buttocks in taut green silk.

The light is coming in from behind Miriam as she stands between me and the window.

'You know, I get the feeling I can see straight through that frock.'

'You can't, can you? Do you think it's a bit much?' She stands back and surveys herself in the long wall-mirror. 'I've not looked from so far away. But you can't really see through it, you know.'

'If you think you can the effect's the same.'

'D'you think it's a bit much?' she asks again.

'That's hardly for me to say, love.'

She turns away from me, a little smile playing on her lips, and, for a moment, takes the weight of her right breast in her left hand in a movement almost identical with that of the bar-girl in Wanchai, but, unlike hers, loaded with erotic intent. Miriam's breasts were what first drew my eye to her: flattish, low-slung and bra-less, with nipples that can protrude through three layers of clothing. And she knew within seconds that I was looking, giving me that same almost-the-ghost of a knowing smile as my gaze flicked up to her face. I'd spotted the cluster of rings on her wedding finger, of course, and it struck me that she was probably no more or less than a normal faithful wife who nevertheless couldn't resist showing off wares reserved for her husband. Nor could I resist manoeuvring myself next to her, a little later, and offering to refill her glass.

'You're Vic Brown, aren't you?' she said as I handed her a hefty vodka and tonic.

'That's right.'

'My husband pointed you out to me earlier. Hedley,' she said as I was obviously not catching on. 'Hedley Graham.'

'Oh, yes, of course . . .'

For – another confession – Miriam's husband is one

of my colleagues, which does nothing to lessen the guilt I feel in making love to a married woman at all. The only factors that make our relationship possible are that Miriam is a very determined lady indeed, and Hedley Graham, not even a close colleague, let alone a friend, is a type I've found it easy all my life to dislike on first acquaintance – a cold, arrogant, sarcastic man, with a sneer for a smile, a snigger for a laugh, and an emotional make-up which seems to be turned on only by the profit and loss in a balance-sheet. That I have little to do with him, and am not junior to him either, probably saves me from exposure to the worst side of his personality, which sometimes leads him to bully anybody vulnerable in reach. I'd not met his wife before because he'd not been with this branch of the company very long.

'I'm sorry,' I said. 'I arrived too late for the introductions.'

We were giving a cocktail party for three representatives of a Belgian company who were interested in manufacturing one of our products under licence, the main problem to be thrashed out being whether we should make more profit by exporting under Common Market conditions, or through receipt of royalties from them.

'You seem,' Mrs. Graham was saying, 'to be something of an odd man out here.'

'Why is that?'

'All the others have wives with them. Couldn't yours come?'

'I'm not married.'

'Oh?' She looked me over thoroughly without seeming to do so.

'I was once, a long time ago.'

'You seem much too young to be able to say that.'

'I was much too young at the time, and it didn't last long.'

'And since then . . . nothing?'

It was said with a deceptively soft sympathetic innocence, but when I replied, 'Well, not marriage, anyway,' she knew what I meant, and she knew that I knew she knew.

'You're a Lancashire man, aren't you?'

'Please!' I raised my eyebrows. 'Yorkshire.'

'Sorry. My ears aren't attuned to so fine a difference. I could tell you were from the north, though.'

'Is it still so obvious?'

'Does it bother you?'

'Not as much as trying to say 'larst' and 'barth'. That makes me sound awfully phoney. To my ears, at any rate.'

'And you wouldn't want to be thought phoney, would you?' she said, giving me again that quick flick of a once-over.

'There's a difference between making the most of what you've got, and trying to be something you're not.'

It was several weeks later, when our relationship had progressed as far as my bed, that she said to me:

'You know, I can't understand how you can appear so young and naive and at the same time so experienced and knowing.'

'I'm never quite sure myself which is protective veneer and which solid substance,' I told her. 'Anyway, is that some kind of implied criticism?'

'No. You're knowing enough in here.'

'More instinct than experience.'

'I'll believe you, darling, where thousands would doubt.'

She was quick to twig my uneasiness about Graham, and equally quick to try to reassure me.

'He no longer really cares, sweet. His idea of making love is a grunting quickie every other week-end.'

'He's got a highly developed sense of keep off the grass, though.'

'The lawn he can't be bothered to tend and nourish properly must have care and attention from someone else.'

It was all very well for her to say that, but if I knew anything about Graham it was that he considered his property his to care for or neglect as he chose.

'It wasn't always like that,' Miriam said. 'We were quite passionate and close at first. But I suppose boredom eventually creeps into the best of relationships.'

'I've never known the best for long enough to judge.'

'Poor you.' She snuggled closer into the crook of my arm and ran her sharp fingernails lightly down my back. 'We shall have to do something about that.'

I wondered if she was just talking, or really did think that what we were embarking on was some Grand Passion.

The lad I once was would have said with glee to his mates of Miriam: 'She fucks like a rattlesnake.' I've never bothered to find out with what enthusiasm rattlesnakes do copulate but the boys would have known precisely what I meant by that colourful, if crude, description. It is, I think, all she's really interested in, apart from a change of company to eat out with, and it suits my book well enough, since I don't love her, would not miss her for very long if I never saw her again, and feel safe from any danger of lasting entanglement; though I do know an occasional twinge of apprehension when I think how the combination of her hot pants and wilful independence might lead her to some indiscretion that will shop us to her husband and involve me in a divorce case.

I'm thankful that she comes quickly and several times during any session as I withdraw and ease my weight down beside her.

'Well,' she says after a moment or two, 'I wouldn't call that the best ever, but it'll do to be going on with.'

'Jet-lag,' I say drowsily.

'Where are you going to take me to dinner?'

'How long have you got?'

'Till about ten.'

'Plenty of time, then. Mus' just have a little nap . . .'

It's as positive and irresistible as a dentist's whirlpool and as unassailable as any prolonged anaesthetic. Dreamless, too, apart from the distant dreamlike awareness of someone moving about the room, of being shaken, of my name being said over and over again, and a light somewhere being inexplicably snapped on and off, on and off. When I wake, at three in the morning, Miriam has gone, leaving a scribbled note on the pillow beside me, which is still dented with the imprint of her head: 'I can get *that* kind of thing at home! I'll ring you tomorrow.'

I feel that I ought to eat something, but I have no appetite. My hand is on the bottle to pour myself a tot of whisky when I think better of it and go into the kitchen to make myself a hot-milk nightcap, a habit I've retained from childhood and adolescence. I spoon Bournvita on to the surface of the milk and stir, thinking of music appropriately soothing. What I put on the hi-fi is Schwarzkopf's recording of Richard Strauss's *Four Last Songs*, lowering the stylus on to the *Beim Schlafengehen* track. Strauss and his adoration of the soprano voice . . . I think a little as I stretch out on the sofa of what it must be like to look back over a long lifetime of good work well done, and face the end with the serenity that this music epitomizes. I neither finish my drink nor hear the end of the record, but wake again at seven to the soft click of the stylus as it swings to and fro in the middle of the disc.

The *Guardian*, with Donna's interview in it, is crumpled under me. I open it and fold it back at the features page, smoothing it out and wondering as I do so just how far, after all, the years have taken me.

7

I'm at the office early and already behind my desk, sorting my papers in preparation for writing my report, when my secretary, Janice Wheeler, comes in. She's been caught in a shower and she fusses for a while with her raincoat, the transparent plastic hood she's worn over her hair, and a wet umbrella before, looking up from examining the back of her stockings, her gaze focuses through the open connecting door and she sees me.

'Oh, good morning! Nice to see you back.'

'Good morning, Janice.'

'Was it a nice trip?'

'Lovely.'

'Thanks for your postcard. Funny to think you've been all the way round the world while I've been sitting out there.'

'Yes, all the way round. Twenty-four thousand miles, I should think.'

'Golly! And I thought going to Minorca was an adventure.'

Janice is a girl who faces life permanently agog. Wide-eyed and expectant, she's even excited when her husband phones her unexpectedly and says he's taking her out for a meal and to the pictures. Not long married, she's obviously wonderfully happy, and though I don't fancy her that way myself, her pleasure in simple uncomplicated everyday things has led me to wonder idly what her sex life is like; whether, for instance, she's amply satisfied with the missionary position and would be shocked if her husband suggested variations. She's certainly not the young woman who thought that VAT 69 was a tax on soixante-neuf – she'd more likely guess it was the Pope's telephone number – and I don't somehow, when I think about it, like to imagine my fall in her esteem should she find out about Miriam and me.

'I hope you've not been bored to death, twiddling your thumbs, without me.'

'Oh, no! I've had plenty to do. You know what they're like when they find a secretary free. "Will you type me this? Would you mind doing that?" '

I reach down and bring up a parcel. 'Here's present for you.'

'For me?' She takes it, her fingers probing its softness. 'Can I open it now?'

'Of course.'

The sight of the silk Chinese housecoat, in silver, with gold embroidery, makes her gasp. 'Oh, I say!' She holds it up and away from her.

'Do you like it?'

'Oh, it's lovely. But it's far too much.'

'It isn't. They were so cheap in Hong Kong I couldn't resist buying it.'

'It wouldn't be cheap here. Oh, I don't know what to say.'

'Try "thank you". '

I smile as she colours up. She's too literal a person for jokes like that.

'Didn't I already say that? Thank you very, very much.'

Now she's beginning to embarrass me.

'I hope it's the right size. I had to guess.'

And a job I had, too, looking round the Chinese women assistants and realizing the impossibility of finding any comparison with Janice's willowy build.

'If I can just try it on and see . . .'

'Go ahead.'

She slips the coat on over her sweater and skirt and turns, looking down at herself and running her palms over the sheen of the silk.

'It's absolutely gorgeous. What a pity I haven't got a mirror.'

'You can admire yourself later. But it fits okay.'

'It's one of the grandest presents I've ever had.'

'Well, I tell you, it didn't cost the earth, and if your husband starts wondering I'll show him the bill.'

It's true I couldn't resist it at the price, and there was no one else I could buy one for.

'You should have saved it for somebody special.'

'You're special, love,' I tell her. 'I'm glad you like it.'

'Oh, I do. I want to run round showing it to everybody.' She turns on me a sidelong look which has in it the nearest she'll ever get to guile. 'But I think I'll just wrap it up and take it home.'

'Well, then. What's been happening that I ought to know about?'

She likes a good unmalicious gossip, Janice does, the frailties of human nature being a constant source of surprise to her, or I shouldn't invite her into the one-way process of dishing the dirt to me when all I can offer her in return is the poker-faced neutrality that befits my station. And as my mother has been heard to say: 'If you don't ask you often don't get to know.'

'Nothing much, really. A girl from Mr. Graham's office asked for her cards and left, after he'd made her cry. Pat Fraser. Do you remember her?'

'Can't bring her to mind. What did she do to upset him?'

'What does anybody have to do to upset Mr. Graham?' A moment's pause, as if she's waiting for me either to agree or reprimand her for criticizing one of her elders and betters. I do neither. 'She made some silly little accounting mistake that threw a lot of other figures out. Anybody could have done the same but he was the wrong side out and he went on and on at her, as though she'd cost the firm thousands of pounds, calling her a stupid little half-wit who wasn't fit to add up on a bead frame. In front of the whole office, too. Anyway, she finally burst into tears and ran into the cloakroom and wouldn't go back.'

'He didn't sack her?'

'No, she sacked herself. Miss Frogget from Personnel tried to calm her down but she said she didn't need their job and she wouldn't work for any firm that allowed people to treat her like that.'

'She sounds like a little ball of fire.'

'Well, then Miss Frogget went to see Mr. Graham and he said he'd be obliged if she'd leave him to handle his staff in his own way, and what she was asking him to do was – what did she say he said? – oh, yes, tantamount to making an apology. So then Miss Frogget went to see Mr. Kendall and Mr. Kendall called Mr. Graham in. Nobody knows what was said between them, but Mr. Kendall told Miss Frogget afterwards that he couldn't interfere, and Pat could go back to her job if she wanted to. But then Pat said that that was tantamount to expecting *her* to apologize, and she wasn't going to do that. So she went to the wages office and got her insurance card and left.'

'And while all this was going on she'd been sitting in the cloakroom?'

'Well, there and in Personnel.'

'Hmm . . .'

I'm a bit disappointed that the story doesn't include the appearance of Clive Jenkins on a white horse, waving the union banner, but decide that to say as much to Janice would seem decidedly facetious.

My non-committal 'Hmm' takes us as far as we can go, since Janice can hardly expect me to say that I think Hedley Graham a dog, and that Pat Fraser's husband, if she has one, ought to lie in wait for him and punch his face, though privately I think he probably did.

'Hmm . . .' Janice echoes. She clutches the housecoat, which she's rewrapped, and a small smile of pleasure comes to her face as she looks down and becomes once more aware of it.

'Is there anything special you want me to do?'

'No, just hang about till I get my things in order. You might give Mr. Kendall's secretary a buzz and tell her to tell him that I'm back and in my office writing my report if he wants to see me. The same with Mr. Taggart.'

Answering to nobody below director-level is a mark of my status which always pleases me, reminding me as it does of the extent of my rise in the world; a rise which still has the power to surprise me in the reflective hours of the day. It's solidly based – let's make no mistake – on ability; but I also had the luck to be in the right place at the right time. The North London firm I joined as a development engineer shortly after getting my degree was taken over within a couple of years. I survived the subsequent shake-out and was promoted, then, soon after, promoted again. It was the older men who suffered, the young ones who gained, and my secret reluctance to believe I was really on the way up was mostly a hangover from my adolescence, when it was always understood that advancement was bound to be a long and gradual process, since age and seniority counted for more than flair. My experience was, of course, limited to two companies, neither of which was typical of modern business methods: Dawson Whittakers, an old-fashioned stolid family concern which paid a great deal of lip-service to the virtues of loyalty (but which was never known to let this inhibit its cutting of costs by reducing its work-force) and Joyce and Walstock, who were too much of a small fringe enterprise to serve as an example of anything but small fringe enterprises.

To imply that my present employers recognize ability and value it above all else is not to suggest that they don't also give a living to their fair share of bullshit merchants, piss artists, arse-lickers and time-servers, as well as pushers and thrusters of varying skills; but when, occasionally, I become exasperated by somebody taking home good money whom I personally wouldn't pay out in washers I console myself with the thought that my ability is my long-term security. Talent is not always justly rewarded and the phoney do sometimes appear to prosper to an unfair degree; but that I know I can always get another job means I need play no game except doing a good day's work for a good day's pay.

And that piece of paper, which cost me so much in sweat, tears and midnight oil, is a great consolation, conferring as it does the right to status shorthand after my name: V.A. Brown, B.Sc. It's done; I've got it; it's mine; nobody can take it away.

I've got my expenses for the trip listed and on their way to Hedley Graham by the time Ben Taggart buzzes for me. Ben is Sales Director of this division and inhabits an office decorated with charts and graphs which have blinds he can pull down when there's anybody in who he doesn't want to see them; though how much they mean to anyone but him has always been something of a mystery to me. I pass through the outer room and give a wink to his secretary, possessor of a button-straining bosom that brings a tingle to the palms of every normal heterosexual male in the building, and find Ben standing at the window, smoking his pipe. He so obviously enjoys the pipe, and it's such a permanent feature of his face, that I'm tempted every time I see him to take one up myself. A very dark, stocky chap, Ben; swimmer, tennis-player, ex-Rugby Union three-quarter and, like a lot of athletic types, nearly bald in his middle forties.

'Ah, Vic, how did you find the Antipodes?'

'Everything the right way up, despite rumours to the contrary.'

'Natives friendly?'

'They make exceptions for Yorkshiremen.'

'You mean they do when they see they're not peddling horse-shit.'

'Something like that.'

'Maurice Kendall wants me to take you along for a chat.'

'Okay.'

Ben glances once more at the clutter of the North Circular Road beyond the window than turns moodily away. 'Bloody English weather.'

'It's spring down under,' I tell him. 'Blue skies, and temperatures like a good English summer's day.'

'Which good English summer's day was that?'

99

Well, there's no arguing with someone who condemns the English weather, because it's less weather than an attitude of mind, and no amount of figures for hours of sunshine will convince a man who can't, or doesn't want to, remember.

'It took me one and a quarter hours to drive here this morning,' Ben says. 'If I'd been you I'd have been tempted to write home and say I wasn't coming back.'

'Eucalyptus trees are very boring.'

'Are they?'

'And you get snakes in your garden.'

'You can't have everything.' He opens a drawer in his desk and finds an indigestion tablet. 'I think it must be the male menopause. Pick up any good stories?'

One of Ben's quirks, seemingly at odds with most other things about him, is a passion for dirty jokes. I sometimes put it down to his rugger-playing background.

'Two blokes in a bar in Melbourne. "Tasmania?" one says to his friend. "Don't talk to me about Tasmania. There's nothing there but whores and footballers." He feels a tap on his shoulder and looks round to see another bloke, about eight foot twelve, standing behind him. "I come from Tasmania," says this bloke. "Oh, do you, cobber?" says the first bloke. "And what team does your mother play for?" '

It makes Ben smile. 'You should have saved that for Maurice Kendall.'

'Oh, I've got a better one for him. This body-builder type is swaggering along Bondi Beach, all brown skin and bulging pectorals, when he sees a sheila in a bikini lying on her back with her eyes closed. So he goes up to her and kicks sand over her face and when she looks up at him he says, "D'you fack?" "Well, I down't usually," says the sheila, "but yer silver-tongued chaarm jest turned me on." '

This time he laughs out loud. 'I dare you,' he says. 'I just dare you.'

'You know he likes a saucy one. He takes them to his club.'

'Reminds me,' Ben says, 'of the old earl eighty-seven and long past it, who wakes up one morning to find himself the possessor of a most enormous erection. He calls for his valet and throws back the bedclothes. "Look at that, Barker," he says. "What d'you think of that?" "Congratulations, milord," says the valet, and gives a deferential little cough. "Er, should I call her ladyship?" "No," says the old boy. 'Get the car round. I'll smuggle this one into town." '

He walks across to the dictaphone, chuckling, out of his earlier mood now. 'It's good to see you back. We'll have a jar across the road later and you can tell me all about it. In the meantime, you can give Maurice Kendall a prelim.' He presses a button. 'Oh, Maurice, Ben here. I've got Vic with me now . . . Yes, we'll be right up.'

Vic and Ben, Ben and Maurice, Vic and Mr. Kendall is how the protocol runs between us. I always feel that Kendall, since he encouraged and never blocked my promotion, must have rather more respect for me than I have for him. Not that I dislike the old boy; it's just that he's one of the less effectual members of the pretty hard-nosed family who founded the original firm and, according to rumour, he had security of tenure written into the takeover agreement, his chief value to the combine apparently being his chumminess with all kinds of people in influential places, including several members of both Houses of Parliament and a couple of merchant bankers. Rosy-cheeked, white-haired, and thoroughly upper-crust, he sometimes makes me feel that my boots are too big and the carpet between us is littered with my dropped h's; though I do my best not to show it.

He's all amiability as Ben and I walk in, getting up from behind his big desk and coming round in his courteous way to shake my hand.

'You're looking well, Vic.'

'It's all that Australian sunshine,' Ben says sourly.

'Well, as much as filters through factory roof-lights,' I say.

'We could all do with a little sunshine,' Kendall says.

You'll have to wait for your two weeks in the Bahamas in January, I'm thinking, which will be more than the rest of us get.

'I've had a letter from Thomas McKinnon,' Kendall says, taking a sheet of headed paper from the only folder on his desk.

'Beaten me home.'

'Yes. He says he found you amiable and efficient.'

'I hope he's not being premature with his compliments.'

'In what way?'

'All I'd time to do was supervise the basic installation. Any teething troubles in full working they'll have to take care of themselves.'

'You're not expecting any real difficulties, are you?'

'No, but on a similar job at home we make a couple of follow-up visits as routine.'

'You'd brief their chaps fully, of course.'

'Oh, yes. And they're good men.'

'Quite. They will be if they work for McKinnon. I served with him in the Highland Division in North Africa, you know. That was before he emigrated.'

'Yes, he told me about it at dinner one night.'

'First rate chap. From quite modest beginnings. Father a minister in the Church of Scotland. McKinnon came up through the ranks. Wouldn't have known it. Had quite natural authority. Can't keep men like that down. What was that line of Barrie's? "There are few more impressive sights in this world than a Scotsman on the make"?' He chuckles. 'Doesn't sound exactly complimentary put like that, but he knew the breed. How did you find Wal Dearnley?'

'He seemed in fair fettle.'

'Still lifting his elbow?'

'We had a glass or two one evening. I didn't notice anything excessive.'

'Oh, no, no. Doesn't let it interfere with his work, I'm sure.'

Despite his disclaimer, Kendall was fishing. Wal

Dearnley is agent in Australasia for us and several other non-competitive companies; a widower and a rather world-weary man on whose breath I did, as a matter of fact, catch a whiff of the hard stuff at an unseemly hour of the morning. No longer at his reputed best, and not a lot of help to me, if the truth be told. I nevertheless took a liking to him and as he's in his early sixties and on the way to retirement I'm not prepared to queer his pitch with Kendall.

'I expect he'll be reporting when he knows everything's okay.'

'Yes. Well, I'm pleased to know you didn't run into any insuperable problems. And, of course, we shall have your full report in due course.'

'I'm working on it now.'

'Have you any questions for Vic, Ben?'

'Nothing pressing. I'll sit down with him for an hour later on.'

'Good. Good. Let me offer you a glass of sherry, since it's getting on towards lunchtime.' He goes to a cupboard in the long sideboard that occupies one wall, takes out a bottle of Harvey's Bristol Dry and holds it up to the light. 'Dear me, that won't serve us. Let me see.' He pokes about among the other bottles and finds a full one. 'Ah! That's better.'

'It reminds me,' I find myself saying, 'of the Australian wedding. At the height of the reception a voice suddenly calls, "Everybody aht. We've run ahta booze and somebody's facked the bride." They all move towards the doors, then suddenly the same voice pipes up again. "As you were. We've fahn some more booze and the bloke's apologized." '

As Ben chokes over his first mouthful of sherry, Kendall stands with the beginning of a smile frozen on his features. He blinks rapidly several times, then clears his throat.

'Very irreverent, the Australian sense of humour.'

'Oh, very.'

Outside, as we leave, Ben says, 'You bugger. You saved the best till last.'

'I just couldn't resist it,' I tell him. 'When I saw his face I wondered if I hadn't gone too far.'

103

' "First rate chap, Brown",' Ben says, giving a passable imitation of Kendall. ' "Streak of vulgarity in him that betrays his origins; but first rate chap".'

'Mr. Graham's been asking for you,' Janice tells me when I get back to my office. I go into my own room and get him on the inter-com.

'Hedley, Vic here. Do you want to see me?'

'I'll come along now.'

That guilty part of me always half-expects whenever I meet Graham that he'll start off with, 'Look here, what the hell do you think you're playing at with my wife?' and I'm completely incapable of planning any adequate answer in readiness for a confrontation which my occasionally trembling conscience tells me is sooner or later bound to take place. So when Graham marches into my office I greet him with a wary amiability through which I hope shines an impression of unassailable innocence.

'Morning, Hedley. What's on your mind?'

'This list of expenses for your trip.'

'Oh, yes?'

'I see you've charged up hotel bills and meals on stopovers in Sydney, Hong Kong and Rome.'

'On my way back, yes. I did the outward trip in one long hop via North America. I believe they advertise it as to Australia overnight. But it's a bloody long night, believe you me. So I thought I'd have a less punishing schedule on the way home.'

'But the stopovers were made at the company's expense.'

'You don't think I should have paid for them myself?'

'Well, no, but don't you know that on journeys of more than a certain duration the airline itself is obliged to offer you overnight stops?'

'I wish somebody had told me. I could have sampled New York and Honolulu as well. As it was, I went straight through to save the firm time and money.'

'It's unfortunate.'

'Well, what did the stopovers cost? Eighty, ninety quid in all? Against the total expense of flying me out there and back and keeping me. Wasn't a charge to cover it written into the estimate for the job?'

'It's a pity that we have to foot the bill for something you could have got free.'

I'm getting tired of his penny-pinching.

'Look, Hedley, I brought you back my reserve traveller's cheques, and I'll tell you what I did yesterday. I took the airport bus from Heathrow to Cromwell Road, instead of a taxi.'

'There was no need to economise to that extent.'

'Maybe not. But it just struck me that I couldn't thoil paying six or seven quid for me to ride in solitary state.'

'Thoil?'

'It's an old northcountry word. It means "abide". We're so tight with brass up there, as you might have heard – other people's as well as our own – that it now applies solely to spending money. When the Danes first brought it in it referred to people as well. "I can't thoil people who quibble about my expenses," we might have said.'

I give him a little smile which I know full well I can't make reach my eyes and watch him come near to flushing.

'Nobody's questioning the accuracy of your claims.'

'Hedley, they're not claims. They're statements of what I've already spent. I'm not *claiming* anything. I've brought you money back.'

'All the same, I –'

'Yes, I know it must make your accountant's heart bleed, but if you speak to the people who booked my flight and suggest they get boned up on airline rules and obligations then whoever goes next time can get the perks I missed.'

I'm sorry I've let my exasperation show so plainly. On the other hand, not to stand firm with Graham is to give him the advantage. Firm, though. Firm and reasonable. Not irritable. No need to let a man see he gets under your skin. That makes it personal.

The telephone rings. The girl on the switchboard tells me there's a Mrs. Wilson on the line.

'Wilson?'

'She says she's an old friend.'

'Put her through, then.'

The moment I recognize Miriam's voice I press the receiver hard against my ear, convinced that her clear penetrating tone must reach Graham, who's now lingering by my drawing-table, though as far as I'm concerned the conversation between us is over.

'Oh, hello,' I say brightly. 'I couldn't place you for a second. How nice of you to call.'

'I expect you're mad with me, really –'

'Not at all, not at all.' I am, though. Livid. Apart from the possibility of the girl's recognizing her voice from calls made by Graham to his home and vice versa, if she should be listening in she'll know by now that I'm not speaking with someone I haven't seen for ages. 'It's just a little bit inconvenient at the moment. How are you, by the way?'

'Have you got someone with you?'

'Yes, yes,' I say, still bright. 'I'm fine. Just excuse me a moment, would you?' Only pretending to cover the mouthpiece with my hand, I speak across the room, 'Does that wind it up, Hedley?' and hear Miriam take a breath in my left ear.

'Well, I suppose so.' He moves towards the door.

'If there's anything else perhaps I can pop along and see you after lunch.'

'I'm going down to South Wales this afternoon. I shall be away for a couple of days.'

'Anyway, it's all pretty clear, isn't it?'

'I suppose so. We'll leave it as it is, seeing it's done.'

'Good.' I lift my hand to him as he goes through the door.

'Was that –?' Miriam begins, and I interrupt her quickly with 'A colleague,' hoping she won't say 'My husband,' over the open line. My heart's already thumping like a pneumatic hammer.

'I'm free this evening,' she says. 'I wondered if –'

'What a pity. I'm engaged this evening. How long

will you be in town?'

'Really –'

'Why not give me a ring at home tomorrow evening. Say about seven. I'd love to see you again.'

'I should hope so,' Miriam says.

'Have you got a pencil and paper? I'll give you my number.' I recite the figures she already knows by heart and as she breaks in with 'Is all this performance really necessary?' throw my voice across the room again, calling 'Come in,' and say to her, 'I'll expect to hear from you, then. Goodbye,' and put down the receiver.

My heart's still pounding and I straighten in my chair and take several deep breaths. Miriam, I say to myself, you may not realize it but you've just made it plain to me that you'll have to go. It won't do, Miriam. It won't do. I'm just not cut out for this kind of thing.

8

I remember a limpid early morning on Fiji. We'd flown in over low, intensely green terraced hillsides. One or two native Fijians with their great frizzy bonnets of hair waited on passengers at the gifts stall in the tiny airport terminal which, under extension, was open on one side to the runway and beyond that the sea. It was the most foreign place I'd ever been in and I could gather together in my mind no conception of how the people lived, what kind of living they made, what kind of society they upheld. Where did they come from to staff this airstrip, a staging post in the middle of nowhere?

It was our first daylight since we'd overtaken the night somewhere above the western United States. In Los Angeles, from the air a pattern of glittering diamonds on black velvet, the jewels abruptly absent as the velvet changed from land to sea, it was eight in the evening, though somewhere around five the next morning by the time I'd carried with me from London.

I'd adjusted my watch so many times I'd no accurate knowledge of how many hours we'd spent on the way, and here now, in the South Pacific, we'd crossed the International Dateline and I was no longer sure even what day it was. The air was pure and refreshing, with a promise in it of great heat as the sun rose higher. We were due in Melbourne for lunch, but by local time, so it was going to be a long morning. I looked forward to a bath and a kip between sheets, a change of clothes and a meal which didn't come wrapped in polythene on a plastic tray.

Wal Dearnley met me at the airport and drove me into the city. A small lean man with a good head of grey hair and a complexion like crumpled leather.

'You've missed a night's sleep,' he said as I sat, quiet and bemused, looking out at the strange suburban landscape. 'But take a tip from me. Don't go to bed this afternoon. Wait till nightfall, then get in a good eight or nine hours, or you'll keep on being out of synch for days.'

Good advice, which nevertheless didn't stop me from waking up on the floor of my hotel room at three a.m. the sheets and pillows pulled down round me, out of a dream that I was still flying through the Pacific night, below which was sunlight and a view of the endless arid hills of northern Queensland. Which was odd, because I was not to see that untrodden moonscape until my journey home. A woman was asking me to stop snoring as I was disturbing her, which again was curious, since I couldn't sleep on the plane and was slumped, trying to stretch my legs as I read under my seat light while, up front, Donna and Ingrid were singing a song to the passengers and beside me Clive Carter was shaking with laughter. I'd never seen him laugh and I wanted to ask him, 'What the hell's amusing you?'

'What the hell . . .?'

The woman with blue rinsed grey hair and expensive glitter-framed glasses looks down with cold disapproval and says, 'I'd like to pass you.'

That north American short 'a'. Not at all like its Yorkshire counterpart.

Unable to collect myself quickly enough to stand, I swing my legs into the aisle in what must seem like grudging acquiescence and she and the trim-suited, trim-haired, trim-bespectacled man with her push by. 'Drunk' is the only word I catch from what he says to her as they pass out of earshot.

The curtain's down. Other people follow the American couple out of the row. I stand up and, feeling slightly dizzy, go along with them into the stalls bar, where a

Scotch (when I finally get served) and a cigarette make me feel better.

I have fallen asleep in the theatre. I have fallen asleep during Donna's play. Was she on stage at the time? No. I was waiting for her and could keep awake no longer. I put my elbow on the arm of my seat and rested my chin on my hand and shut my eyes, listening to the voices, knowing I should know her voice when I heard it. And fell asleep. Now she must have been on without my knowing. While I was asleep, and a snoring nuisance to the American couple and God knows how many others nearby.

('To pay out money for a ticket and then sleep through the show.'

('Like I said, he's probably drunk.'

('And he's drinking some more now. If he's a bother after intermission I shall call the attendant.')

With my glass to my lips I catch the woman's gimlet glance through the crowd. Perhaps they think I'm not drunk but stoned. What did the notices at Kennedy Airport say? Asking for patience – 'a drug-free America comes first'. And a gun-free America comes last. The customs officers wore guns. The reality of a gun on a man's hip is very brutal. The reality of New York seen only from the air was very disappointing. With the blood and mayhem of *The Godfather* resting on my knee I searched for the famous skyline and finally found it, a small spiky kernel in the great brown spread of the city's agglomeration.

Well, these two gallivanting Yankees will surely understand my present problem; or do they take their standards from their cool-headed Kissinger, who flies between countries as other men drive from town to town, ready to tackle the problems of the world at each touchdown, and not a drooping eyelid in sight except as a convenient racially provided guard on expression? I've never really learned not to care what people think of me, which I think is sometimes a weakness, and I weave through the standing drinkers until I reach the couple.

110

The woman looks at me as I approach, then looks away.

'Excuse me,' I say, and she takes a defensive step slightly closer to her husband. 'I must apologize for being a nuisance during the performance. I've just made a long journey by air and I haven't caught up with myself yet.'

'Oh, jet-lag!' The woman's expression at once becomes open and interested. 'My husband and I know about that. Why, we spent most of our first day here in London trying to adjust. Didn't we, Orville?'

The man responds with what I can only describe as 'Yup,' but the final 'p' held back between the lips and almost silent.

'Have you been in England before?'

'My husband was here with the Army Air Force, in '44, but this is my first trip. But, say, we ought to introduce ourselves. We're Mr. and Mrs. and Orville Forrest.'

'Victor Brown.'

'How do you do, Mr. Brown. Well, like I was saying, this is my first trip, though my mother was born here, you know.'

'Was she indeed?'

'Yes, she came over in nineteen-o-five with her parents – my grandparents – found a fine young third-generation American, and married him. All my grown life I've been promising myself to take a look at where she started from but, well, when you're young and making your way you're not always as well-to-do as you get to be in later life, and what with my husband building a business, time kind of slips by. Now my husband's passing more of the load on to our two boys and so I said to him this spring, "Now, Orville, it's this year or maybe never." So, here we are at last. And I must say I find it all so fascinating. You English are so polite and helpful. Why, you ask the way of a man in the street and he'll take you by the arm and guide you.'

'Even here in London.'

'Why do you say that, Mr. Brown?'

'I come from the north. Up there we rather tend to

111

think of Londoners as being wrapped up in their own affairs.'

'The north, you say? Forgive me, but I was trying to place your accent. Now, my mother came from the City of York. Would you be familiar with that?'

'I have been there. I'm a Yorkshireman myself.'

'You don't say so! D'you hear that, Orville. Mr. Brown hails from Mother's part of the country.' Orville half opens his lips as if to say 'Yup' again, then decides it's not worth the effort as his wife carries on, 'Well now, we're here in London for another four or five days, then we're going north ourselves.'

'You'll enjoy York. It's a very beautiful town.'

'I've seen so many pictures of it. Those amazing walls, and the old buildings. It must make you feel you're in direct contact with centuries past.'

'If you can ignore the traffic.'

'Well, I guess that's a hazard any place now.'

'What business are you in, Mr. Forrest?' I ask, turning to the silent Orville.

'Leather. Animal hides.'

'Just curing, or manufacturing?'

'Both. We take in the untreated hide at one end and bring you out a pocket book or a pair of shoes at the other.'

'That's a coincidence. I went to Australia to instal a ventilation system in a tannery and shoe factory.'

'Is that so?'

'I suppose you're already well equipped, or have engineers locally who can service you. I'll give you my card, though, if I may. You never know when we might have an opportunity of being of use to you.'

I hand him my business card which he glances at briefly and pockets with an unencouraging 'Thanks.'

'I guess we should be getting back,' says Mrs. Forrest as the second bell is heard. I stroll along with them and we take our seats.

'I hope you'll feel free to poke me in the ribs if I nod off again,' I tell Mrs. Forrest, and she chuckles.

112

'Well, now that we've been introduced I might at that. In any case, you shouldn't miss it; it's a very amusing play. So typically British.'

'I'm annoyed with myself because I know one of the cast.'

She's all ears now. 'You do? Which one would that be?'

'Donna Pennyman.'

'Wait a minute . . .' She looks at her programme. 'Yes, I have her. And is she really a friend of yours?'

'Well, she was years ago. I haven't met her for a long time.'

'How interesting! She's really very good.'

'I'll tell you better when I've seen her.'

'Yes, of course.' She chuckles again as the house lights dim.

The play's a modern comedy that opened to rave reviews and is already playing to capacity houses. I got a full-house reply when I phoned for a seat, and nearly changed my mind. Then I came anyway and hung about in the foyer till there was a cancellation. Short on plot and long on double-takes, pauses and gone-out reactions, it's all middle-class misunderstandings, acted out in the garden of a small country house which at one time I'd have called a mansion, and which everybody in the cast refers to as the 'the cottage', and full of lines like 'But Edgar said Welwyn Garden City', which make the audience fall about and might mean more to me if I hadn't spent the first act miles away in an aeroplane. Donna plays a character called Freda, whom everybody else spends a lot of time talking about, but who's conspicuous by her absence for the first ten minutes, as in fact she was in the first half. Then suddenly Mrs. Forrest taps me lightly on the knee with her programme, giving me a little sidelong smile full of shared knowledge as she nods towards the stage ('I danced with a man who'd danced with a girl who'd danced with the Prince of Wales'), and there she is.

She's wearing a wig – or at least, her hair's not as I

remember it – and I can't make out her features with absolute clarity; but what she's not disguising, the way she moves, the plant of her feet and the set of her legs as she stands, gives me the remembered totality of her with an impact that takes my breath away. I once, years ago, followed a girl with Donna's legs and Donna's walk, glimpsed in a heartstopping moment at a distance in a London street, only to find, when I came alongside, a stranger's face. Now I fumble for a shilling, slip it into the gadget on the seat in front, and extract the opera glasses. They're fixed-focus and I tilt them at my eyes till what I want to see comes up sharp and clear. Donna's face. Older? Made-up? Still Donna's face. But a Donna whose experience through all the years I've not known her means that I can't see through the part to the real woman.

I can only remember the Donna I knew and the times we had together. That last time, which I didn't know was the last time, but which afterwards seemed to have had in it the agony of imminent parting. I made some remark about the electric blanket and she kidded me, as she liked to do when the puritan in me peeped out, 'Would you rather we sinned in discomfort?' What was the look on her face, the thought in her mind, as she moved gently under me, her hands tender on my back in the dark? Did she know already then that it was over, that with Carter back in her life there could be no place for me? How much did it matter to her? How much had any of it mattered? 'It's not a world-shaking act when two people go to bed with each other,' she said, speaking of the world she lived in. 'They can do it simply because they're lonely and want to give each other a little warmth.' Maybe that she saw anything in me was why I thought she must, must see more than she did. At the time. For soon enough, afterwards, I was ready to wonder that she'd seen anything at all. Oh, Donna, there was a sweet moist tunnel into your body which in the moment of my penetration drove care from every corner of the world. There's been nothing like it, ever, since. But was it ever like that for you?

I can't sit still. Only isolated sentences of the play get

114

through to me. The audience laugh and I've no idea of the line that made them. Mrs. Forrest is enjoying every minute, and probably wondering where my sense of humour is, because my restlessness must look like boredom. Even Orville, at one point, lets out a huge guffaw.

With the curtain down, after half a dozen calls, I take my leave of the Americans, shaking hands with both of them, and find the quickest way to the street. Outside, I look for the stage-door and linger on the pavement some way from it, jostled by the leaving crowd but keeping my eyes all the time on where Donna must come out. I have no idea what I'm going to do, and as the crowd thins and nobody appears I begin to wonder if the cast have already made a quick get-away. Then a man whose face I recognize comes out, throwing a 'good night' back into the passage before walking briskly away towards Trafalgar Square. He's followed by a group of three, which leaves two more to come. They appear together, Donna and the young male lead, chuckling over something as they step into the street.

She's wearing a casual coat of some kind of fur fabric over sweater and jeans. Her hair seems darker, and the ash blond strands I remember are gone. For a moment the light from a street lamp falls directly on to her face. It's thinner, sallower somehow, with ten more years of living etched into it. Something makes me turn my own face slightly away as they walk towards me. I could almost reach out and touch her as she passes, but she doesn't glance my way. I follow them as they stroll up towards the main road. They stop outside a pub and look as though they're thinking of going in. But it's the man who does so, leaving Donna with a little pat on the upper arm. She moves off, at a quicker pace now, and I follow her to the corner. If I didn't know where to find her again, I tell myself, I'd hurry and catch her up and speak to her. But I let her go and watch her till she's lost to view. Who is she hurrying home to? I wonder. Who's waiting to ask how the evening went, to chat with her over a drink, discuss plans for tomorrow and the next day; to hold her close in her bed, or even stretch beside her, companionable but not bothering to touch? I wonder.

I smell Miriam's perfume as soon as I enter the flat. I hang up my topcoat, hoping she's not still here, and thinking of how to handle her if she is. She's sitting in the living-room, drinking whisky, and she turns on me the bright bold gaze I've seen before when she knows I shall think she's gone too far but she's set on her own course of action.

'Hello.'

'What are you doing here?'

'Waiting for you, of course.'

Ask a silly question . . . 'Do you know what time it is?'

'Oh, the night's young. Hedley's away.'

'Oh?'

'In South Wales. Or North Wales. Or somewhere in Wales. For a couple of days. More important, a couple of nights. Didn't he tell you?'

'I don't keep his diary.'

'He was with you this morning, though, wasn't he? When I rang you?'

'Yes, he was, and a right bloody turn you gave me. Don't you know better than to take a risk like that? Suppose the girl on the switchboard recognized your voice? Suppose she was feeling nosy, and listened in?'

'Oh, suppose, suppose . . . I saw you yesterday for the first time in over six weeks, and when Hedley said he had to go away I thought it too good a chance to miss.'

'I thought I told you I'd something on this evening?'

'Well, you're back now and we've got the rest of the night.'

'And what if I'd brought somebody home with me?'

'Oh, you mean I might have upset your plans?'

'I mean how would I have explained you sitting here if I'd walked in with a friend. I have got some friends, you know.'

'No, I thought you spent six evenings out of seven

116

sitting here playing patience and listening to your gramophone. Don't be stupid, Vic. I don't care what you do when I'm not with you, but –'

'Don't you? I can just imagine the kind of fire you'd spit if you thought I had other women up here.'

'Can you? Well, we won't argue about hypothetical cases.'

'You mean you don't think I do have other women?'

'I certainly don't mean to waste time bothering about it now. What I was going to say was if I don't care what you do when I'm not with you I certainly expect a friendlier welcome when I do manage to get away.'

'Look doesn't your old feller phone you when he's off on business? Suppose he rings up tonight?'

'If he does, depending on what time he does, I shall either say I was out or I'd taken a sleeping-pill.'

'And what if he can't get you tonight and tried again first thing in the morning?'

'I shall just have to make sure I'm having my corn-flakes where I can hear the phone, shan't I? I should have thought that gave us plenty of time together. I'm not greedy.'

'Not much, you're not! Christ! but you do push the boat out, Miriam. You really do.'

'And it quite cools your ardour, doesn't it?'

'Cools it? It bloody cripples it.'

'Come on, let me give you a drink and we'll see what a little friendly persuasion can do.' She reaches for the bottle and pours into a glass she's got ready waiting. 'Here . . . Anyway,' she says as I take the glass and light a cigarette, 'he doesn't always telephone. Not the first night, in any case.'

'Not to let you know he's arrived without mishap? Not to find out if everything's all right with you?'

'Not now. He used to. But I've told you, we've been married a long time.'

'And in all that time he's been able to leave home without the slightest suspicion that there was any hanky-panky going on while his back was turned?'

117

'Why not? He hasn't the least idea that you and I have ever met other than in public.'

'I wasn't specifically referring to me.'

'Then what were you referring to?'

'The others – before me.'

'What others would they be?' she shoots back, her chin going up, her eyes ablaze with a passable imitation of outrage.

'Come on, Miriam. Act like the experienced woman you are and not a slighted virgin.'

She climbs down a little. 'What – or who – happened before you is none of your business.'

'It's my business if Hedley starts looking for somebody to carry the can and drops on me.'

'So that's what's worrying you?'

'It's not exactly news, is it?'

'I thought we'd agreed to let me take care of that side of it.'

'But you see, Miriam, I don't trust you, love.'

'Thanks for your confidence.'

'I mean, being you, one of these days you'll go too far.'

'And you don't want to be involved.'

'It was never part of the arrangement.'

She goes quiet, reaching for a cigarette herself. The box on the table is empty. I pass my packet and lean across to give her a light.

'Now be fair,' I say, 'Was it?'

'It was never part of the arrangement that I should fall for you as I have.'

'You're fooling yourself, Miriam,' I tell her, gently.

'Am I?'

'I'm a good screw, love; and amusing enough company when the mood's on me. Why blow it up into more?'

'Is that all I am to you – a good screw and amusing company?'

'Isn't it enough? Why wish it into something else, with all the pain that comes with it?'

'You know about that kind of pain, do you?'

'Yes, love. And I've had enough. You want things you

118

can't find in your marriage – without busting that marriage up – and *I* don't like living like a monk. So, there's an arrangement.'

'And if the arrangement gets out of hand?'

Arrangements imply agreement. When you can't agree – end of arrangement.'

'You're a cold devil.'

'No, I'm not. I'm just trying to be sensible for both of us.'

She reaches for the bottle and stiffens up her drink.

'Have you got the car?'

'Yes, it's along the street.'

'You'd better go easy on the Scotch.'

'Does that mean my departure is imminent?'

'I didn't say that.'

'You implied it.' She throws back the drink and stands up. 'I'll go, anyway.'

'No, don't.'

Tell the truth, I'm suddenly a little scared for her. She's capable of trying to work off her present mood with an all-out sprint down the motorway. She has to pass me. I stretch out my hand towards her. She contemplates it for a second of decision then takes it, subsiding on to the arm of my chair.

'That's twice in two days you've not been pleased to see me.'

'Yesterday I was knocked out by travelling.'

'And tonight I've managed to upset you.'

'It's only sensible to take as few risks as possible. Suppose he did cotton on? Where would we be then?'

'I sometimes find myself wishing he would. It might shake him out of some of his smug, complacent assumptions.'

'Don't make me a pawn in your games with Hedley. Lomax's would be too hot a place for both of us, and I'm not thinking of changing jobs just at present.'

She slips down on to my knee and puts her face in my neck.

'We could always run away together. I've got my own

119

money, you know. We couldn't live the way we do and put the boys through boarding school on Hedley's income.'

'Come to mention it, I've always fancied being kept by a rich older woman.'

'I'd see you out, don't worry.'

'Yeh, in plenty of time to lure somebody else.'

'Did I lure you? I thought it was the other way round.'

'You mean I seduced you from your marriage vows? Honey, if your roving eye hadn't been plain to see I'd never have thought of making a pass. After all, you *are* older than I am –'

'So you keep reminding me.'

' – and a hell of a sight more sophisticated.'

'Am I?'

'Knowledgeable. Worldly wise.'

'A little corrupt?'

'Corrupting, or corrupted?'

'Have I corrupted you?'

'If you consider that you're the only married woman – or other man's wife, shall we say – I've ever been to bed with, I suppose you have.'

'Is that the truth? That I'm the only one, I mean?'

'It's nothing to lie about. I've always steered clear. I've never had the bad luck to fall in love with a married woman, and I'm not one of your randy young Lotharios who take special pleasure in screwing unsatisfied wives. When you interfere in a marriage you never know what delicate balance you could be upsetting.'

'Then why did you make an exception for me?'

'Well, in the first place, I wanted to go to bed with you the instant I laid eyes on you.'

She likes that. She murmurs 'Mmmm . . .' and rubs her nose under my ear.

'And in the second place, I caught on pretty quick that you were dying for it, and if it wasn't me it would be somebody else.'

She draws her head back and looks at me. 'I don't think that's a particularly nice thing to –'

120

I put my finger across her lips. 'Ssh! We've done striking attitudes. So I thought it might as well be me as some young stud who'd pick you up, use you, and then drop you with a thud.'

'God! you're arrogant. So you did it to save me from myself! To stop me wandering the streets like a bitch on heat, ready to follow the first willing cock that showed itself!'

'Don't be vulgar. It shocks me in cold blood.'

'And you stop talking like a bloody missionary and admit you saw something you couldn't resist: an easy lay who wouldn't give you any trouble simply because she *was* married.'

She's on her feet again now and over at the table, taking another cigarette from the packet that's still lying there.

'If you want the truth, I rather thought *you* might use *me* for a while.'

'Did you?' She turns, exhaling smoke. 'Did you really?'

'I mean like married men use single girls. You know the routine: "Sorry, love, but things have got a bit dicey at home. It was nice while it lasted, but I've run out of excuses." Shrug, shrug. "Anyway, no harm done, and I'll see you around." '

'I see.' She sits opposite me and pulls thoughtfully on her cigarette.

I don't know why I've let the conversation run into this channel. For although it seemed better that she should stay here tonight than leave and risk smashing herself up through pique, better also she should stay than leave me to go to bed alone with my thoughts of somebody else, I've already decided that after this I shall have somehow to retrieve that key, somehow let the affair die as gentle a death as she's prepared to allow.

Oh yes, I was evading serious consideration of that apparently lighthearted suggestion that we scarper together. I say 'apparently' because I'm afraid now that Miriam has come to feel for me more than she should. Or, at least, *think* she does, which could be just as dangerous in the immediate damage it might cause.

She looks across at me with a quick, uncertain, almost shy glance. 'I don't think you know how – how fond of you I am.'

'Oh, I think I do, love. I was talking about the beginning of it, not now.'

And I'm thinking that now, in fact, might be the moment to break it to her. That it's run its course and is better finished. Now that the outrage has left her. But soft tears can't mark the end of our relationship, whatever feeling she lays claim to. No, anger will show that for the pretence it is. And angry is how I daren't send her away. So I tell myself, and it is a genuine part of the truth, the rest being that I want her one last time, a time she might even, if she knew, ask for herself, to show me once more how good it is, something too good to lose.

I stand up and go to her, resting a hand on each arm of the chair and bending to kiss her on the mouth.

'What time shall I set the alarm clock for?'

'Make it six.'

Miriam, though she can give me five years and is the mother of two children, has a body she need feel no shame in revealing. But tonight, when I follow her into the bedroom, I find her with the sheets drawn up over her, and lying facing the edge of the bed, as though suggesting that her desire to be with me through the night can be something other than carnal. Though when ever, meeting at intervals as we do, have we denied ourselves when alone? Tonight as well, when I turn her to me, she's quiet, receptive, waiting, like a girl on the wondering brink of some enormous experience she's only had described before. Slowly she receives me, slowly she mounts the wave with me, waiting as if holding herself back. And silent; no whispered words tonight to keen the edge of excitement. I begin to sweat, cursing her for not being as she always has been, needing her greed to goad my own climax, and wondering for the first time ever with her if I might fail to reach it. I labour over her, conjuring up erotic images to quicken me:

122

remembered sexual episodes, the superb flaunted shape of a girl glimpsed briefly in the street. Anything. But not Donna. There was never anything of masturbatory fantasy in the totality of my feeling for her.

The telephone rings.

'Oh! God,' Miriam gasps. 'Not now.'

I relax on her.

'Leave it,' she bids me. 'It's probably some drunk, got a wrong number. Don't stop now.'

It shrills on, an arm's length away.

'I'm sorry,' I say, and Miriam sighs as I lift myself off her and reach for the receiver.

'Vic? Is that you, Vic?'

'Yes.'

'This is Christine. Were you asleep?'

'Yes . . . It's okay.'

'It's Mother, Vic . . .'

'Mother? What –?'

'She's had a heart attack. A serious one.'

'She's not –?'

'No, but she's very ill. They rushed her into hospital and revived her, but I'm afraid it looks bad.'

'When was all this?'

'Earlier today.'

'And where are you?'

'I'm ringing from the call-box in Meadow Lane.'

'Have you rung Jim?'

'I'm going to when I've finished talking to you. It won't be quite as much of a shock to him. He came over last week, when she'd had the first one.'

'The first one? Last week. But why –?'

'She seemed to come round all right from that and she said I wasn't to go making a fuss and bothering everybody.'

'Everybody being me. The only one who didn't know.'

'You were in Australia, Vic. When did you get back?'

'Yesterday.'

'There you are. I think you ought to come now.'

I glance at the bedside alarm-clock. 'I'll be there

before morning. Will there be anybody up to let me in?'

'Yes. I'm coming out to ring the hospital every so often. You'll take care, won't you?'

'I'll take care.' The pips are heard and I shout over them, 'See you later,' and hang up.

'Bad news?' Miriam asks.

'My mother. I've got to go home.'

I get up and go into the bathroom and splash my face with cold water. When I come back, Miriam is almost dressed.

'Do you think you should drive all that way tonight?'

'I'll be all right.' I'm opening and shutting drawers. 'Blast it, most of my stuff's at the laundry.'

I take a roll-neck sweater and pull it over my head, put back on the underpants I've worn all day, and bundle what other clothes I can find into my grip.

'Is there anything I can do?'

'I don't think so.' I manage a wry little smile. 'I'm sorry I left you high and dry.'

'Don't be silly. There's always time for that.'

Ah, but is there, love? I'm thinking. What if I were to tell you that this has been the last time?

I stand still, looking round and trying to gather my thoughts. My mother . . . But we all expected her to outlive the Old Man by years . . .

'Now where did I park the bloody car? The street was full when I came in after work.'

'Haven't you been out in it this evening?'

'No, I used the Underground.'

'I'll walk round with you till you find it.'

'Yes, just stick around, will you, till I see if I've got enough petrol to get me to an all-nighter.'

It's cold down in the street and I feel the sweat from my labour with Miriam cooling on me. We walk round into the square where I spot my car. I get in and start the engine and check the fuel gauge.

'I'll be okay till the first M1 services.'

'When will you be back?'

'I've no idea.'

'I'll try ringing you in a couple of days.'

'Yes, do that.'

She leans in through the open window and offers her mouth. I make a token peck at it, say good night, and move off, realizing as I change up through the gears that in my mind my relationship with Miriam is already a thing of the past.

9

At least I don't have to wait for trains nowadays, I tell myself as I slip on to the motorway and gently put my foot down. None of that Longford to Liverpool Street, Liverpool Street to Kings Cross, Kings Cross to Wakefield, Wakefield to Cressley and a bus out of town routine. I can travel door-to-door in my own good time, and as many or as few times as I wish.

I haven't been as often as I should, partly out of idleness, partly because the Old Lady has never really forgiven me for breaking up my marriage – though Ingrid has been married again for some years now, as far as I know happily, to a chap who works in a bank – and my not 'settling down' again in her terms gives her every excuse to look askance at my way of life. If anything, my degree and my good job only make her more disappointed that I haven't found another wife and produced a couple of grandchildren to add to Bobby, and Jim's twin girls.

Why won't I conform, fit to pattern?

'Nay,' I can imagine her saying, 'he's got a grand job, and no worries about money, but he just doesn't seem to want to settle *down*.'

As though I were living in a tent and moving from town to town, job to job, as the whim took me.

The trouble is, I know what she means. I can't laugh it off because what she wants for me is what I want for myself. To her it's easier to find, that's all. You just work harder at it when you've got it; learn to be content; accept your lot. But I've been through all that. Oh, I'm no loner; my present life is not a pattern I've consciously created; it's something that's come about from living one day and then the next. I don't see it being like this for ever more. But I've not seen any alternative that's tempted me for longer than it's taken me to consider the hell of getting it wrong a second time

Rosie, the Canadian girl who moved in with me for a couple of months, used to tell me there were no cast-iron certainties in this life, pronouncing it as the collected wisdom of her twenty-two years. I had to agree. She was near the end of her time in England when I met her and she finished her post-graduate course at London University and went home to Montreal. I think if I'd asked her to marry me she'd have stayed. Or am I flattering myself? Anyway, I didn't, and she left. I don't expect many relationships as good as mine and Rosie's. She stripped like the centre page of *Playboy*, her body drawing other men's eyes in a way that made me positively glow with the pleasure of temporary possession. She was lively, intelligent, shared a lot of my tastes, and was buoyantly accommodating between the sheets and on top of them. She made me laugh often and when she went I suddenly thought I would miss her like hell. But no, that faded soon enough, until I could think of her with sweet and gentle pleasure, and no regrets. So why couldn't what we had have been enough? Why didn't I accept all those pleasurable ingredients as being the best I was likely to find?

Damn it! I want something I can't bear to be without, because anything less must be in constant jeopardy.

With my petrol tank topped-up, I forge on. It's a dry clear night, which is one small blessing. Here, south of the Birmingham link, there's quite a lot of swift-moving heavy traffic on the road, and I'm up to eighty and passing it in the middle and third lanes before I realize that I'm going too fast, putting too much strain of concentration on someone who started out far from fresh. I pull over into the slow lane and ease off to sixty-five, letting who wants to pass me. My haste might be seemly but that's all that can be said for it. More sensible, I think, to have stayed put, where Chris could phone me with news. Because if the Old Lady is all that poorly they won't be letting anybody see her, and now I'm out of touch. I should at least have asked Chris where they'd taken her so that I could ring up for myself.

I switch on the radio and wind down the window as my eye-lids begin to droop, and suffer the inrush of cold air till my right hand goes nearly numb on the wheel. My privates feel heavy with my unshot load, on the edge of aching with the orgasm that first Miriam's response then Chris's phone call thwarted. Tenderness, Miriam wanted, tonight of all nights; Miriam who usually grabs sex like a kid stuffing its face with chocolates. Short, sharp and often is her usual style. Let's get it done with and then we can do it again. I've forgotten, of course, to get back that key. But it was no time to ask her for it, even if I'd remembered.

About the half-way point is the service area at Leicester Forest East, in my experience one of the few purporting to offer refreshment to the weary traveller along the motorways which doesn't put you off food altogether. God knows what foreign drivers make of them, faced with endless soggy chips, hot pies with crusts like wet cardboard and sausages overcooked and then kept warm till they're as hard as dog turds grilled by the sun. I pull in, park and go upstairs to the Buttery. There, over a cup of coffee, I can look out and see the headlights swooping on the carriageways.

My mother . . . Women are tougher than men. They outlive them. The world is full of widows. The Old Lady was all set to be one of them, soldiering on into her nineties, until she became a similar fixture to her great-grandkids. That's the thing about parents: they *are* fixtures, fixed always at the age they are now, changing only when your back's turned long enough. You can't remember what they were like when they were young, and you can't imagine how the world will close over them and carry on as before when they're gone.

Until . . . And then . . .

I go back down. As I pass the telephones I think through the process of getting Directory Inquiries for the number of the hospital, finding enough coins for the call, inquiring if that is the hospital she's in. My mother . . . keeping it from us till it couldn't be hidden any longer. Keeping it from me, at any rate, because I don't go often, haven't been lately, am not her favourite, the one she would naturally tell. In the gents there's a machine offering french letters moulded in a variety of surface forms. Times change. Imagine! I could have given Ingrid not only protection but thrills the naked penis couldn't. And what different person would that have made me by now, if I'd never married her, if none of it had happened? What would I be doing ? Where would I be? Coming home for the same reason but from farther away? Driving across the town? Walking round the corner? Bringing somebody with me? Leaving somebody behind? Only last week I was in Australia, on the other side of the world. And what difference does that make? Well, I'm glad I've been, aren't I? And better off in that way than those who haven't.

I reckon a good deal must have been written and said about human beings' capacity to absorb and get used to improvements in their conditions. It's not an original thought: I must have picked it up somewhere. But I know it's true, because it applies to me. What I mean is, we're so quick at taking for granted what we've got, we only know the pleasure it gives us when we stop and think how miserable we'd be without it.

Once, in the summer, with my car off the road for a couple of days, I found myself on a main-line railway station early on a holiday evening. A fault somewhere miles away delayed a train for well over an hour. The platform was packed with parents and kids who'd been visiting a nearby zoo and pleasure-park. The kids got restless and began playing-up. Some got hungry, some wanted to run about, some wanted to pee. All of them wanted to be anywhere and doing anything rather than waiting for a train which got later every time an announcement was made. I could feel the parents' plans for a quiet evening with the telly or at the pub when the kids were in bed, going for a Burton, and I suddenly thought to myself, 'They're victims.' They were at somebody's mercy every day of their lives, and this time the failure of the system they depended on had buggered-up their day.

So, although not one hundred percent my own man, I am at least a sight better off than them. I've got a job that I like, do well, and get good money for. I'm going on thirty-six years old, sound in wind and limb, white, Anglo-Saxon, nobody's butt, and carrying no chip. I have a car and there's nobody even to call me selfish because it's a two-seater and not a family saloon. So why don't I want it to stay like this for ever? Oh, dear God, don't let it get worse! But how long do you have to live waiting for something round the corner that will make you sit up and shout, 'Yes, yes! This is it!' And what a rotten joke to reach the end of a life, look back at a time, and say, 'Ah, yes! If only I'd known, that *was* it.'

What is my mother thinking – if she's not beyond conscious thought – as she faces a possible end? When was her time? Has it all fulfilled itself, or been too disappointing to contemplate with serenity? Is she ready? Does she mind? Is she fighting it or gracefully giving in?

As I hold my hands, brown from Australian sun, under the hot-air dryer, I see the white shape of a scar on one of my fingers: something I've not noticed for years, the memento of a childhood mishap. It must have been a deep, wide-open wound, but I have no memory at all of how I got it. Did I cry, and did she comfort me? Was her comfort the most important thing in the world to me at that time? Ah! Why can't she wait till I can get it all together and then tell her how it all should be? Because now, perhaps, she'll never know. There's so much she'll never know.

*   *   *

Jim's white Triumph Stag, status symbol of the with-it young GP, is parked outside the house. He answers the door and lets me in.

'Ah, Vic . . .'

'Jim . . .'

'You've made good time.'

'Yes. Hang on a minute,' I say as he walks away from me along the hall. 'What's the news?'

He half-turns and shakes his head. 'I don't like it. Chris'll tell you better. She's the one who's been ringing the hospital.'

In the living-room my sister is sitting forward in an easy-chair, drawn up to the fire. She squeezes my hand as I go over and bend down and kiss her cheek. As I straighten up I catch the flash of light on the first silver in her hair.

'I hope you drove carefully,' she says to me.

'I'm here, aren't I? In one piece. How is she?'

'Not good. They've got her in intensive care.'

'Shouldn't somebody be up there?'

'There's nothing anybody could do if they were. And we're only a few minutes' walk away. I've been phoning every hour.'

'Is my dad in bed?'

'I made him go and lie down. I don't suppose he's asleep.'

'You got here pretty quick, didn't you? Or were you here already?'

'I've been here since Dad sent for me, last week.'

'You mean when she had the first one? Or has she had others before?'

'She's been having treatment for six months.'

'I didn't know that.' I turn to Jim. 'Did you know?'

'She couldn't keep it from me.'

'She bloody well kept it from me.'

'Oh, Vic,' Chris says, 'she didn't want to worry people.'

'People? I'm not people, I'm her son. I don't come often enough to ferret it out for myself, so I suppose it doesn't matter that I don't know.'

131

'Whose fault is that, if you don't come?' Jim says.

'Now don't you bloody start. You're just at the other end of the M62; you can pop over in an evening.'

'When I haven't got a waiting-room full of patients.'

'We all know how overworked you are, over there among the Cheshire fleshpots.'

Jim's face tightens. 'Now look here –'

'Vic!' Chris breaks in. 'Stop it, and stop it now. If all you're going to do is cause bother it were better you'd not come at all. We've got enough trouble,' she adds in a minute as I grunt and move to a chair and feel for my cigarettes.

She's right, of course. I don't know what it was that made me flare so quickly. Perhaps a combination of my uneasy conscience and a feeling of being shut out that finding them together brought on. Add to that a habit Jim has of rubbing me up the wrong way. The truth is that for some while now I've not been able to number my brother among my favourite people. His wife, Claudine (how the hell did a Lancashire lass come by a name like that?), is a snob, and his two little lasses precocious brats. Which can't be altogether his fault. After all, we all make mistakes. But there's a certain type of North-country educated know-all, who talks down whenever he opens his mouth and lets out that characteristic supercilious voice, with three-quarters of its accent pressed out of it, that I cannot abide. And Jim, I'm sorry to say, belongs in that category. It wouldn't matter what his politics were, either (God knows, I'm no crusading ideologist), but that he's made the grade and turned arch-reactionary to support it doesn't help me to like him any the more.

I seem to remember we had a little set-to the last time we met. He said something about the state of the country and if I was asked to sign as many sick-notes as doctors were nowadays for men who just wanted to skive, I'd know where the trouble lay. So I asked him when was the last time he'd talked to a working man. All he did was treat riding-blisters on the arses of the daughters of

Cheshire business-men. Which was a bit hard on him, and which he didn't like. Nor did his missis, who shot me a look with daggers in it. But that's how it often is in families.

I apologize. 'I'm sorry. I'm tired. And it's been a shock. I mean, me dad . . . You're sort of half-prepared for something to happen to him . . .'

'But Mother,' Jims says, 'was going to live for ever.'

'Something like that.'

'Would you like a hot drink?' Chris asks, and I suggest that coffee will be the best thing, seeing we've the fag-end of a long night still to get through. As she gets up to go and make it I see how the solid flesh is gathering on her hips. Quite the figure of the young matron, she's becoming. She must be forty-two now; never any sign of more kids after Bobby; comfortably happy with the bloke she married and the life they've built together. I used to look up to her a lot, like some chaps idolize an older brother who's got it all sorted out. But a lot of ale's turned to water since then; though I do still envy her her gift of contentment.

I quiz Jim, as the medical man, about the treatment they'll be giving my mother and he runs through the standard drill and the alternatives. I'm just about to ask him for an honest opinion of her chances when the Old Feller appears, wearing his thick woollen dressing-gown over shirt and trousers.

'Dad.'

'Hello, lad. I thought I heard a motor car pull up. I was just dozing.'

I vacate the chair. 'Here, come and sit down.'

'Nay, nay, I'm right for a minute . . . It's a bit of a capper, this lot, isn't it?'

'Aye, it is.'

'Aye. Been me, there'd ha' been a bit o' sense in it.'

'Don't say that, Dad. We don't want anything wrong with either of you.'

'Can't pick an' choose, though, can we? Can't pick an' choose . . .'

133

He's half convulsed for a minute by his wheezing bronchial cough and I take his arm, with the feeling that I could make my fingers and thumb meet through the skin and gristle above his elbow, and press him down into the chair.

He fiddles with the skirt of his dressing-gown, then:

'Haven't you brought Ingrid?' he asks all of a sudden. 'You ought to bring her with you when you come.'

I shoot an astonished look at Jim, who narrows his eyes and gives me a slight shake of the head. Chris comes to the door.

'I'm making a drink, Dad. Do you want one?'

He gives a little wave of the hand that could mean anything, and I follow Chris back into the scullery.

'Jesus! Chris, he's just asked me why I haven't brought Ingrid.'

'He's started having these lapses of memory.'

'Lapses! How long has this been going on? I'd no idea.'

'I didn't really know myself till this last week, when I've been with him all the time. He was talking about writing to Uncle William the other day.'

'Christ!' Uncle William, my father's elder brother, has been dead for years.

'It comes and goes,' Chris says. 'Most of the time he knows exactly what's what. Apart from the usual patches of forgetfulness old people suffer from.'

'You mean his memory just sort of slips out of gear, without warning? What did me mother say about it? I mean, did she talk about it?'

'Yes. She was more worried about him than herself. She said he'd need to be looked after. We mustn't let him live on his own.'

'I should think not. At his time of life things like that get worse, don't they?'

'Yes,' Jim says quietly, by my shoulder. 'Senile decay usually does.' He's come softly through from the other room. 'Keep your voices down a bit, will you? There's not much wrong with his hearing.'

'Take him this cocoa,' Chris says to Jim, pouring hot

134

milk on to the paste she's mixed in a cup, and stirring. 'It'll soothe him, perhaps we can get him back to bed.'

Jim takes the cup and leaves us.

'What if the worst comes to the worst, then, Chris?' I ask her.

'You mean if Mother doesn't pull through?'

'Yes.'

'Even if she does she'll have to take things very easy. She'll really need help herself.'

'And if she doesn't?'

'Somebody will have to take him.' She turns a tight little smile to me. 'And there's only one obvious candidate for that, isn't there?'

I think about it. There's nothing I can do as far as offering the Old Feller a home is concerned, and I can't see him fitting into Jim's ménage. Apart from anything else, it's the woman of the house who will have to carry the load, and Christine *is* his own daughter.

'Don't you fancy it?' I ask her. 'If it's a question of room, me dad would have to sell this place anyway, and he could help you to buy a bigger house.'

'Oh, I've thought it all out. It wouldn't matter in the normal run of things. He's no bother and I'd take him as a matter of course. It's funny, though; David and I have been talking quite a lot lately about emigrating.'

'Emigrating? Emigrating where to?'

'Wherever propects and conditions are better for teachers than they are here. And where there's a better future for Bobby.'

'What's wrong with Bobby's future here?'

'You must know as well as I do that this country's in for a rude awakening. It's been coming for some time now. People wanting everything for nothing. Behaving as though money comes out of a bottomless well. And Bobby takes his eleven-plus next year. Or he would if there still was such a thing where we live. But there isn't. And no grammar school for him to go to. We can't afford to send him away to school so he'll get lumped with all the rest and go to the local comprehensive.'

'And what's wrong with that?'

'You want to spend as much time in them as David has and you wouldn't need to ask.'

'How can you, a collier's daughter, begrudge working-class kids a decent education?'

'But I don't. I don't begrudge it for those who want it, who can make the most of it. Look at us three, you and Jim and me. What made us different from the kids of other families round about? Brains, and the ability to work and use them. That's why all three of us went to grammar school when other kids were kicking their heels in secondary moderns and waiting to find a job in some factory or shop. It's why I went to a teacher-training college, why Jim went to university and medical school, why you took a degree in your spare time. Nobody laid anything on a plate for us.'

'A couple of generations before there'd have been no grammar school places for us.'

'Then why take them away from us again?'

'To give more of a chance to everybody.'

'And less of a chance for the bright ones, who are held back by those who wouldn't know a chance if it was covered in diamonds.'

'How many fee-paying pupils were there in school in your time?'

'A few. Why?'

'Were they specially bright or specially stupid?'

'They were mixed. Some of each.'

'But there shouldn't be any stupid kids in grammar schools according to your reasoning. How many bright kids were without a place because your fee-payers had bought what their brains couldn't with them?'

'It's a man's privilege to use his money to buy the best he can for his children.'

'At the expense of the less privileged, though?'

'Look, Vic, why do you think we always had decent school uniforms when kids from similar families went about scruffy? Why did we have things like bikes to go to school on, when other kids went without? Why have we always had full bellies and everything else we needed, within reason? Because we had a mother who cooked and baked and mended and a father who worked a full week and didn't waste what money he had on booze and gambling.'

'Lucky us.'

'Because we had parents with guts and character?'

'Yes. And should kids who haven't be made to suffer accordingly?'

'People who have it in them will make their way whatever.'

'Oh, Chris, Chris! What the hell's happened to you?'

'All right, then, we'll try to help them make their way, but not at the expense of everybody else. Ask Jim if he wants some coffee.'

I stick my head round the door and ask him.

'He says no, thanks.'

'Drink yours, then. It goes cold quickly.' She looks at her watch. 'I must go and ring up again in a few minutes.'

It's none too warm in here, away from the fire, but neither of us seems to want to go back into the living-room yet. We lean opposite each other and sip our coffee. It's been a night of shocks, and as if that weren't enough I've got also now a feeling of a kind of creeping dismay. For a moment I have a longing to be back in the old days, when the family was all together, the Old Feller and the Old Lady were in their prime, and we kids were still working towards some kind of place in the world, when all kinds of things looked possible but we were content to build on the basis we had and weren't torn by greed, restlessness and hopelss longing. We were all in it together then; the assumptions we shared were more important than the differences between us. But I think I might be kidding myself: making the standard mistake of people who look at the past from a present that suddenly seems sour.

Jim comes in.

'Dad's gone back to bed.'

'Oh, good,' Chris says.

'I think I ought to go up to the hospital,' Jim says. 'Get hold of somebody who'll talk to me.'

'Will you go and telephone again first, though?' Chris says. 'Then we shall know if there's any change.'

'Okay.' he checks his pocket for coins, and goes out.

Chris and I move through into the living-room and take the easy chairs on either side of the fire, which I mend with the smokeless fuel that's all we're allowed to use now. It burns with a red glow, not the leaping, stretching flames of the old coal. But the results of the clean-air act are showing themselves in the town, in the sandblasted stone of the older buildings, pale honey-colour after three-quarters of a century of black grime. If they'd do a bit more of that, and altering and modernizing, instead of knocking everything down and replacing it with concrete which weathers with dingy stains and looks slummy before it's been up ten minutes, we might at last have a town that both kept its character and was good to look at.

I light a cigarette and Chris, who hardly ever smokes, takes one when it's offered. Waiting, we seem now to have run out of things to say.

'Where were you thinking of emigrating to?' I ask her after a while.

'What's Australia like?'

'Six weeks don't make me an expert. The people seem fairly well-off, and they're friendly enough if you don't give the impression that you think of them as colonials or second-class Britishers. Is that where you were thinking of going?'

'We'd talked about there, and South Africa.'

'You *what*?'

'South Africa. It's a beautiful country, with a good climate and plenty of opportunity.'

'I thought part of the problem was Bobby's future.'

'It is.'

'What kind of a future do you think he'll have in a society that's built on false pretences? The blacks won't prop up the white man's affluence for ever, you know. Sooner or later they'll ask for their share. And they'll take it. If it doesn't come in your time it'll come in Bobby's. Jesus! Whose idea was South Africa, yours or David's?'

She doesn't answer, but says instead, 'Where do you suggest we go, then – Russia?'

Oh, dear! That creeping dismay rears itself and washes over me in a great wave.

'I'm not suggesting you go anywhere, love. I like it here.'

'It's probably all right for you. You're doing well enough.'

'Okay, so I am.'

'But circumstances alter cases.'

'And broken noses alter faces,' I say, automatically.

Chris allows herself a little reminiscent smile. 'I haven't heard that for a long time. One of Dad's, isn't it?'

'Yes. But you're right, of course. If you want to go, go. It's up to you and you know your own know best. But I don't like to hear people always using the excuse that this country's washed-up.'

'It's not what it was; you can't pretend it is.'

'In many ways it's a damned sight better. And I think it's going to be better still. What we've got now isn't the end. It's only a stage in the change we're going through, the transition; and education's one of the fields where it shows most.'

'I think you'll allow that David and I know rather more about education than you do.'

'Granted. But I think you'll allow that there are people who know as much about it as David and you do, and don't think like you think. So who's right? Are we going to the dogs or gradually moving to something better than before?'

'It's a matter of opinion.'

'And South Africa's a matter of common sense. Unless you want to help skim the last of the cream and then move on somewhere else. What sort of bloke are you wanting to turn Bobby into? One who takes it for granted that his standard of living will be supported by a pool of exploited labour? Apart from anything else, it can't last, can it? The world's running out of places like that.'

Chris sits leaning towards the fire. Her face appears slightly flushed, I don't know whether by the heat or because of the way I'm talking. But she can't be more upset than I am. You can hear a similar reasoning to hers all the time in business. The attitude that as long as I'm making my profits everything's all right with the world. And if it isn't, at least it's all right with me. I just never expected it of Chris; and neither did I expect her implication that anybody who questions it must do so standing under the Red Flag.

Jim comes back. He looks out of temper. We both turn our faces to him and Chris asks him for the news.

'I don't know,' Jim says. 'All I could get out of the silly bitch I spoke to was that she's as well as can be expected.' he looks at his watch. 'I'm going up there.'

'Do you want me to come with you?' I ask him.

'No, you stay and keep Chris company. I'll find the man in charge and have a chat with him. At least *he* won't be able to fob me off with "as well as can be expected".'

'You'll let us know if there's any change?' Chris says.

'Yes. Damn and blast not having a phone in the house. I've been trying to persuade them for years. It would have cost practically nothing if we'd clubbed together to pay for it.'

'Yes, I know,' I say. 'Still, if you could talk to them on the phone you'd have even less to make you come and visit.'

'You speak for yourself.' he says.

'I was, actually,' I tell him.

'I'll go, then.'

He goes.

'I wish you and Jim got on better,' Chris says.

'You mean you wish I wouldn't needle him so much.'

140

'What is it you've got against him?'

'His king-size ego, mainly. The world revolves round him and his.'

'Who does your world revolve round? You do pretty well for Number One, don't you?'

'I try to do it without trampling on everybody else.'

'I thought you'd done some pretty fair trampling in your time.'

'Oh hoh! I didn't pass the test, did I? And nobody's ever forgotten it. Well, you and Jim were never put to that particular test, were you?'

'You don't know what tests we've had to face.'

'They must have been stiff ones for you to still feel sanctimonious about my sins.'

'I just don't think you're in any position to preach to people who want to make the best lives they can for themselves and their families.'

'Then I won't any more.'

I shut my eyes. Apart from that involuntary nap in the theatre I haven't slept for nearly twenty-four hours. Worried as I am, there's no resisting its pull now. I don't know if Chris says anything else, because in what seems like seconds I'm fast on.

I wake up in what seems exactly the position I fell asleep in. I gingerly straighten my stiff neck. There's a smell of frying bacon coming from the kitchen, and a hollow feeling of anxiety in my guts. The curtains are still drawn and the light's on. My watch says seven forty-five. I stand up and stretch my limbs.

Chris is standing over the gas-cooker. She looks at me as I appear in the doorway.

'They say she's out of immediate danger,' she tells me at once.

'Ah!'

'So we can all breathe again.'

'Yes. Where's Jim?'

'He's had some breakfast and gone to bed for an hour. I thought you were going to sleep for ever.'

141

'Does me dad know?'

'Yes, he's asleep as well now.'

'What about you? When do you sleep?'

'When you and I have eaten. We can visit this afternoon. Do you want one egg or two?'

I realize I'm famished. 'Two, please. Is there anything I can do?'

'Lay the table, if you will. Jim just had coffee and a bacon sandwich. And make some toast. There's a pot of tea already mashed.'

When I've put a cloth on the table and laid out the knives and forks, I take a mug of tea to the fire and toast slices of bread on the end of the long old-fashioned toasting fork that I remember us having all my life.

'Do you have to go back today?' Chris asks me, when we're eating.

'I ought to be back in the office tomorrow. I haven't written my Australian report yet. What about you? Can they manage without you at school?'

'They'll have to. I don't see that I can do anything but stay here till Mother's on her feet again. I expect David will come up with Bobby at the week-end. Which reminds me, I must phone him before he goes out to school, and tell him the news. He'll be wondering.'

'Are they both okay?'

'Bobby's fighting fit. The only problem is getting him to sit still for five minutes.'

'And what about you?'

'Oh, there's nothing much ails me. I'm overworked and underpaid, that's all.'

'But appreciated, eh?'

'Cherished, even.'

'That must be nice.'

'It is.'

'Then what's the real trouble, Chris?'

She sighs and thinks for a minute before answering. 'Well, it's all right for me because the kids I have, in junior school, are mostly a joy to be with. They're outgoing, trusting, receptive. I sometimes think they're

142

almost like blank slates that you can write on. Unfortunately, though, that doesn't last long. They grow older, and something happens to them.'

'Somebody must be writing the wrong things on the slate.'

'Perhaps so. Perhaps we're not getting it right. Perhaps it's in the nature of the animal. Or perhaps it's the system. More tea?'

'Please.'

She tops up my cup, then her own.

'I get worried about David. He's living on his nerve-ends all the time. They expect too much of teachers nowadays. They want us to be parents, social workers, psychiatrists – the lot. That's apart from trying to drill some academic knowledge into a lot of heads that don't want it. There's no authority any more. Parents have stopped exerting it just at a time when we're prevented from doing so. We have no sanctions to apply. We can't draw meaningful lines and say thus far and no further. The kids are expected to do it for themselves, and it's asking too much of them. Self-discipline is only possible once you know what discipline itself is.'

She gets up, pushing back her chair. 'I must go and phone, or I'll miss him.'

She takes her handbag from the sideboard and looks for coins. I feel in my pocket and find a couple of ten-pence pieces.

'Here, take these.'

'Thanks. I shan't be long.'

I've cleared the table and washed up the few dirty pots by the time she comes back. The clatter of the brass handles as I open the sideboard drawer is one of the sounds I associate with this house and the life we all used to live here together. As I slip the folded cloth into the drawer I see the edge of a photograph mount sticking out from under the other things in there and I lift them and take it out. It's a group picture of Chris's form at the grammar school, and when I look again I find one of Jim's year and one of my own.

'Look what I've found.'

Chris peers over my shoulder. 'Good lord! It's a long time since I saw those.'

'Me too. Can you remember the names of everybody on yours?'

'I shouldn't think so.'

'Neither can I.' I identify a few at random: Clegg, Austin, Jackson, Foster, Widdop, Lucas, Mitchell, Greaves, Pickering, Sheldrake, Mellor, Lockwood . . . 'And of course none of us even thought to write the names on the back, because we saw them all every schoolday for five years and never dreamed there'd come a time when we couldn't remember some of them.'

Chris points to the open smiling face of a pretty blonde girl on her picture. 'Kathleen Waterford. She's dead. Cancer. A couple of years ago.'

'I've got a tight-mouthed suppressed grin on my face, as though I can't obey the photographer's command to smile without cracking out in untimely laughter. I can't remember why, though I notice I'm standing next to Rufus Widdop, who was a prodigious farter, dropping the most pungent raspers and reekers with a blue-eyed innocence that had the rest of us in fits. We used to blame it on his passion for baked beans.

'Be an interesting little exercise, searching them all out and finding out what they're up to.'

'It's usually disappointing trying to resurrect the past. You've changed, they've changed, the situation's changed. If your memories are good ones, keep them as memories, I always say. Can I beg a cigarette?'

'I shouldn't encourage you,' I tell her, offering her the packet.

'Oh, I shan't even think about smoking once this lot's over.'

'Why don't you go up to bed and get some sleep?'

'I will, when I've finished this . . . We need some groceries. The cupboard's just about bare.'

'Write me a list and I'll go.'

In the end, I find pen and paper and write the list

144

myself to Chris's dictation, then read it back to her.

'I think that's everything.' She can hardly keep her eyes open now. 'You'll need some money.'

'Got some. Come on, now, off to bed with you.' I take hold of her hands and pull her up.

'Don't forget the latchkey. It's on the sideboard.'

'Okay.'

Suddenly she puts her arms round me and presses her head into my shoulder.

'God! It's a relief.'

'Aye . . .'

I'm touched that she wants my comfort. It's a comfort in its turn. We can live our separate lives, not seeing each other for months, have differences of opinion, and bicker sometimes, when we do meet, but find times like this when comfort comes from all we know about each other, all we've shared. And it makes me realize what true loneliness must be: not when you can't have what you need, but when you look round and find that there's nobody, nobody at all, who needs you.

The mechanical hardware standing outside the house must be evidence to the neighbours that the Brown kids are doing well. My mother wouldn't dream of looking down on anybody who hadn't got a car, but that her children can muster three stylish models between them has, I know, always given her quiet satisfaction when they've had occasion to be parked out there all at one time.

I roll the MG back from behind Jim's Triumph then move in first a hundred yards up the hill, thinking I'll turn round at the next side street. It occurs to me when I get there that I can cut through. I thought all the property behind here had been pulled down, but I find that on the top side of this street of old broken cobbles there's still a dozen or so terrace houses left standing and occupied. It's so long since they had a lick of paint, some of the doors are through to the bare wood, and its obvious that nobody's going to spend money on them when they're so near to demolition. A street, in fact, similar to the one Willy Lomas was living in when he moved my furniture for me. It's the windows that tell you about the people inside: some are curtained with fresh clean nylon lace, others have only the filth on the glass to stop you seeing in. They mark the difference between people with pride and those who couldn't care less, the kind of difference Chris was talking about, between our family and others round about, not a difference in jobs and income, but that between tidy working-class and squalid, a difference that boils down to nothing else but character. With the tidiness, of course, come the rules, ways of living that stop you sinking to the level you can see all round you: drunkenness, scrapping in the streets on Saturday night, wife-beating, broken marriages, kids from different fathers in one house, kids who roam in gangs, turn to vandalism and petty crime, father bastards, keep the cycle going, round and round, never up and out. To my parent's generation it must have never seemed far to fall, because they'd seen it happen all too often, even among members of one family. The renegades and black sheep are always with us.

It's market day. The streets where I thought I might park are already chockablock with traders' vehicles and cars and I have to drive round for a while before I find a space. Walking back, I pass what was Mr. Van Huyten's music shop. Out of curiosity I go inside. I can't recognize it as the place I worked and spent some happy hours in – that I thought, in fact, would one day be mine. They've remodelled the interior. They still sell television sets, radios and record-players, but even fridges and vacuum-cleaners as well now; and the record department which was my pride and joy has been whittled down to not much more than a selection of cheap-label LPs in a couple of revolving racks. It's still quiet, being early, and a young bloke comes over and asks if he can show me anything. I resist the temptation to tell him I want to see something that was lost more than ten years ago, and leave.

Back at the market, I wander down through the first area of open-air stalls, my nose picking up the scents of fresh fruit and flowers, and begin to think about the items on my list. I buy lamb chops, bacon, sausages, eggs, cheese, butter and vegetables, stopping the caper of a bloke who wants to sell me poor tomatoes from the back of the stall instead of good ones from the front, then go on into the other part where they're displaying kids' clothes, bolts of end-of-run and reject fabrics, shirts, pots, pans, crockery, wonder gadgets that peel potatoes, open bottles, cut glass and remove corns – everything except write the letter of complaint when they don't do all they're claimed to do – secondhand books, and paperbacks returnable in good condition for a half-price refund.

The number of times I've walked through here, holding my mother's hand. Mostly in the early dark of winter afternoons, it seems to me now, with pools of shadow and the lights on the stalls shining on heaps of red and yellow fruit and the multi-coloured mountains of unwrapped sweets; glinting on glassware, cheap jewelry, trinkets and toys, so that each and every alley was an Aladdin's cave of treasure. First me alone, then Jim and me together, because Chris, when she was there, was already the little woman, sworn in as my mother's deputy to help check two greedy-eyed lads. 'No, you've had all you're getting, so shut up and behave!'

But I don't belong here any more. The present here is just echoes of the past, and the future's somewhere else.

10

My mother has been moved from intensive care into an annexe at one end of a public ward. We're allowed in to see her two at a time. We let the Old Feller stay in most of the period, but at one stage Chris and I are on our own with her. She's had a fright, but she's not one to feel sorry for herself and the look in her eye is the kind of dry expression she might turn on somebody else who's taken a bit too much for granted.

'It'll stop me gallop for a while, I expect,' she says.

I haven't realized how upset the sight of her in bed, weak and under orders, would make me, because I can't remember, apart from the occasional bout of 'flu, when she was laid up before. Fretting about the Old Feller won't help her to get her strength back in peace, either. She must have expected for a long time that he would go first. It's bothering her now that there's a real possibility she won't see him out, making sure of his creature comforts to the end. All this lot was never part of the plan, not to her, nor to us either.

Both Chris and I suggest they'd be better off selling the house and buying a bungalow, which would be easier to run. They'd get a good price because property values have rocketed. But she doesn't like the idea of our losing our old bedrooms, which she's kept furnished and ready for our visits home.

I feel I'm copping out by leaving her; but I've got to get back, and there's nothing I can do if I stay. It's woman's work and Chris will have to cope, as she expects to, as I suppose it was written into her future that she would one day.

Promising to come up again as soon as I can, I say good-bye to them all there at the hospital and drive straight through the town to the nearest motorway access. I'm in London by half past seven. I open a tin of what claims to be Spaghetti Bolognese – the only food I have in – and sip a stiff Scotch-and-water on the rocks while I wait for it to heat up. I phoned Janice this morning and told her to let those who'll be wondering know where I was, and now, I think, I could save part of the lost day by getting on with my report. I could, that is, if all my papers weren't at the office. I eat off a tray, sitting in front of the television set, which is showing an episode of a cowboy series. I wonder who's working out what by turning all these gruff, silver-haired patriarchs of the Old West into white liberals, always persuaded to give someone who's strayed from the straight and narrow a pat on the head and a chance to do better next time, instead of stringing him up or shooting him out of hand, which was more likely the way they actually settled such problems.

It's nine o'clock by the time it finishes. I take stock of the evening. I'm usually contented enough with my own company. I don't always feel the need to be gallivanting and I've spent many an evening here alone. There's a couple of hefty paperbacks I keep meaning to get stuck into, the second half of a concert on the radio, plenty of gramophone records. I could go round the corner for a couple of pints, have a long soak in the bath, go to bed early, catch up on myself with a good night's sleep.

The trouble is though, that after ten years of pushing her out of my mind I know now exactly where Donna is and what she's doing while I'm fidgeting about the flat like a dog in a heatwave, that can't find a cool place to lie. And it could be the same every night for as long as the play runs. If I don't do something about it. And if I do do something about it, what then? I'm knackered either way, that's what.

I take a shower, dress again and go downstairs. It's drizzling now and there are haloes of mist round the street-lights. A night to be indoors with your feet up, instead of chasing lost dreams.

When I've parked the car I still have a little time to spare so I go into the pub near the theatre, a Victorian place of brass, red plush and engraved glass, and drink half a pint of beer. I get an odd feeling, standing at the bar on my own, and then I realize that one or two fellers, also drinking alone, are quietly sizing me up. So it's a place where you need never be without a friend; if that's the kind of friend you fancy. In the gents, which I visit as an insurance against being taken short at an inopportune moment later, I find among the graffiti the carefully written question – more a complaint, really – 'Where are all those Guards at 30p for 20?'

The obvious thing is to send a note round to Donna, asking her if she'll see me; but I have reasons for not doing that. Not that I think she'd refuse; I just want the get-out, a way of saving face, that bumping into her accidentally-on-purpose will leave me, and that my openly wanting to meet her again wouldn't. Or, I tell myself, as I wait in the street, with one eye on the stage-door again, I could go and get into my car, drive home and go to bed, willing her out of my thoughts as I did before. Right out. I mean, I have done it before, haven't I? It could be another ten years before I pick up a newspaper with her picture in it, and I ought to be well armoured by then. This little setback is only a temporary breach in my defences. Why should I go out of my way to widen it? But what I don't know is whether the reality of her now matches the reality I knew; and that's what I've got to find out. Because although I see no hope, my stomach is hollow with all the newly remembered wanting, and what could be more hopeless than pining again, only this time for someone who no longer exists?

They come out in different groupings this time. The man who was first is first again, but now he's got the oldest of the three women with him, and they walk away together. Then three more appear: the younger feller and two women. They stroll slowly off the other way, towards the pub, where they linger on the pavement for a minute, until the older of the women breaks away. The others go into the pub as Donna comes out of the stage-door on her own and follows at a brisk pace. I could easily cross over and pretend I'd just recognized her; but I'm after more than an awkward encounter in the street which she can bring to an end as she likes unless I push harder than I'm ready to seem to be pushing, and I mutter under my breath as she nears the pub: 'Go in, go in, go in.'

She goes in.

I take a deep breath and let it out, waiting a minute before I move. There'll never be another moment like the one where we meet for the first time after all these years, and I'm scared to death of muffing it, of doing it all wrong, of giving the game away straight off and finding she couldn't care less.

I use the other door, on the corner. The place is full enough now for me to look round and see before I'm seen. When I've managed to get served, I stand back, pint in hand, and begin to edge farther into the room between the tables and the standing drinkers until I spot them, round the curve of the bar. A chap drinks up and goes and I slip into the space he's left at the counter. Now she can see me any time she looks my way, but I find that I can watch her without seeming to in a mirror fixed at an angle to me, on a buttress behind the bar. She's chuckling as the bloke they're with gives out with the patter, talking away, his hands making shapes in the air. He's got tight black curly hair and with that and the round gold-framed glasses he's wearing he looks like the young Franz Schubert in washed-out denim tunic and jeans. The other girl is black-haired too, but I can see no more than that and an occasional glimpse of a snub-nose profile as she turns her head and picks up her half-pint glass of lager.

The light, as she steps back once, is harsh on Donna's face, picking out the bone structure and darkening the cavities of her eyes, so that suddenly she looks older still.

It's gone as she moves again, but the curious vulnerability of her in that moment stabs me to the quick. My heart beats faster. I've got to do something before they decide to go, and rob me of the chance. But Donna's got money out of her bag. She turns to face the bar, catches the barmaid's eye, orders refills, waits, glances idly round. I switch my gaze to the mirror as she looks my way. She looks again, her eyes narrowing. The barmaid brings their drinks and speaks to Donna, who inclines her head slightly to catch what she's saying. She counts coins into the girl's hand than passes the drinks to her friends. When she's resumed her previous stance she brings her gaze round in my direction, a little frown between her eyes. She's seen me.

In something like panic, I empty my glass, ask for another drink, and feel for cigarettes. When I glance in the mirror again I can't see her. I look directly across at where she was standing. She's gone. Her drink, untouched, is on the bar.

Christ! no, I think. She can't have . . .

I feel a touch on my elbow, from behind.

'Hello, Vic.'

Should I pretend surprise? Well, well, well! Hello, hello, hello! After all these years!

What I do is simply turn and face her square on and say quietly, 'Hello, Donna,' in a way that surely tells her I've seen her first and let her make the first move. What might tell a stranger watching that there's unfinished business between us is that neither of us smiles, and our eyes are shy, unable to hold for long.

'How are you?' I ask her.

'I'm well enough.'

But you look tired, love, I'm thinking. Is it permanently taking so much out of you, or am I seeing no more than normal post-performance fatigue?

'You're looking very fit.'

'Oh, I'm fine. I don't ail a thing.' Except something that medicine can't cure, something that's picking me up and bouncing me along in great drowning waves. Every

152

muscle, every nerve in my face feels tight with the strain of not letting it show.

'What are you doing in here? Do you get in often?'

'I've never been in before.' I glance round. 'Looks to me like the sort of place, if you drop anything you kick it to the door.'

Now she manages a little laugh, even. 'I expect you can still look after yourself.'

'I haven't always found that I could.'

That's too near the bone. She says nothing.

'What are you up to these days?'

'I'm in a play, down the street.'

'Oh? The big time, eh?'

'The security will be nice, if it runs.'

We're lost for a minute. Awkward. Am I playing the part too well?

'Can I get you a drink?'

'I've got one, thanks. Over there.'

'Don't let me keep you from your friends.'

That's right, you bloody fool. Let her think you're freezing her off. Give her every excuse to go, and say, 'See you around, in another ten years.'

'Oh, they're all right.'

'You must have a drink, then. Let me get you one.'

She hesitates, looks towards the other two, seems to be deciding between breaking it now and letting it carry on for a while. All in a second, before she says, 'Come over and join us.'

She's taking a risk. I could snub her straight out now; show her that I don't want her crumbs of politeness after what she did to me.

'Actors, are they?'

'Yes. Two of the company.'

'Don't mind. Long time since I met any actors.'

I follow her as she edges through the crowd, wanting to reach out and touch her, let her lead me by the hand. They've grabbed a table that's suddenly come vacant and I sit down beside Donna as she squeezes into the semi-circular alcove.

'This is Vic Brown, an . . . old friend. Millie Verity, Michael Lucas.'

The younger feller nods amiably and the girl gives me a friendly wide-mouthed grin that shows about a dozen more big white teeth than the normal human complement. 'Hello.'

'I was just telling Millie about something I read in Pascal,' the young chap says. ' "The silence of those infinite spaces terrifies me." Might be a comment on Pinter, don't you think?'

'Yes.' Donna takes his point with a smile.

I don't know who Pascal is, though I do know some of Pinter's plays, so I keep quiet as Lucas turns to the girl and picks up what he was saying before we joined them:

'You see, I'm quite sure that when an intuitive writer like Pinter begins to accumulate such a body of comment, that tries to tell him what he's doing and why he's doing it, it can analyse him into a crippling self-consciousness.'

'Oh, but Michael, don't you think he's much more aware of what he's up to than he lets on? A lot of his public statements about his work are just a defence, surely?'

'No, no. You see . . .'

'Where are you living now, Vic?' Donna asks me.

'Here, in London. I've got a flat in St. John's Wood.'

'Do you see anything of Albert Conroy these days?'

'Not a lot. We sometimes have a drink when he comes up from Southampton. He's been with a company there for two or three years.'

'Did he ever get married?'

'Not Albert. He seems to be prefer the bachelor life. And I've completely lost sight of Fleur.'

'Oh, I can tell you about her. She did get married, to a Portuguese businessman. She lives abroad most of the time now.'

'Landed on her feet, eh?'

'She's certainly not short of creature comforts.'

A pause. I try to time it.

'I ran into Clive Carter the other day.'

I'm sitting more or less sideways on to her and I can't read her expression as I tell her this.

'I haven't seen him in years.'

'No, I know. He told me. I asked him.'

'Where did you meet him?'

'On a plane, coming from Rome.'

'Had you been on holiday?'

'No, I was on the last lap from Australia.'

'Oh? What were you doing out there?'

I tell her, keeping it brief, simple, factual. She smiles.

'Big time yourself, by the sound of it.'

'Well, let's say I'm doing well enough for the present.'

She fishes a pack of Gauloise out of her big, soft leather bag and offers me one. I refuse, take one of my own and light us both up. She smokes quickly, nervously, reaching out after every pull to tap off ash with a hand that's not quite steady. So she's either living on her nerves nowadays or something's thrown her. And that, I guess, can only be meeting me again. Maybe she thinks I'm just waiting my time to reproach her, that the years have hardened me so that the only feeling I have left is a memory of the injury she did me. Well, let her think so.

Lucas finishes his drink and gets up. The girl starts to gather her belongings.

'Must be off, Donna.'

'Oh . . . all right.'

They leave together. 'See you tomorrow. Good-bye.' The girl flashes that battery of teeth at me. 'Good night.'

''Night.'

We're alone. What am I going to say? 'Another drink?'

'No, thanks. I must be going, myself.'

'Where have you got to get to?'

'Barnes.'

'I've got the car. I'll give you a lift, if you like.'

'Oh, it's much too far out of your way.'

'How do you usually travel?'

'Underground to Hammersmith, then either bus or taxi across the river.'

'Well, I'll take you.'

'No, really . . .'

'Come on, don't be silly. It's no way at all.'

'Is there nobody waiting for you?'

'No.'

It invites a similar question from me, but I hold it back, thinking I'll get to know all I want to know in my own good time.

The two-seater MGB is not a car for keeping your distance in. We're almost as close together as we were in the pub, but alone now, cocooned from the world outside. I have to reach across her to fasten her safety-belt for her, and though there's nothing in the world I want more at this moment than to put my arms round her and hold her tight, I manage the operation with as much decorum as if I were buckling in an elderly maiden aunt.

Leicester Square and Piccadilly Circus are, as usual, full of crowds spilling off the pavement into the road, taking their lives in their hands. We're both quiet till we're clear of all this and heading down Piccadilly itself. I've been to bed with this girl. I know – or knew – the shapes and scents of her body. What pattern in life is it that gives me that, keeps us apart for ten years, then puts in my way a newspaper interview that leads, two days later, to our driving alone together like this through the London night? What is it in my nature, more like, that leads me to build patterns where there are none, to play with fire, get burnt, come back for more, and want to call it fate?

'Knightsbridge and Ken High Street?' I ask her as we come on Hyde Park Corner.

'Yes, then straight through to Hammersmith Bridge.'

Not many minutes later, leaving the Albert Hall behind on the left, I realize that we're about to pass within two hundred yards of the hotel where we spent a couple of nights together one week-end when we were escaping from the Longford crowd.

'Do you remember that place?' I ask her, pointing to the lighted canopy down the side road.

'Yes.'

'What it is to be young and foolish.'

There's a pause.

'*Did* you and your wife split up?'

'Oh, yes. She threatened to name you, but it went through as desertion in the end.'

'Perhaps she wanted to give you time to change your mind and go back to her.'

'I didn't, though.'

'I'm sorry.'

'What for? That I didn't go back?'

'I meant for my part in it.'

'You needn't be. It was on the cards. Ingrid's married again now.'

'What about you?'

'No . . . You're not either, are you?'

'How do you know that?'

'You're not wearing a wedding ring.'

'That doesn't mean much nowadays.'

'Am I right, though?'

'Yes.'

'What about the baby? There was a baby, wasn't there?'

'A boy. He'll be ten in December.'

'What do you call him?'

'Tom.'

'Tom Pennyman. Is that after somebody?'

'My grandfather.'

'What did you tell him about his father?'

'Oh, that he was somebody I didn't want to marry.'

'Or who didn't want to marry you?'

'Why should I say that?'

'I thought it might be a better explanation of why he wasn't around. Why he never saw the lad.'

'How do you know he doesn't see him?'

'You've more or less told me he doesn't, haven't you?'

She's quiet for a second, thinking back. 'Yes, I suppose I have.'

'Well,' I say then, 'it's nothing to do with me, but I just

don't understand a man who doesn't want to see his own kid.'

'People aren't all alike.'

'I've noticed. My mother always says the world would be a dull place if they were. It must have left you with a bit of a problem, though, bringing him up on your own.'

'Oh, my parents were wonderful. I stayed at home for quite a while, helping around the place in any way I could.'

'Mucking out the pigs, for instance?'

'What? Oh, you remember the pigs, do you?'

'Yes.' I remember everything, love.

'Then when Tom got walking I began to pick up the threads. I did a stint at the Northcott at Exeter, then a spell with Bristol Old Vic – both within striking distance of home.'

'But didn't you feel frustrated ever? I mean that you'd been losing ground at a crucial stage in your career?'

'Not really. I was glad in a way of a chance to take stock. In any case, I didn't feel I was depriving the world of a great talent. And I never had the kind of astonishing good looks that must be exploited before they fade.'

'What about the boy? Is he a happy lad?'

'I think so. He's always had plenty of affection.'

'So . . . It's not turned out too badly, then?'

'Oh, no. You make your life with the ingredients to hand, don't you?'

'Yes . . . Yes, you make your life.'

Beyond Olympia we're into the ring of less elegant boroughs which encircle the West End, full of long roads with those flat-roofed London-type pubs you never see in the provinces: Islington, Camden Town, Shepherds Bush, Hammersmith, Fulham . . .

'You and your wife never had children, did you?'

'No. We got married because she was pregnant, then she fell down the stairs and brought on a miscarriage. She had another a couple of years after that. The doctors told her she had a good chance of carrying the full term if she took special care; but, well . . . we decided to leave it for a while. Maybe it was me who did the deciding. I was getting more and more restless and a kid would have been another chain.' She knows all this, or did. 'Ingrid has a child now, a girl, I've never seen her.'

'Don't you feel that you'd like children?'

'Inside a stable relationship, okay. Otherwise it's the children who carry the can, isn't it? I mean, I don't go about wanting to populate the world in my own image. It's not so much wanting a child as wanting some particular woman to bear your child. An . . . an extension, or an expression, of your feeling for her.'

'With the child as a by-product.'

'A by-product of happiness. What better reason for existence than that?'

At the end of the long straight road beyond the bridge she directs me right. Soon we pass by a kind of stray, with a pond.

'Pretty.'

'Yes. The Green.'

'How do you come to be here? Are you in some sort of digs, or a flat?'

'We have a house – next turn left. Sorry.'

'We? Who is we?'

'My father died a couple of years ago. My mother felt like a change from Cornwall, and I thought it was time I tackled London again. You can pull in anywhere here.'

We're in a street of small terrace houses with dormer windows in the roofs and bays on the ground floor.

'Hmm. Cosy.'

'We were lucky in our timing, actually. We bought just before house prices started to take off.'

'They're beyond all sense and reason now.'

'Quite.'

'So you live here with your mother and the lad?'

'Yes.'

'Nice convenient arrangement.'

And if there is anybody special he's not, I gather, living in. That, I find, is a bit of knowledge that makes me almost lightheaded with relief.

'Well, thanks for the lift.'

'Don't mention it.'

'I feel I've left you with an awfully long drive back.'

'Oh, there's nothing to it.'

'Can I offer you a cup of coffee before you go? Or a drink?'

'Tell you the truth, I'm a bit fagged. If I come in and sit down I might not get up again. It's all this flying. It takes you days to catch up, and I had to make an unexpected trip up to Yorkshire last night.'

'If you're sure.'

'Yes. Thanks all the same. Another time, perhaps.'

You'll never know that I'm really dying to come in with you, I'm thinking. And I'm calling on more willpower than I ever thought I could muster to stop me asking if I can see her again. How do I know I'll ever have another chance like this? But something tells me not to rush it; that playing it cool is the only way.

She's fumbling with the seat-belt lock. I click it open for her.

'You will drive carefully, won't you?'

'Window down all the way.'

She opens the door. 'Thanks again.'

'You're welcome.'

'Good night.'

'Good night, Donna.'

She's out. The door shuts. I gun the engine and move off as soon as she starts to walk.

Part Three

11

Talking about a friend can sometimes seem to prompt him to turn up. Conroy gives me a ring at the office the very next day.

'Vic, I've got some business in town. Are you doing anything this evening.'

I tell him no.

'Let's have a jar and some nosh, shall we?'

'Okay. Are you staying over? Do you want a place to put your head down?'

'Got one, thanks. On the firm. What time do you leave your office?'

'Oh, any time after half-past five. Six at the latest.'

'Look, then, do you know the Cumberland Hotel, Marble Arch?'

'I know where it is.'

'Meet me in the cocktail bar there, about half past six. Is that okay?'

'It'll be nearer seven. I'd better drop the car off if we're having a few.'

'See you, then.'

He rings off. He sounds on top form, and I'm delighted at the prospect of seeing him. I haven't made many what I'd call close men friends in the last few years. There are some chaps at the office whom I'm chummier with than others, and whom I see outside; but the danger for a bloke my age living on his own is that he'll become dependent for companionship on men whose first priority is their wives and families, or that he'll be out all the time looking for amusement: frittering his time away,

163

scared to sit down alone and contemplate his navel. So I learned to be happy outside working hours with my own company, apart from that of whichever girl was currently engaging my attention, making the flat into a home where I could relax reasonably contentedly with a book or some music, from which I could wander round to any one of the local pubs that took my fancy for a couple of late evening pints, and to which I could thankfully retreat and shut my door when the bores and glib putters-of-the-world-to-rights were too thick along the bar.

It's nearly seven by the time I've stop-started through the rush hour, found a space for my car, had a wash, changed my shirt and made my way by Underground to Marble Arch. I was held up for five minutes by a phone call from Miriam, timing my arrival home to a nicety and taking advantage of the fact that Graham needs longer for his journey.

'When did you get back?'

'Last night. But it was very late.'

She asks about my mother, then we agree that she'll phone again, in a day or two, when she knows how the land lies. I've already decided it's over, and I want to let it drag on even less now that I've met Donna again; but I doubt if there's any way I can finish it without telling her to her face, and doubt even less that she'll accept the fact and not try to hold on. But I push that problem to the back of my mind as I walk into the foyer of the Cumberland, suddenly aware that I'm more consciously happy than I have been for a long time, and look for Conroy.

There are people wandering in and out of a dim blue cavern in the bend of the L-shaped lobby and I go and stand in the doorway, adjusting my eyes to what appears to be an almost total absence of light, until I finally see an arm lift at one end of the bar counter and recognize my man.

'What are you doing lurking in here, Albert? Travelling incognito?'

'My last appointment was just round the corner. What'll you have?'

164

'Well, I won't show you up by asking for a pint. Scotch on the rocks.' He orders. 'They don't fix you up with digs like this, do they?'

'Nothing like so splendid. Anyway, I thought to myself, seeing as how I'm to be alone in the Great Wen I might as well try to see my old buddy Brown and bring him tidings of great joy.'

'Come up on the pools, have you?'

'I'm getting married.'

'You *what*?'

'Don't look as if I'd said I was having a sex-change. I said I'm getting married, espoused, spliced, wed.'

'Christ!'

'No, it won't be a church ceremony, but I'm glad you're pleased . . .'

'Oh, I am, Albert,' I feel my face crack open in a huge grin.

'. . . because I want you to be my best man.'

'Do you? Do you really?'

I'm knocked out by surprise. I'd taken it for granted as something he'd never try again. I thought his sex-drive was almost non-existent. I've wondered from time to time, in fact, if there wasn't a touch of the AC-DC about him, but so mild that one inclination cancelled out the other and left him in a state of contented neutrality.

'You'd better tell me about the brave woman.'

'Her name's Felicity. She's a widow, about my age, with a son away at university and a daughter just coming up to A-levels. Her husband died seven or eight years ago.'

'How long have you known her?'

'Six months. I knew she was right for me after a month, but I had to wait for me to grow on her, if you see what I mean.' His stubby fingers are scooping up and making short work of the salted nuts in the dish on the bar counter as he talks. 'So . . . that's my immediate news. What about you? Are you getting your fair share of everything?'

'Can't complain.'

'You look like an ad for sun-tan lotion. How did you find Australia? Thanks for your card, by the way. I could have killed you. It was pissing down the morning it arrived.'

'I'll tell you all about it.'

I'm grinning again as I look at him. He'll be about forty now, his thick-set body running to extra weight a bit, his hair thinning and receding off what used to be a rather low forehead. Conroy never really could look well-dressed for long; his clothes seemed to crumple on him till he had the appearance of a sleepless bed; but today he's looking easily smart and even sporting a matching waistcoat with his dark blue chalk-stripe suit. There's a bead of sweat on his fleshy upper lip and I guess he won't stand this atmosphere for very long, set at a level of heating designed to suit visiting Americans. I'm enormously happy for him and I think what a strange thing the birth and growth of a friendship can be, because if anybody had told me in my early days at Whittakers' that Conroy and I would come to this I'd have said he was off his head.

'Eeh, Albert,' I tell him, 'Ah'm reight chuffed for thee, lad.'

'Aye, well,' he says, 'don't hang about. Get supped off and we'll move on and celebrate.'

A hundred yards along Oxford Street he hails a taxi, which takes us into New Bond Street, where he pays off the driver and walks me round a couple of corners to a Yates's Wine Lodge with a small crowded room at the back. He works his way to the counter and returns with a bottle of champagne and a couple of glasses.

'Here's fizz up your nose,' he says, pouring for me.

Now when you're basically a beer drinker and haven't had your quota of liquid to kill the thirst, champagne goes down like lemonade, and neither of us has any trouble in keeping the conversation going. What you've got to watch is the temptation to break into a gallop too early and find yourself sloshed before the evening's half over. I'm finding no grounds for objecting to this, but Conroy says 'Food' when we've emptied the bottle and I suggest replacing it with something similar. 'We must have some nosh, and put a lining in.'

'Okay. My turn now to lead the mystery tour.'

We go out and find another cab, which I direct into Soho.

'Here?' Conroy says, at the door of the little Turkish place.

'I know. You wouldn't dream of going in if I weren't taking you, would you?'

'I have serious misgivings, even now.'

'Put your trust in me, Albert lad.'

There's the telly going in one corner, as usual, and the same old lady watching it. The proprietor comes over and I give him an order and ask for a bottle of red wine to be brought while we're waiting.

'Where's the menu?' Conroy asks when the man's gone away.

'We don't need a menu.'

'What's Turkish for egg and chips?' He's looking suspiciously at the cheap bare tables and chairs. 'I was planning white linen cloths and waiters in tails, and you bring me to an Oriental transport cafe.'

'You can't eat waiters in tails.'

'You can boss 'em around when they get stroppy, though, can't you? I mean, I wouldn't want to hurt this old chap's feelings.'

'You won't need to. Just sit quiet and enjoy yourself. You'll like it when you get it. The bill as well. I did hear you say you were paying, didn't I?'

'You did. My treat tonight. You should have taken advantage of me while you had the chance.'

'You'll need your pennies if you're acquiring a wife.'

'But that's the point, mate. We shall both be better off than we've ever been. Fel's got a teaching job which she sees no reason to give up, and a house which I shall move into with her. She's not had any new furniture for a long time and I shall be able to help with that on what I save by giving up my flat. Then it'll be the old story – two can live as cheaply as one. We shall be quids in.'

Fine, I think, as long as the economic advantage is a happy bonus and not the reason for joining hands. Two living as cheaply as one is no joy when they grow to hate the sight of each other. But while I tell myself that the freedom to do as you please is worth paying a lot for, I know in my bones that it's no subsititute for a fulfilling partnership. I realize now that I'm not only pleased for Conroy, I'm sick with envy of the why he's building what he sees as his pattern of happiness.

'So, when are we going to get you fixed up and settled down?'

I grunt. 'There's nothing like a convert for wanting to convert everybody else.'

The Turkish bread and roe paté arrive, followed by the kebabs. Conroy makes appreciative noises as he tucks in. Some time and a second bottle of wine later we're standing on a corner in Wardour Street, mellow and burping. The lighted display windows of the film distributors' offices are full of advertisements for their latest epics. One of them features the blown-up face of a well-known film actress, her eyes glazed over and her lips parted, as though somebody out of shot has got his hand up her skirt.

'Well?' Conroy says. He looks aimlessly up and down the street.

In all the range of talk between us I've deliberately not mentioned the person uppermost in my thoughts. Now, with the booze making inroads on my inhibitions, I say, 'Come on, a little walk'll shake the grub down.'

'Where are we going?' he asks, as he falls in beside me.

'A place I know.'

He grumbles amiably at the distance I'm dragging him as we go through the narrow streets, across Charing Cross Road and into St. Martins Lane.

'We're too late for this,' he says as he steps after me into the theatre foyer.

'I know.' I point to one of the stills of the production. 'Look there.'

He peers at the photo. 'Is it "Spot the Ball"?'

'Do you see anybody you know?'

'Ah!' he says now. 'Ah!' He stands back, looks round, then reads the cast list of a poster. 'I see.' He looks at me. 'Have you seen her?'

'Yes.'

'Has she seen you?'

'Yes.'

'And?'

'And what?'

'You know what.'

All I can manage is a shrug, which gives the game away completely.

He shakes his head. 'You're a glutton for punishment, aren't you, lad?'

He's probably wondering why I've made him a witness to it; but I'm thinking that having him with me tonight can be useful in taking another step. I find a business card and write on the back of it: 'Am in the pub with an old friend. Come and have a drink?'

'Hang about,' I say to Conroy.

I nip round to the stage-door and find the man.

'Give this to Miss Pennyman, will you?' He turns it over, looks at it, looks at me. 'I'm a friend of hers. You will make certain she gets it, won't you?' On a thought, I fish some change out of my pocket and offer him a fifty-pence piece. 'Here, have a drink.'

The last of the big spenders . . .

'Will she come?' Conroy asks as we stroll up to the pub.

'She will if she wants to.'

'Suppose she comes though she doesn't want to?'

'I don't get you.'

'We're not kids in school any more, Vic. She might feel she owes you a bit of civility. Can you stop yourself wishing it into something else?'

'I still want her, Albert,' I tell him simply. 'I thought if I saw her again I might find I'd grown out of it. But I haven't. I want her more than I want anything in this whole wide bloody world.'

'Does she know that?'

'I don't think so. I don't think she can quite make me out now. When I knew where she was I made it look as though I'd run into her by accident.'

'When was this?'

'Last night.'

'And here you are, back already, with your tongue hanging out.'

'Look, I mentioned I'd seen her, didn't I? And you said you must come and look her up.'

'Okay. Is there any serious competition at present?'

'No.' I hold up my hand with the first two fingers crossed. 'I don't think so.'

'What about laughing boy – her old flame? What was his name?'

'Carter.'

I tell him about meeting Carter, what he said, what Donna said about him.

'If you can carry a torch for ten years, so can she. Especially when she's got his kid to remind her. There was a kid, wasn't there?'

'A boy. He's knocking ten now.'

'Fancy taking him on as well, do you?'

'I'll cross that bridge when I come to it. *If* I come to it.'

It's an if that refers to a possibility so overwhelming I suddenly can't bear to think about it. I knock back my Scotch, order another round and glance at my watch. The curtain should be down by now. She'll have my message. Suppose that surly sod of a stage-doorman doesn't give it to her and she walks straight past? Suppose she chooses not to come, thinking she'd better choke me off now, at the very start? I turn my back to the door, fighting down a terrific urge to go out and intercept her in the street, knowing that if I do I shan't know whether she came of her own free will. I fumble with my cigarette lighter as it slips in my sweating palm, aware that Conroy can see perfectly well the state I'm in, not wanting his pity, his thinking how bloody sad it is that he's getting what he wants and I'm back at my old game of eating my heart out for what I can't have.

So that I don't see her come in, don't know she's behind me till Conroy says, 'Here she is,' and lifts his hand, when I have no time to prepare myself, to put on any expression for her but the genuine one that's signalled by a rush of blood to the face, burning my ears till I feel they must be as conspicuous as night-time warning lanterns round a road-works.

'*Albert!*'

'Hello, then!' Conroy says. A second's hesitation, then he puts his big hands on her shoulders, dips his head and kisses her on the cheek. I think, how ironic that he can do that and I couldn't.

She's smiling all over her face at him, that frown of last night wiped away from between her eyes.

'I was only asking about you the other –'

'Vic told me. As soon as he mentioned he'd seen you I said I must come and look you up.'

'How lovely to see you.'

'Scotch, Donna?' I ask her.

'Please.' She gives me a quick glance, the first time she's looked at me since she came in, and I turn away to order.

'Oh, but I say, you haven't been out front tonight?'

'No, no,' Conroy says. 'We were too late for that.'

'Thank goodness. It was awful.'

'I'm sure it wasn't. How are you, anyway?'

'I'm pretty well. What about you?'

'Never felt better.'

'What are you doing up in town? Just having a boys' night out, or what?'

'We're celebrating,' I tell her over my shoulder.

'Oh? What can that be? Promotion? A new job?'

I hand her her drink.

'*Albert* is getting *married.*'

'How wonderful! Why, Vic was saying only last night that –' She stops, as if she thinks she shouldn't repeat it.

'And what was Vic saying?'

171

'Well, Donna asked if you *were* married, and I said not you. You seemed too well settled into the bachelor life.'

'You were wrong, weren't you?'

'I was that.'

Donna lifts her glass. 'Here's to you. I hope you'll be very happy.'

'Thank you. I don't see why we shouldn't. We're both of an age when we know what we want and what we don't want.' He flicks a quick glance from her face to mine, and back again. 'So, you're storming the citadels of the West End now?'

'I wouldn't say storming. Well, not me personally. But we seem to have got a success.'

'I can't understand how I missed knowing about it. Except that I do play hit and miss with the theatre reviews.'

'There was quite a big feature about Donna in the *Guardian*,' I tell him, and a second later could bite my tongue off. She's not supposed to know I read that. I see something register behind her eyes as she takes it in. All those questions I asked, in apparent ignorance . . .

'Yes, they were very kind to me. I don't know why they picked on me, but they did.'

'Shows a bit of discernment,' Conroy says. 'I always used to say in the old Longford days that you'd make it.'

'Yes, you did, didn't you? I remember. But one West End part doesn't make a career. The *Guardian* said it was my return, but they got it wrong. It's my first time, and there's no guarantee it'll ever happen again.'

'There's no guarantee of anything, love, except that most of us won't live to a hundred and five.'

Conroy asks about the people he remembers from the theatre in Longford, chuckling when he hears about Fleur, and coming out with some names I'd forgotten. One or two are doing quite well, others managing to keep their heads above water, some gone to ground she doesn't know where. All those hopes and dreams, all that waiting, dependent on the right person thinking of you at the right time.

'Can you tell me of another union that has seventy per cent of its members out of work at any one time?' Donna asks.

'I think you're all very brave,' Conroy says. 'I don't think I could take it – all that putting myself on offer and being refused.'

'But listen,' she says to him, 'you must come and see the play. Bring your fiancée. Will you?'

'When can you guarantee us a night that won't be "awful"?' he asks, grinning.

'Oh, you'll have to take your chance with that. But tonight really was nerve-racking. There was a whole planeload of Japanese in. They're on some kind of package tour, or visiting a business convention; I don't know. They must have made a block-booking weeks ago when the play was first announced. Anyway, they sat in absolute silence until about fifteen minutes from the end, when something, for God knows what reason, finally tickled them. And of course we didn't know at first that they were there. All we knew was that there was a great bottomless hole in the middle of the house that we were throwing our lines into. All the timing we'd learned from previous audiences went for nothing, because there was nothing coming back. We came off like wet rags.'

'Another drink?'

'Well, just a very quick one. I shall have to go in a few minutes.'

'I've got no transport tonight,' I tell her.

'Oh, I wouldn't have expected that, anyway. You did get home without mishap last night?'

'Oh, yes.'

'And how's your jet-lag?'

'I'm back to BST, I think, now.'

'Does your son take after you?' Conroy asks her. 'I mean, does he want to be an actor?'

I curse him under my breath for bringing that subject up, for putting her to the embarrassment of discussing it with him in front of me; because if he knows about the lad it must be because I've told him, and what did I have to say then? Still, he asks the question with casual ease, thinking, for all I know, that he's doing me a favour by getting information I'd be too uptight to ask for myself.

Something like a shyness comes over Donna's manner as she answers him.

'Oh, only inasmuch as it might get him a place in Dr. Who's team. Otherwise he wants to be an explorer one day, an astronaut the next, and a tube-train driver on another.'

Conroy laughs. 'He's just a normal healthy little lad.'

'Oh, yes. There's nothing exceptional about him.'

'Do you carry a picture of him?'

'I don't know if I've ... There's nothing recent, anyway.'

She's automatically going through the motion of looking in her bag, but she's obviously – to me, at any rate – ill at ease now, not wanting, if she has anything with her, to show it.

'Oh, there is this ... It was taken last year, in Cornwall.'

Conroy looks at it, making interested noises, then hands it to me. It's a beach scene, with a house on a cliff in the background. Donna, in a bikini, is bending as the lad, wearing swimming trunks, offers her a large shell. There's not much impression to be got of him and it's her I'm looking at, not with any salacious interest in the exposure of flesh, but dwelling on an added element in my new experience of her: a glimpse of her present world and status.

'Nice place,' I say, passing it back to her. I want to keep it. 'Is that your house?'

'No, ours is a bit farther inland, though we have got a view of the sea.'

'You've still hung on to it?' Conroy asks.

'Yes. We let it for most of the summer. Mother can't bring herself to part with it altogether.' She glances at the time. 'Look, I'm sorry to break it up, but I must go.'

'We'll walk round with you,' Conroy says. 'They'll be

calling time here, anyway. Where do you go from, Leicester Square?'

'Yes.'

We drink up and leave. She and Conroy walk together, me feeling like the spare part as I tag along behind in the stretches where the width of the pavement and the people won't allow three abreast. She hesitates at the entrance to the subway, but Conroy gently touches her elbow and we go down with her and through to the ticket office. She pays her fare.

'It has been lovely seeing you again,' she says to Conroy. 'If you can manage the play be sure and let me know you're in and perhaps we can get together afterwards.'

'I'll do that,' Conroy says. 'Take care.'

'And you.' She accepts the hand he offers. 'Good night.' A flick of a glance at me. 'Good night.'

'Good night, Donna.'

We stand and watch as she passes through the barrier and descends out of sight on the escalator. My sudden deep sigh brings Conroy round to face me. I look at him, sheepish now.

'I expect you think I'm a right hopeless cunt, Albert.'

'I don't know . . . I was watching her watching you, while you were trying not to look at her . . . There was somethng there, in her face. I couldn't read it. But I'd say . . .' He purses his lips. 'I'd say she's interested.'

'You mean . . .?'

'Don't take *my* word for it.'

But I'm already on my way to the barrier. I don't know what the fare is and I haven't time to look, so I shove a couple of coins into one of the ticket machines, shouting back to Conroy, 'I'll phone you.' I beat the escalator, bounding down over its measured speed, and take a quick look at the route indicator as I hear a train come in, stop, its doors open. On the platform, I see her as she steps aboard. I run and throw myself between the closing doors. The carriage is far from full and she chooses a seat facing the other way, so that she has no idea I'm there till I sit down beside her.

175

She jumps and turns her head quickly. What the hell does this man want with her?

'Oh!' She takes a breath. 'Is something wrong?'

'No . . .'

I catch my own breath, thinking now that I've chased her as though she'd step off the edge of the world and never be seen again. I've chased her and let her see that I've chased her. I could have let it ride, run into her again, given her no chance to refuse me, because there was nothing I was asking for. Now she knows more than that and will have to form her responses with that knowledge.

'I thought I'd ride as far as Hammersmith with you.'

'Has Albert gone?'

'Yes. Great to see him so pleased with himself, wasn't it?'

'Yes. I'm glad he's found somebody. Do you know her?'

'No, no. She was news to me. He wants me to be his best man.'

'That must please you.'

'It does. I've known him a long time.'

'Yes, I know.'

I fiddle with cigarettes. She refuses one of mine and takes out her Gauloise.

'Do you always smoke those?'

'I have done for a year or two now.'

'Are they supposed to be less harmful?'

'I don't really know. I don't think so. I don't smoke that much anyway, and I've got used to the taste of these.'

Well, sometimes I like their aroma and sometimes, like now, it gets on my guts. It must be the booze. The Scotch on top of the wine. And the excitement. I'm sweating again.

The stations slide by: Piccadilly Circus, Green Park, Hyde Park Corner, Knightsbridge, South Ken, . . .

'What I was thinking . . .'

She turns her head towards me. 'I'm sorry. What did you say?'

'What I was thinking,' I begin again, 'was that I know

you're tied-up at night and I'm at work during the day, but Sunday, you don't have a performance then, do you?'

'No, not on Sundays.'

'I was wondering,' I say, knowing now that she can, within the next minute or so, give me an answer which will close the door finally and forever, 'if I came over in the car and picked you up we might perhaps go somewhere; have a run out for a meal, or whatever you like.'

I wait, suddenly almost paralysed by fear, as the seconds dawdle by like drawn-out minutes.

'Sunday's the only day I can see much of Tom.'

'Oh, bring him too. I mean, we can go where he wants to go.'

'We may have something planned for Sunday already. They do sometimes make plans, Mother and Tom.'

'It doesn't have to be this Sunday. Or we could make it Saturday. Get you back in time for the theatre.'

'Sunday's better.'

'Sunday, then. That's what I thought.'

My heart soars. She's not turning me down out of hand. Or is she waiting for a time to do it in her own way?

Gloucester Road, Earls Court, Barons Court . . .

'Are you sure about this?' she asks, looking not at me but down at her hands.

'I'd like to see you again.'

'You can catch me most nights in the pub, after the theatre.'

'It's not the same thing.'

Another pause . . . Another station. She looks out.

'We're here.'

I get up with her. We walk along the platform to the exit.

'Can you give me a ring, during the day?'

'Sure.'

'Ring me tomorrow.'

'What time do you get up?'

'About ten, usually, but it varies. Mother lets me sleep till noon if I want to.'

'Midday, then?'

'All right.'

'Are you in the book?'

'No, not yet.'

She tells me the number, which I jot down in my diary. We give up our tickets and walk out into the street.

'What kind of things does Tom like to do?'

'Well, obviously there's more scope for outdoor things in summer. Sometimes I just take him to the pictures.'

'That's fair enough. Will you catch a bus now?'

'Unless I see . . . Look, there's a taxi.'

I jump to the edge of the pavement and wave him down. As I hold the door open for her and she gives the driver her address I'm tempted to get in with her, take her home and then let him bring me back here. But we've gone far enough tonight. I want no more awkwardness between us.

'I'll ring you, then.'

'All right. Good night.'

'Good night, Donna.'

I stand and watch the cab go.

Down on the deserted platform I pace back and forth, then break into a clumsy little dance. I hear the rumble of a chuckle behind me and look round to see that two West Indians have appeared. One says something to his mate and they laugh again.

Okay, fellers, I think. But you should feel like I feel just this minute. You should just feel like I feel.

12

I wake next morning with a slight head and a touch of boozer's gloom. Like a fool, I didn't go to bed straight away, but sat up thinking, to the accompaniment of two large Scotches. Everything seemed wonderful then, with me riding on Cloud Nine and a bright new world opening out before me. Now I can only think again that I've made a tactical error, pushing too hard too soon, giving her no choice but the gentle brush-off. Oh, so gently she'll do it: 'I couldn't tell you last night, but it was all so long ago and I see no point in going over old ground. I'm sorry if it disappoints you, but I think you'll agree that it's better said now, before . . .'

As the clock climbs the last few minutes before noon, I'm talking to the Chief Draughtsman, Ted Roebuck, and Ben Taggart, in Ted's room, which has one glass wall that gives a view of forty draughtsmen working at three rows of boards in the drawing office. Ted's a man who can give me twenty years, an old and reliable hand who's risen as high in his trade as he seems to want to and doesn't, like some I've met, foul up the work by constantly trying to find fault in younger blokes who've come up the ladder faster than he has. He's telling us about a European immigrant, a refugees, he worked with in an office just after the war.

'Actually, he had a very good command of both the English language and the job, but you know what draughtsmen are for taking the mickey. They got him so worked-up one day, he blew his top. It was an office twice as big as this one, with about eighty boards, and he stood at one end and roared down the length of it: "The trouble with you buggers," he said, "is you think I know fuck nothing. But the truth is I know fuck all!" '

I like that, and so does Ben, who turns purple in the face.

'Anyway,' Ted says, reverting to the job we're discussing,'It looks to me to be no different basically from that new weaving-shed we designed for in St. Helen's, last spring.' He shifts drawings round on the top of his desk as he talks. 'And that should give us a good start.'

'I think Vic might have a run up to Bolton some time next week,' Ben says. 'How's your diary, Vic?'

'Clear at the moment.'

'Why don't you give their people a ring and fix a day?'

'Okay.' I look at the time. 'If that's all for now, I have another phone call to make.'

In my own office, I ask the girl on the switchboard for Donna's number, and sit with the receiver to my ear.

'I'm sorry,' she says, 'the number's engaged.'

Damnation! 'Okay, I'll try again later.'

I've hardly put the receiver down when the telephone rings.

'Call for you. Mrs. Wilson.'

This time I really do swear, only under my breath. I'm starting to consider whether I should ask her to say I'm out, when she plugs the line through and I hear Miriam's voice.

'For Christ's sake,' I say, my temper demolishing my caution, 'what did I tell you about ringing me here?'

'It couldn't wait,' she says. 'I've just found out I can be free this evening. Can I see you?'

I want to say no, back off, Miriam, leave me alone, good-bye. But I shall have to see once more, if not tonight then later.

'If you're sure it's all right.'

'Safe as houses. Your place, about seven?'

'Okay.'

Once she's got what she wanted she rings off. Thank goodness for small mercies. I light a fag and pull myself

180

together before asking the girl to try Donna's number again.

'It's ringing now,' she says in a moment.

'Thank you.'

'Hello?' says a woman's voice; an older woman's voice.

'Could I speak to Miss Pennyman, please?'

'Hold on, I'll get her.'

Ten seconds. 'Donna Pennyman speaking.'

'Sorry, love, I'm not casting Alfred Hitchcock's latest; it's only me, Vic.'

'My agent is a woman.'

'Ah! Didn't fool you then. Look, have you thought about Sunday?'

'Yes.'

'And?'

'We've got nothing special planned.'

I don't ask if I might come over. This step by step conversation is a positive torture.

'What time would be best? About twelve?'

'If you're sure it's all right for you.'

'Well, I can make it earlier or later, whatever suits you best.' I realize as I'm saying it that that wasn't what she meant. But how do I know if it's all right for me? Only she can tell me that.

'Twelve will be fine.'

'Oh, you'd better give me the number of the house. I think I can find the street again, but . . .' She tells me the address; I jot it down. 'Ask the lad to think of something he'd like to do,' I tell her.

When I've put the receiver down I get up out of my chair and walk about, singing a tune and beating time with both hands. I realize in a minute what the tune is. At one time I used to read quite a lot of books about music and I was always coming across blokes who said that the big tune in the last movement of Brahms's First was very similar to the big tune in the last movement of Beethoven's Ninth, the Choral. I thought that anybody who thought that must have cloth ears. Then this pop tune hit the charts some while ago, based on a classic. I was talking to somebody who didn't know its origin and clever feller me said it was Brahms's First. But it wasn't; it was Beethoven's Ninth, and I was the monkey after all.

What is thundering through my mind as I walk up and down, beating the rhythm with my hands, is the full version in all the splendour of chorus and symphony orchestra.

It's called the *Ode to Joy*.

I shower and change my shirt as soon as I get home, thinking that if I'm in any state of undress after Miriam arrives she might try for a quickie before we go out. I shall have to take her out, too, though I know my skin will be crawling with apprehension at the possibility of somebody seeing us even more now, when I'm in the process of doffing the new before I don the old again, restored in bright and what I hope will be everlasting colours; because if we stay in I shall have to spend all evening stalling while I try to find ways of saying what I want to say. One of the things that appealed to me about Miriam was her candid reaching for sex without the time-wasting ritual of preliminaries (we both like it so why don't we get on with it and enjoy it?). Now my trying to stop her getting me between the sheets will be a sure sign to her that all's not well.

I've had a letter from Chris to say that my mother is making progress, but that was twenty-four hours old, and I expected her to telephone. It occurs to me that she could have tried: I've not been in the flat much the last couple of days. I get the number of the hospital from directory inquiries. I've dialled that, got through, and am waiting to be transferred to the sister in charge of the ward, when Miriam's key slides into the lock and she comes in. That bloody key . . . I lift my hand to her as she appears in the doorway.

'Hello? I'm inquiring about Mrs. Brown. Lucy Brown. She was brought in on Tuesday, after a heart attack.'

'Mrs. Brown is making good progress. We want to keep an eye on her over the week-end but if she continues to mend she may be able to go home on Monday.'

'How is she?' Miriam asks me when I've rung off.

'On the mend. Will you excuse me for another minute?' I dial Jim's number and get his wife. 'Oh, Claudine, this is Vic. Is Jim still in his surgery?'

'He should be free any time now.'

'It doesn't matter. I've just been speaking to the hospital. They say my mother's picking up nicely and they'll probably discharge her on Monday.'

'Oh, that's good news.'

'Yes, isn't it? The thing is, I'd have driven up tomorrow, but I've got to make a trip to Bolton on Tuesday and I thought I'd leave it till then and run over when I've finished my business. Chris might have been trying to phone me, and I can't ring her as you know, so if she phones you, will you give her that message?'

'You'll be there on Tuesday.'

'Yes. Late afternoon or early evening.'

'All right.'

Her voice is cool, without warmth. She hasn't much warmth in any case and as I don't care for her and she doesn't care for me, there's none to spare for our relationship. Her father owns a couple of hardware shops and she went to what's generally thought to be a good school; but she's a minus as far as real culture's concerned, and received ideas from her own lower middle-class background are what she passes off as awareness of how the world really ticks. She reminds me a lot in some ways of Ingrid.

'How are you?' I ask her.

'Oh, fine.'

'And the kids?'

'They're fine. Are you keeping well?'

'Yes, fine, fine . . . You'll pass on the message, then?'

'Yes.'

'Thanks. G'bye, then.'

'Good-bye.'

I turn to Miriam. 'Well . . .'

'Well . . .' she says. 'I'm in your bad books again, amn't I?'

'Oh . . .' I shrug and wave my hand.

'If it comes to that I seem to have been in them ever since you came back from Australia. You didn't fall for somebody out there, did you?'

'No . . . How many times have I seen you this week?'

'Three. It could have been four, but you had to go up north.'

'Well, three times in five days. And we used to reckon on one in seven, if that. You're pushing the boat out, love.'

'It won't capsize, so don't worry.'

'What fool-proof cast-iron excuse have you got for tonight?'

'A couple of tickets for the Festival Hall. I bought them weeks ago and Hedley suddenly said he didn't want to go. I'm not surprised. He does regard music as something of a penance.'

'Hmm. Who's playing?'

'Adrian Boult and the New Philharmonia. We can just about make it if you're ready.'

'*I* can't go to the bloody Festival Hall with you, Miriam!'

'Who's to notice you and me among all those hundreds?'

'Among all those hundreds there very likely could be somebody who knows one or both of us.'

'But I want to hear Boult.'

'I wouldnt mind hearing Boult myself but I'm bloody well not going to. Christ! Miriam, I sometimes think you're willing him to find out.'

The thing is, if I said okay she'd go out of sheer bravado, but though she must have known I'd refuse she likes to throw out these challenges that put me to the test and make me feel a weak-kneed wet. She pouts a bit, acting disappointment.

'What shall I say if Hedley asks me about the concert?'

'You should ask me! But just be sure Boult hasn't scratched at the last minute. He's an old man.' I get up.

184

'Come on, I'll take you for a meal. Where would you like to go?'

'I'd just as soon stay here.'

'Oh, we must eat, and I've got nothing in but baked beans, till I shop tomorrow. Chinese?'

'If you like.'

We decide on the Lotus House in Edgware Road. Miriam wants to take her car so I let her. She runs a Mini. The first classless motor car. Graham drives a Ford Granada, rather heavy and ponderous-looking, like himself, but not to be handled carelessly. Despite not feeling relaxed in Miriam's company, I find that I'm hungry, and order a good selection of dishes. I'm also feeling dehydrated still after the wine and spirits of last night and I could sink a couple of pints of lager. I compromise by ordering one for starters, and a bottle of Chablis, for Miriam's sake.

Miriam is one of the few women I've known with an uncertain appetite. The others were, and are, nearly all clean-plate ladies, diligent demolishers of everything put before them. Tonight she manages a bowl of soup, skips the spare ribs, and toys with a couple of pieces of duck. Conversation languishes. I guess she's rather unhappy and I'm in no position to cheer her up, planning, as I am, to make her even unhappier before the evening's over.

We've nearly finished when I catch the flash of a silver housecoat in the doorway, out of the corner of my eye. The head waiter moves towards them. Miriam looks at me as I groan.

'What's wrong?'

'That's my secretary just come in.'

'Has she seen you?'

'I don't think so. Not yet.'

'They're coming this way.'

'*Hello!*' Janice says from behind me.

I twist my head, manage to smile – 'Hi!' – as she gives Miriam a quick once-over, seems for a fraction of a second as though she'll enlarge on the greeting, then moves on to sit down half a dozen tables away.

'Who is that with her?' Miriam asks.

'Her husband, presumably. Does she know you?'

'I don't know her.'

'That doesn't mean much. I wonder why she didn't introduce him.'

'She probably took in my rings and decided on discretion.'

'Yeh, p'raps that's it.'

Miriam looks down the room at Janice, who is sitting in profile to us. 'Nice coat she's wearing.'

'Mmm.'

'Very appropriate.' She gives me a mocking look. 'Oh, we can't possibly go to the Festival hall because somebody might see us.'

'All right,' I say, 'it's finally happened.'

Though she can see that I'm itching to run for cover, Miriam insists on having tea after the meal. You bitch, I think. You just thrive on a bit of danger. Pushing every situation to the very edge, knowing that if you do go over your defiance will get you out of it. Get you out of it, but what about me? I'm not playing your game. I'm not going to be your whipping boy. Not ever; but specially not now.

I ask for the bill when I order the tea, hoping that I've enough cash and won't have to spend time palavering with my credit card. I find that by leaving a slightly larger tip than's necessary I can pay without waiting for change.

'Drink up,' I tell Miriam, 'and let's go before she decides to bring him over.'

'Why should she do that?'

'Because he's her husband and I'm her boss and we've never met.'

'Why don't you go and bluff it out, then?'

'What do you mean?'

'Go over and introduce yourself to him while I powder my nose. I'll wait for you in the lobby.'

'That's not a bad idea.'

'Suppose he's not her husband, though?'

'Don't be daft. They haven't been married ten minutes. He can hardly let her out of the house on her own to come to work.'

That mocking look again. 'Go on, then.'

I push my chair back, pull the table out to free Miriam, let her go, then walk to Janice's table. 'Mr. Wheeler?' He's sandy haired and there are freckles on the face he turns up to me. 'I'm Vic Brown, Janice's boss.' We shake hands. Janice is blushing.

'I was going to introduce you, but I didn't want to interrupt.'

'That's all right. I hope you'll enjoy your meal. Have you been here before?'

'No, this is the first time.'

'I'm sure you'll enjoy it, then. I must rush. Nice meeting you. See you on Monday, Janice. G'bye.'

I have to wait for Miriam. In the car, she says, 'What would you have done if she had stopped to talk when they first came in?'

'God knows.'

'You could always have introduced me as Mrs. Wilson.'

'Very funny. The trouble is neither of us can be sure she doesn't know who you are. She likes a gossip, does Janice, and I think she's shockable. I'm not certain how her loyalty to me would stand the strain if she knew I was knocking off a colleague's wife.'

'You'll just have to sound her out tactfully.'

'Yes, fine. But you don't even seem to care.'

'I jump my fences when I come to them.'

'You sometimes seem to enjoy putting fences where there aren't any. Christ! I wouldn't put it past you to come into the office next week and deliberately give her a sight of you.'

'What kind of idiot do you think I am?'

'I don't know. But I think it's time we called it a day.'

A silence.

'Do you really mean that?'

'We've had our fun, Miriam, but now it's run its course.'

'Not with me it hasn't.'

'We neither of us intended to let it go on indefinitely.

187

It's surely best to pack it in now before somebody gets hurt.'

'You're absolutely terrfied of a scandal, aren't you?'

'Look, if Hedley walked into my office and said "Leave my wife alone." I'd do it. I'd do it because I'm not prepared to stand the consequences of not doing it. So why don't we stop now before he does find out?'

'Because he hasn't found out, and he won't. God! One glimpse of your secretary and you're shaking in your shoes. Are you going to let a little . . . a little nonentity like her put you in fear and trembling?'

I say nothing; but it surely demonstrates what a false position we're in when somebody like Janice *has* the power to do us damage.

'But that's only part of it, isn't it? You've been building up this, haven't you?'

I don't deny that. 'Perhaps it was Australia. Being on the other side of the world. Seeing things from a distance. Who was it said a sea-change always had a curious effect on people?'

'Is there somebody else?'

'Why does there have to be?'

'Because you like what you get from me and I don't think you'd give it up without having something to put in it place.'

'I've managed without before.'

'If I know you you won't go without for long. You'll soon be on the look-out for a bit of fresh.'

'A change is as good as a rest.'

'You shit,' she says, low and with feeling. 'You hard-bitten selfish shit.' She looks straight ahead, her face set, driving with a kind of murderous caution.

There's an empty space not far from the house. She pulls into it and kills the engine. 'I suppose I can come up for a minute?'

'Of course you can.'

Inside the flat, she drops her handbag on to the low table and looks at me. 'You might offer me a drink.'

188

I fetch a small jug of water from the kitchen, pour two Scotches and put the bottle back in the cupboard.

'That's your ration,' she says, looking at the glass.

'You've got to drive.'

'Oh, quite. We musn't have me doing anything foolish.' She slumps down into an armchair, her body twisted slightly sideways. 'I often used to wonder how it would end. And I knew you'd be the one to finish it.'

'I used to think it would be you.'

'Why?'

'Because you're the one with the ties and the problems.'

'And you've got neither, have you? You can just pick people up and drop them as the fancy takes you.'

'You're not being fair, Miriam.'

'Whenever did I pretend to be fair? And don't you start saying it'll all look different in three months' time, or I'll scratch your eyes out.'

We sit for some time without speaking. I light a cigarette and swing one leg over the arm of my chair. She broods opposite me, her face sullen.

'I've hurt your pride, haven't I?'

'Oh, is that all?'

'I'm sorry.'

'You won't do it again, don't worry.'

She puts down her glass, takes a little make-up case she carries out of her handbag and goes into the bathroom. I sit there for several seconds before I register the open bag on the table in front of me. I reach into it, lift out her purse and search its compartments. I find the key in a zip-up pocket at the back.

When she comes in again she finishes her drink without sitting down. I get up as she takes her bag and moves towards the door.

'Miriam . . .'

She looks at the hand half-reaching out to touch her. Her top lip draws back, stiff with contempt.

'Want it the easy way, do you? Can't we still be friends . . . Not bloody likely, chum.'

She walks across the passage, opens the outer door, shuts it firmly behind her. I knew she wouldn't slam it; it's not her style. I pour myself another drink, but it doesn't altogether kill the taste of shame.

13

'I always find something very touching about them as they come in to land. They're like big game birds.'

'You mean something that somebody shoots at?' Tom asks.

'No, I mean in the sense of plucky, brave. They're so sleek and graceful in the air, like something that should never have to touch the ground. But they're under orders so, very patient and obedient, they let down those big clumsy wheels and come in and sit there till they're allowed to fly again.'

Tom's request was to see the air traffic at Heathrow, and now he's standing between Donna and me on the observation terrace outside the intercontinental terminal as a breeze with a cold nip in it pinches our faces.

'Where has that one come from?' He points to a 707 that's taxying to a halt below us.

'Japan. More customers for the play, perhaps, Donna?'

'What?' She smiles. 'Oh, yes. God forbid.'

'Have you ever been to Japan?' Tom asks me.

'No, I haven't.'

'It's a country with a very high density of population.'

I grin at Donna over his head. 'Oh, is it? Did they tell you that at school?'

'No, I read it. I wonder what will happen when it gets full. Do you know?'

'I don't think that's happened in any country up to press. Perhaps if it does they'll go to Australia. There's a lot of room there.'

'It's big, isn't it, Australia?'

'Vast. You can't imagine how huge till you fly over it in daylight for hour after hour.'

'Why aren't there more people there?'

'Well, it's not an ancient country like Japan or Britain. It was only discovered fairly recently. And there are thousands of square miles in the middle which are desert, where hardly anybody lives because it's so hot and there's no water.'

'They'll find a way for people to live there eventually, though won't they?'

'I expect so.'

'They'll have to do before all the Japanese can go.'

'Perhaps the Japanese will find a way.'

'They're a very clever people, aren't they?'

'Oh, yes. In fact, the Australians were scared that the Japanese were going to invade and conquer them in the last war.'

'They're not a warlike people now, though, are they?'

'Not now. They were then, though.'

'Your grandfather fought the Japanese in the jungle, Tom,' Donna says.

'Yes, I know.'

'He was a prisoner for a time. They didn't treat him very well.'

'Are you warm enough, Donna?'

'No, not really.'

'Let's go inside, then. We can still see from there.'

'Look,' Tom says, 'there goes one now.'

It is, I think, the Air India flight for Delhi, called just after we arrived. We watch the steep climb, the undercarriage retraction, the turn into flight path. A group of well-to-do Indians, the women in brightly coloured saris, watch with us.

'There, she's herself again now.'

'Are aeroplanes men or women?' Tom asks.

'Well, ships are women, so I think aeroplanes must be.'

'Do you know why that is?'

'No, I couldn't say offhand. I could probably find out. Are you feeling hungry yet?'

'No, not yet.'

'He had a good solid breakfast,' Donna says. 'He should manage for a while.'

We find a table in the lounge. The broad wooden cross-member of the tall window is just at eye-level when you're sitting down and relaxed.

'Isn't it marvellous?' I say to Donna. 'The guy who dreamed that up couldn't have planned it better if he'd meant it.'

Tom, standing, can see over it. I go to the bar and get some drinks. When I come back Tom is asking for the lavatory.

'There's one just over there,' Donna says.

'I'll go with him.'

'He's quite capable of –'

'I'm sure he is, but I want to go as well.'

'Have you known my mother a long time?' Tom asks me as we stand at adjacent stalls.

'I used to know her before you were born.'

'I can't remember that,' he says.

'No,' I say. 'It's funny when you think about it, isn't it?'

I think how easily I get on with him. He's what my mother would call old-fashioned in his ways, which probably comes from long contact with Donna's parents, people two generations older than himself.

As we go back across the lounge the sight of Donna sitting on her own sends a pang through me. Again I'm struck by her seeming vulnerability, as though what she's most in need of is care and protection. But that, I guess, is just fancy on my part. She's brought up this boy without a father and spent all those years in a tough and demanding profession. She's furnished her life, and why should I think there's an empty room in it for me? There's a reserve about her that I can't break through, a veil she brings down at any hint of a frank and open look between us. Yet the way I could make her laugh is one of my vivid memories of the old days.

*   *   *

The pub on The Green was just opening as I passed this morning. Twelve noon. The boy answered the door.

'Hello.'

'Hello. Are you Tom?'

'Yes.'

'I've come to see your mother.'

'Are we going out with you today?'

'I hope so.'

He goes off along the hall, calling for Donna and leaving me standing on the step until a plumpish woman in her fifties, dark hair drawn tightly back into a bun, wearing a caftan, and a medallion on a chain round her neck, appears from the back of the house.

'Come in,'

'Mrs. Pennyman? I'm Vic Brown.'

'How d'you do?'

We shake hands. Is it my imagination, a trick of the light, or does she really give me a curious look, doing almost a double take on me, as though she thinks she's seen me before? Perhaps, I think, she's shortsighted and too vain to wear her glasses all the time.

'Donna's getting ready now. We had a late breakfast. I like to let her have her sleep in the morning, after the theatre.'

'Yes, of course.'

She shows me into a small cosy front room, where one bar of an electric fire glows. On the wall over the fireplace hangs the painting of Donna's mother's that I always thought of as the fried egg: a great ball of orange against a ground of varying greens, the paint laid on thick and lumpy. It's something I never thought to see again, a direct link with the room in which I made my first declaration to Donna.

'One of yours, isn't it?' I say.

'Yes. Have you seen it before?'

'It used to be in Donna's flat, in Longford.'

'Oh. You knew Donna then?'

'Yes.'

She gives me that odd quick weighing-up look again.

'Donna likes it. It's not one of my best, which is why I never offered it for sale. I've just made some coffee. Will you have some?'

'Please.'

She leaves me. The *Sunday Times* and the *Observer* are strewn across the sofa, mauled in the way only women seem to treat newspapers. I find the colour magazines and am leafing through them when Donna's mother comes back.

'Help yourself to milk and sugar.'

As she bends with the tray I notice there's a mole on one of her cheeks, with a couple of hairs growing out of it. Her perfume is heavy for the time of day, giving me a sudden almost tangible sense of the plump flesh under the long robe. I wonder what Donna's told her about me, and how many other men have visited to take out her daughter and grandson; what she said and felt when Donna went home pregnant and told her she'd have the kid but bring it up without a father; if Donna has had any regular lovers since then; if there's anybody she goes off to sleep with now; if there's anybody, even, who comes and stays here. I'm a long way from home, on strange territory. Mrs. Pennyman's not the same breed as my mother, though I expect she has her standards. I wonder if she herself has any sex-life since her husband died. She's not pretty – hardly what you'd call handsome, even – but she has this strong physical presence you find in a lot of Latin women.

Donna comes in, carrying a cup of coffee and followed by the lad. I try to read something into her quiet hello. She's wearing a heavy sweater, and jeans, which I think is a pity because they deprive me of the sight of her legs. I love her legs; there's nothing you could objectively call outstanding about them, but they were always a part of her appeal for me.

'Is Mr. Brown taking us to Heathrow?' the boy asks.

'You'll have to wait and see,' Donna says. 'He's just been on a trip to Australia, so perhaps he's seen enough of aeroplanes.'

'Is that what you want to do today, Tom?'

'Yes.'

'Well, I don't mind looking at aeroplanes for a while. But see here, if I'm going to call you Tom, perhaps you'd like to call me Vic.'

'All right.' He looks round at Donna and smiles before coming to sit beside me, on the sofa.

'Have you never been up in an aeroplane?'

'No, never.'

'I've been in lot just lately, and there's really nothing to it.'

'What do you mean by that?'

'Well, they're so big now, and they fly so high above the clouds, it's really not exciting at all. Watching them land and take off is much better; thinking about all the far-off places they're going to.'

'I've never been to any far-off places. Only Cornwall and London.'

'Well, Cornwall's a fine place, and many people think London's the best city in the world.'

'Where have you been to?'

'Australia, like your mummy just said. And Hong Kong, and Italy and France and Holland and Belgium.'

'Why did you go to all those places?'

'Because of my job. I'm an engineer. I help to design things and then I go and show people how to install them in factories and other buildings.'

'You mean some kind of machines?'

'No, not exactly. I mean systems that ventilate buildings, keep the temperature even for people to work in comfortably, and systems that take dust and other obnoxious things out of the atmosphere.'

'That sounds interesting.'

'It is. What do you want to do when you grow up?'

'I don't know yet.'

'What subjects are you good at?'

'Oh, history and arithmetic.'

'Well, you'd need arithmetic if you were going to become an engineer. And history is always useful because it tells us where we came from and why we're like we are. They say history repeats itself, don't they?'

'Yes.'

'And if you don't know what's gone before you're apt to make the same mistakes twice.'

'Get ready, then, Tom,' Donna tells him. 'You'd best wrap up warm. There's a sneaky chill in the air.'

'I'd offer to take your mother, Donna,' I say, 'but the car's only –'

'Oh, don't worry about her. Sunday lunchtime's the one occasion in the week when she goes across to the pub. She stands there, drinking beer and talking politics and world affairs, then comes back and snoozes over the papers.'

'Well, then, we'd better not keep her from it.'

Tom has finished his soft drink and wandered away to look out from another vantage point.

'Is your mother foreign, Donna?'

Her mother was Italian.

'Ah! She still paints, does she?'

'Not so much recently. She's been designing jewellery. She finds it more immediately lucrative, which is something she's had to think about since my father died.'

'He couldn't have been very old. Was he?'

'Fifty-eight.'

'That's no age.'

'No. It was lung cancer. Quite rapid.'

'Were he and Tom very close?'

'Yes, very. You can't always tell with young people, but I think he still misses him.'

'He must miss adult male companionship generally. I mean, a man about the house gives a sort of balance to things.'

She shrugs. I wonder if she thinks I'm prying, or trying to make out a case for myself. 'It happens in a lot of homes.'

'Yes, there's a lot of it about: divorce, widowhood . . .'

I look round after Tom. He's now writing things in a little notebook.

'He's happy,' Donna says.

Does she mean at this moment, or generally? Ludicrous to think now that she might have aborted him. Not that it would have been killing *him*. Still, if she had done he wouldn't be here now. Neither would he be if she hadn't had another try with Carter while she was temporarily away from Longford and me. Or what I thought was temporarily. What was she doing then; having a go at retrieving what was between them before or simply giving in to a passing temptation? Typical of her to see that it was no use pointing her pregnancy like a pistol at his head. Like Fleur said to me at the time: it didn't work out before so what difference would a wedding ring make? Or a baby. And I, having been through it in circumstances where it seemed I had no choice but to conform, couldn't blame them for bucking convention. But all the same, not to be interested in your own flesh and blood . . .

We're drinking lager. I fetch another couple of halves and ask her if she wants a sandwich. She sits opposite me, quiet until I initiate conversation. Though Tom appears contented enough I feel sure he wouldn't object to leaving; and I wonder if Donna is bored. I begin to feel like an interloper, that the trip is something designed not for Tom's benefit but mine; that I'm someone they're politely humouring and the sooner I go the earlier they can slip back into the comfortable routine of their own lives.

I've flattered myself that I've become experienced with women. A fair share have fancied me enough to let me please them while I was pleasing myself. What I took from Ingrid was a bonus for which I paid too high a price in respectability. Donna for a while showed me what completeness might be. In the years between then and now I learned to play a game in which not too much was either asked for or given. There were women, I found, who wanted me for myself, not as a passport to marriage or security; who neither tied nor wanted to be tied. But what does all that signify when the one you want all of doesn't want you, when you are, as I am now, crippled by love? You hang on a word, a look, and might as well be untouched sixteen again.

'I do feel we're robbing you of your lunch,' she says, as I finish my ham sandwich.

'Oh, I shall manage till later.'

'Can you stay and have something with us this evening?'

But of course I can!

'If you're sure I'm welcome,' I force myself to say.

'You're quite welcome.'

Her eyes hold mine for longer than any time before, and when she looks away I seem to see a faint colour flush her cheeks. Something moves in me. I'm lifted on a great surge of new hope. If I can't make her out, I think, all I need is patience. Let her be sure of my position, then she can sort out her own.

'Would you like to go?'

'It's up to you and Tom.'

She calls him over. 'Have you seen all you want to see, Tom?'

'I think so.'

'They're pretty much of a muchness, aren't they?' I say.

'What does that mean?'

'They're all more or less alike. The bigger ones, anyway.'

'The different colours and signs are interesting.'

'Yes, there is that. I'll tell you what: I'll give you all the flight literature and whatnot I picked up on my travels, if you like.

'Yes, I'd like that. Thanks.'

At the top of the stairs Donna stumbles and I grab her elbow. I reach for her hand as she recovers herself. A charge of pure delight runs through me, like something injected into my bloodstream, as she lets it rest lightly in mine till Tom, bounding ahead, reaches the hall and looks round for us.

He squeezed into the narrow occasional seat on the way out. Now he wants to sit with his mother, in front. I lengthen the safety-belt and strap them in together. Tom approves of the MG, and likes me to drive fast. We have a discussion about the relative merits of various models and he decides that none of them has the all-round advantages of mine. I conclude that he wouldn't bend the facts so much in my favour if he weren't trying to show he likes me.

'I ought to drive a company car really.'

'What would they let you have?'

'A Ford or an Austin. Something like that.'

'Oh, no,' Tom says, 'this is much better.'

'I think so. And they very kindly make me an allowance against running it, so I don't lose much and I get to drive the car I want to drive.'

'Does it make you feel good, driving an MG?' Donna asks.

'Yes. A bit of the delayed adolescent coming out, I suppose. I never owned a car till my late twenties, remember. Haven't you got one now?'

'No. I ran the A40 I had in Longford till the bodywork was finished, then I used the family car. My mother sold that when we came up to London. We thought it would be more of a nuisance than a convenience here; though there are times when I miss it.'

We're too late for the pictures, even if we could think of a cinema nearby that opens on Sunday afternoon, so we decide to go back via Kew Gardens and take a walk. The sun's come through now, reflecting gold in the curved glass walls and roof of the huge Palm House. Tom asks me about Australia and, answering his questions, I'm surprised how much information I picked up in the few weeks I was there.

'And so are all the Australians descended from convicts?'

'Oh, no. They've had a lot of immigration since those days: Italians and Yugoslavs as well as British. But a lot of the *real* Australians are. They joke about it. They say you should never inquire too closely into a real Australian's ancestry because you never know what you might dig up.'

'I don't know who my father is, you know.'

The candid way he comes out with it makes me gasp.

'Oh?' I throw a quick sideways look at Donna.

'He was somebody my mummy didn't want to marry and he went away before I was born.'

'Does it bother you, Tom?'

'Tom, all this is very personal,' Donna says.

'Oh, I can talk to Vic about it. He understands. Don't you, Vic?'

'Well, I'm not shocked, if that's what you mean. Do you find anybody who is?'

'Every now and again I have to hit somebody – '

'You haven't told me that, Tom,' Donna breaks in.

'Well, it's nothing. People mostly don't care. It's just every now and again, when somebody tries to be nasty.'

'You don't actually make a practice of telling people, do you?' she asks him.

'No, but if they get newsy and ask me I don't tell lies. I mean, I always think that makes it worse, if people think you're trying to hide something. I don't mind not having a father. Not if he's not a good father. But I sometimes wonder about him. Let's see if there are any fish.'

He darts off to the edge of an ornamental pool. Donna is biting her lip. She's upset, and so, if it comes to that, am I.

'That piece in the paper can't have helped him, you know,' I tell her.

'I've always tried to be as open and honest about it as possible.'

'Yes, that may be all right for you, but what about him? I should have thought a few healthy lies were the best thing all round.'

'And have him reproach me for them later? I thought we lived in an enlightened age.'

'Try telling kids that sometimes.'

'Anyway, you knew all about if before you asked if you could come today, didn't you?'

'Yes, I did. And it's none of my business, is it? I'm

upset, though, all the same, hearing him come out with it like that.'

'I've tried to do my best for him.'

I can't stand her distress.

'All right, love. I know you have. I'm not trying to get at you. He's such a grand lad, though.'

'Do you like him, then?'

Then? She asks with a note of defiant pride, her chin suddenly up, as though Tom's been on test and she's challenging me to fail him.

'Yes, I do. He's a grand lad,' I say again. 'I'd take him on tomorrow. And you.'

She turns quickly away and calls out to him. 'Tom, we're going now.'

Patience, I said. If I push too hard I reduce her options. But all I can think of is how much I want her, and the lost years when we could have been together.

Back at the car I offer her the keys. The concentration in driving an unfamiliar vehicle might, I think, calm her.

'I couldn't.'

'Go on. Have a go. Keep your hand in.'

'Can I sit with you, Vic?' Tom asks.

''Course you can.'

I get into the passenger seat and let him climb on to my knees. I fasten the safety-belt and hold him lightly round the waist. Donna starts the engine and puts the gear lever through its positions.

'Okay?'

'I feel very low down.'

'Just take it easy for a few minutes. You'll soon get used to it.'

I remember her as a good positive driver in the treacherous conditions of that atrocious winter of 1962-63, and quickly now she's handling the car as if it were her own, though she won't go as fast as Tom wants her to, chiding him mildly as he urges her to put her foot down. I give her little sideways glances as she traces the route home. Once she turns and looks at us, our heads close together as Tom relaxes against me.

There's a rich spicy smell coming from the kitchen when we get back to the house.

'Mother's at it already,' Donna says. 'I'd better give her a hand.'

Tom and I sit in the front room. He switches on the television set for the late afternoon programmes. I divide my attention between that and the review sections of the newspapers. In a while I ask Tom where the lavatory is. As I pass the kitchen I can hear Donna and her mother talking. They sound to be having a difference of opinion about something.

'. . . it's only right and proper.'

'But it's not the right time, Mother, and I forbid you to – '

At this point one of them firmly shuts the door as I go on upstairs.

Round the table later there's polite conversation but a kind of constraint, an atmosphere, which I can't see having anything to do with me, but which I can't help uneasily feeling wouldn't be there if I weren't present. I chat mainly with Tom, feeling every now and again Mrs. Pennyman's eyes lingering on me, weighing me up, or perhaps already passing judgement. I wish I knew what she's thinking, what's going on between her and Donna. Is it that Donna already has some chap whose place her mother sees me trying to take over? Or am I in her eyes not the type to be encouraged anyway? The working-class lad who's never far below the surface in me begins to feel all too rawly obvious. She doesn't like me, and she'll like me even less the more I try to win her round.

They serve me coffee in the sitting-room, drinking theirs in the kitchen, having decided to clear the table and wash-up straight away. I suggest that Donna and I should do it and let her mother sit down, but they won't hear of it, and so once again I find myself on my own with Tom, who's eager to see a wild-life programme about penguins on TV. I light a cigarette, drop my lighter, and when I'm picking it up find a book sticking out from under the sofa. It's a new Graham Greene novel. *The*

203

Honorary Consul. I open it at random and a passage takes my eye: ' "That word love has such a slick sound. We take credit for loving as though we had passed an examination with more than average marks." ' They're talking about their fathers, and a different kind of love from the sexual, but I reckon that a lot of people who do fall in love, have that love returned, and don't fall out of love take the same kind of credit, as though what they feel is the same thing as loyalty. 'I've never wanted anybody else,' they say, as though that were an achievement due to some great praiseworthy feat of character.

'You can be in love with someone you hardly know,' my sister said to me when I walked out of the Rothwells' house and left Ingrid for a few days, that first time, ' – all romance and rapture and starry eyes . . . But you can't *love* a person till you know him or her inside out, until you've lived with them and shared experience . . . you've got to share living before you can find love . . .'

Well, all I know about my feeling for Donna – love of the kind Chris was talking about though it can't yet be – is that I fell in love with her once ten years ago and if I thought that seeking her out again after all this time would make me ask myself what I'd seen in her, I was wrong. So at least I know what I want. Or I think I know what I want. Or I know what I think I want. And I should be happier if I didn't want it. But, ah! suppose I were to get it? Suppose, suppose. Just suppose . . .

A giggle from Tom brings me back. 'You snore,' he says with great glee. 'And you've been catching flies in your open mouth.

'Tom, don't be rude,' Donna says. 'He has every right to take a nap if he's tired.' She's sitting in one of the armchairs, looking as though she's been there a long time, and the penguins have given way on the television screen to *Sunday Night at the London Palladium.*

'I'm sorry,' I say, pulling myself up on to the edge of the sofa and feeling distinctly sheepish. 'I didn't mean to drop off. Have I been away long?'

'About twenty minutes.'

'I thought I'd got over the habit.'

'It's probably the fresh air this afternoon, and now the warm room.'

'Somebody's going to give me a nickname – Forty Winks.'

I grin at Tom as he rolls about on the sofa, laughing. 'Forty Winks,' he splutters, and then says it again, 'Forty Winks.'

Suddenly sensitive again, I look at my watch, thinking that I'm turning into the visitor nobody can get rid of. In a second's silence before the commercials I catch what sounds like the screech of something being held against a grindstone upstairs.

'Mother's doing some work,' Donna says, seeing the cock of my head.

And waiting for me to get my big feet off her hearth-rug, I shouldn't wonder. It would make a change, and be a help, I think, if one of these times I were to fall for a girl whose mother thought I was the bee's knees. I sit forward in the attitude of someone whose departure is imminent, idly looking at a commercial for canned beer and trying to identify the familiar voice doing the spiel. I glance at my watch, clear my throat. 'Well . . .'

'Would you like a stroll across to the local?' Donna asks.

'Well, yes,' I say, bounced to the top of the seesaw again.

'Will you be all right on your own, Tom, if Vic and I go to the pub for an hour?'

'Sure,' Tom says. 'If I get lonely I can go up and see Granny.'

It's the first time we've been alone together today, I think, when, a few minutes later, we're walking along the street. And if I'm to creep back into her life through the steady growth of familiarity I shall have to improve as a companion on the dull dog I feel now as, searching for safe small talk, I toy with one topic after another and reject them all as not being worth her attention. Well, there's no harm in a bit of companionable silence, as long as she's not bored out of her mind and thinking – even if she's ever let herself remotely consider the possibility of it – that a lifetime of me would be pure hell on earth. I mean, how do I know that she doesn't think about me as I used to think about Ingrid, when sometimes a kind of stupefying glaze would slide over my mind and I couldn't muster enough interest even to ask her to pass the salt?

'Are you warm enough?'

'That's about the fourth time you've asked me that today.'

'Well, it's a funny time of year. Where will your public be if you catch a chill?'

'Watching my understudy.'

'Do you ever feel like ducking out and letting her take over?'

'Yes, every night, just before I go on.'

'It's a curious sort of job, isn't it? Most other people can have good days and bad days, make mistakes and either cover up or correct them; but you're out there in the spotlight every minute.'

'Most other people don't get the same instant reward, though, do they? The reassurance, like a prize, every night.'

'Does it make living easier, all that reassurance?'

'We're no more satisfied with ourselves and all of a piece than other people. Less so, if anything, or we wouldn't do it in the first place. But think how inadequate we'd be if we didn't do it.'

'You always struck me as one of the more level-headed examples.'

'Did I? I sometimes wonder, believe me.'

A bloke sitting on a stool at the bar hails Donna as we go into the pub. He looks to be in his fifties. He's got a neat haircut and he's wearing a well-cut blue blazer, and a cravat in the open neck of his shirt.

'Ah, Donna. How goes it?'

'Pretty well.'

'The play bringing 'em in?'

'Yes, we're enjoying good houses.'

'Must make an effort to get up to see it. Not highbrow, is it?'

'I don't think you'd call it that.'

Donna introduces us, but I don't catch his name. I order a couple of Scotches. 'Can I get you a drink?' I ask him.

'Very kind of you.' he empties the half-pint silver-plated tankard, with engraved initials. 'A half of bitter, if you don't mind.'

I don't mind. I'd a sudden feeling on asking him that he might be drinking something expensive, like Pimms No.I. I look round. They're doing a good trade. There are no empty seats, and few places you can stand without being shunted about to make way for people passing.

'Far too much of the highbrow about these days,' Cravat says. 'People want to be entertained, not made miserable or preached at.'

'It depends what you call highbrow and what entertainment,' I say to him.

'Oh, quite. The good old public at large knows the difference, though. Always trying to change the world, these chaps, but the world goes on its own sweet way when they've all done shouting.'

I get the strong impression that these are statements he makes and remakes several times a week to whatever audience he can pin down. After which, he probably goes home and says he's had a good conversation. I wonder if we can get out of his way before he starts on politics.

'Cheers!' He waves his little tankard at me.

'Cheers! You'd say, then, would you, that the best policy is to leave well enough alone?'

'Beg pardon.'

'I mean and let the world go on its own sweet way.'

'Oh, without a doubt. Interfering only makes things worse. No offence to people in your profession, of course. You amuse people, give them pleasure in their idle moments, and that's a useful enough function, so long as you remember that that is your function.'

He talks in almost a drawl, with an airy wave of his hand. It must be my denims and being with Donna that have fooled him.

'I'm not an actor,' I tell him. 'I'm an engineer.'

'Oh, my mistake. You'll understand what I mean, then.'

A man comes between us to get to the bar. I lift my eyebrows at Donna and she makes a little mouth in return. Seeing a sudden reshuffle take place as a couple leave, I ease her away till she's standing against the wall.

'Who did you say your friend was?'

'Oh, forget about him. He's an idiot, really.'

'I'd come to the same conclusion.'

'He likes people to think he's familiar with actors, but in fact he despises the profession. He's a dentist, you're an engineer. You both do a real job of work while we just clown around taking money for make-believe. That's when we're behaving ourselves, of course, and not ramming seditious nonsense down people's throats.'

'Not much in the way of prizes and reassurance coming from him.'

'It's all part of the game.' She shrugs, then smiles. 'I once brought an actor called Tony Flynn in here. Have you heard of him?'

'Who hasn't?'

'I had to get him out, quick. If he'd stopped another minute he'd have hit him.'

I drink off. 'Same again?'

'Please.'

'Should have let me,' Cravat says when he sees me with the fresh drinks. 'My turn.'

'Another time,' I tell him.

He's happy enough, I guess, to be let off two Scotches for a half of bitter. Donna and I stand in silence for a time, me looking at her while she looks past me at the people in the pub. Once our glances meet for just a second and she gives me what is almost a wary little smile before her eyelids lower and hide her expression. Oh, I wish I could resurrect the old Donna who used to laugh with me, straight into the eyes.

'Well . . . it's been a funny sort of a day so far.'

'Has it?'

'Enjoyable, though.'

'Yes.'

Have you enjoyed it, love? I want to ask her. Has it meant anything at all to you or was it just a pleasant enough interlude which you've no particular desire to repeat?

'Will Tom get himself off to bed?'

'Oh, yes. And I'll look in on him when I get back.' She glances at her watch.

'Look,' I say, 'next week . . .'

'Yes?'

'Well, Tuesday I've got to make a business trip up to Lancashire and I'm planning to run over and spend the night at my mother's. She's been rather poorly.'

'I'm sorry to hear that.'

'She's coming round now, apparently. But that means I shan't be back till sometime on Wednesday. I don't know how late, so I'd better count that out. But Thursday, I thought I'd come and see the play.'

'Would you like me to leave you a ticket at the box office?'

'I don't mind paying for my own.'

'It's not so much that, it's whether you'll get in. We're getting the house full boards out.'

'All right, then, thanks. But listen, I've remembered that Thursday's also my birthday.'

'Oh?'

'Not that I make much of 'em nowadays, but what I was thinking was that if I brought the car in so that you could get home afterwards, perhaps you could stay up in town for a while and we could have some supper after the show.'

She's quiet for so long that I'm suddenly on the edge of panic, my heart thumping so fast in the certainty that she's preparing to deliver the final no. Then she says, looking down at the glass in her hand:

'You'd already read that piece in the *Guardian* when we met in the pub, hadn't you?'

'Yes. I read it on the plane, just a few minutes before I recognized Clive Carter sitting across the aisle. Quite a co-incidence, I thought.'

'Had he read it?'

'I showed it to him.'

'What did he say?'

'He just grunted a couple of times and said he hadn't seen you in years.'

She says nothing to that, but stands, still looking down and running one finger round the base of her glass in exactly the way she did it on a night in the Mitre in Longford, the night the realization came to me out of the blue that I was falling for her.

'I've been to the play once as well,' I tell her, thinking that since I've admitted so much I may as well confess that too.

'Oh?'

'That was the night before I . . . before I ran into you in the pub.'

'I see. And you still want to come again?'

'I didn't see much of it. I fell asleep.'

'Oh, Vic . . .'

She says the two words with such a direct, gentle expression of concern, of caring, that for a moment I feel I can't breathe. As her eyes flick up to mine for an instant I'm astonished to see that they're bright with the sheen of tears.

'I waited outside the stage-door that night and saw you walk up the street. I could have stopped you and spoken to you then, but I didn't want it like that. I wanted to meet you by accident, on my terms, try to find out if you were the girl I remembered, if you'd any time at all for me. I didn't want to make a bloody fool of myself again. I've managed it, though, haven't I? I'm doing it now. I know I am. But I don't care as long as I think there's any chance. And if there isn't it's better to know for sure, once and for all, than walk about with some daft hopeless dream tormenting me.'

'Oh, Christ!' she says now. She's got one hand up to her face, the fingers spread; the other, holding the glass, begins in a moment to wave in front of her in a blind searching action, as though she's looking for a flat surface in pitch darkness.

She lurches for the door as I take her glass and turn to put that and mine on the bar counter.

'Is she all right?' Cravat asks from his stool.

'Had a funny turn. Needs fresh air,' I tell him as I follow her out.

I see the shape of her, already some distance away, moving through the dark towards home. I run and catch her up.

'Donna.'

No answer. She keeps going, her head down. She's weeping. I don't know what I've said.

'Donna, what's wrong?'

She won't stop and she won't talk. I hold her under one elbow, going along with her, till we reach the house. My car is parked in the road, by the gate. There I take her and turn her round.

'Donna, what is it, love? Was it something I said? What have I done?'

She shakes her head with a fierce jerk. 'Nothing. let me go, Vic.'

'I can't, like this. I want to know what –'

'It's too late. I've done it all wrong. It's all too late.'

'What's too late? Tell me about it. I want to help.'

'No. Just let me go. Please. Let me go.'

She twists free and starts up the path. While I'm standing there, stunned and baffled, she's got the door open and is inside.

14

'It was our wedding anniversary. Our first,' Janice is telling me. 'Robert said seeing I'd got a new Chinese coat why didn't we go to a Chinese restaurant.'

'Did you enjoy your meal?'

'Yes, but they tell me the more people there are together the better when you're eating Chinese food, because you can order a greater variety of dishes.'

'That's true. Four or six is smashing.'

'Anyway, I hope you didn't think I was rude, not introducing Robert when we first came in.'

'Not at all.'

'I didn't want to butt in.' She twinkles. 'Robert said if he'd known you were so young and good-looking he'd have thought twice about letting me take this job.'

'Oh, hoh!' I say. 'Now then! And a divorcee,' I add, pushing the boat out to test her, 'who likes to dine out with the ladies. You are living dangerously, Janice.'

She thinks she hears a serious note under my banter, and flushes a little, wondering if she's gone too far.

'He was only joking, of course.'

'Of course he was, love.'

'And your personal life's your own business, isn't it?'

I shake my head in sorrow at the way of the world. 'But some people just can't help minding other people's business.'

She colours a little more and I think that I'm going too far myself, as though warning her that I've got something to hide and she'd better keep her mouth shut.

'A good secretary knows better than that, though.'

'Yes, I dare say she does.'

I let her go, thinking that although I haven't handled the situation very well, it's pretty certain she didn't know Miriam. Which is one consoling paragraph in a sorry chapter. I'm feeling somewhat raw-eyed this morning, having spent a mostly sleepless night puzzling about Donna's behaviour, wondering what could have made such a hopeful day end in such inexplicable disaster. And then this morning, when I went out of the house . . .

I buzz Ben Taggart and ask if he's free.

'About this trip up north tomorrow, Ben,' I say to him when I've walked along to his office. 'I'm going to need a motor.'

'Oh?' he says, sucking at his pipe.

'Some bastard jemmied my car window open during the night and nicked the radio.'

'I hope his conkers shrivel.'

'I didn't know you cared.'

'You today, me tomorrow. Did he do much actual damage?'

'Jiggered the window lock, knocked the dashboard about a bit, and ripped out some of the wiring. I thought it best to get it in and seen to.'

He has a word with the garage foreman.

'They've got an Allegro in for service. If you'd like to pop down about five they'll have it ready for you.'

'Good. Will Wednesday midday be okay for clocking back in?'

'I didn't think this trip called for an overnight.'

'I don't need expenses, but I'd like to slip over the Pennines and spend a night at my parents'.'

'Oh, yes, your mother. How is she?'

'Reported on the mend.'

'I'm glad to hear it.'

He fills another pipe with firm movements of his fingers. They've got tufts of black hair on the back between knuckle and fist joint. I've seen Ben stripped-off under the shower after he's pasted me at squash and thought

213

how odd it is that some men are hairy practically every-
where except on top of the head.

'Maybe you could make a courtesy call at Mellors' at
Rugby on the way back down. Help justify the extra time.'

'A good idea.' I get up to go.

'By the way,' Ben says then, 'I've got a bit of news for
you.' I wait. 'Not for general release yet, but Hedley
Graham has started a month's notice.'

'You don't mean he's . . .?'

'Got the push? No. He gave Maurice Kendall his resig-
nation on Friday, apparently. Maurice tried to talk him
out of it, but he's set on leaving industry and going into
partnership with a firm of accountants in the City.'

It's a surprise to me, and I'm wondering why Miriam
said nothing. Or does Graham play his cards so close to
his chest even where his wife is concerned?

'Well,' I say, 'I can't pretend I shall shed any tears.'

'No.' Ben lights his pipe, giving me a very funny old-
fashioned look through the smoke. 'It could make things
easier for you, I suppose.'

'I don't follow.'

'I mean not having him around to bump into every day.'

God, he knows! The realization that he knows hits me
even as I'm saying, 'I still don't know what you mean.'

'Well, it's none of my business, Vic, except insofar as it
could disrupt relations between two senior men in the
company. But we don't have to worry about that now, do
we?'

I feel for cigarettes and sit back down.

'Who's been gossiping, Ben?'

'Nobody. Or not to me. I spotted you myself. You can tell
me it was an innocent encounter, if you want to.'

'Where was it, and when?'

'You mean I've had more than one chance?' He looks at
me sardonically as my ears burn and I try to keep my face
impassive.

'Say what you've got to say, Ben, and stop playing
games.'

'It was in a little restaurant off Ken High Street, just

214

before you left for Australia. I opened the door, saw you, took a quick decision, and backed out.'

'Was Louise with you?'

'Yes.'

'Did she see me as well?'

'Yes. She was ahead of me into the place.'

'What did she say?'

Ben shrugs. 'She doesn't care much for either Graham or his wife. And you know she's not a prattler. She was a bit concerned for you, though.'

Yes, she probably was. I like Ben's wife and I think she likes me. 'What about you?'

'He's not high on my list of favourite people, either.'

'That doesn't exonerate me, though, does it?'

'I'm not judging your morals.'

'Why have you waited till now to mention it?'

'Well, you were off beyond the blue horizon, so I thought I'd let it simmer till you got back.'

'But why just now, when Graham is leaving?'

'It seemed an appropriate moment.'

'And which hat have you got on, the sales director's or the friend's?'

'Now that he's going, the friend's. And all I want to ask you before I take my nose out of it is don't you think you might be behaving foolishly to yourself? Even out from under your feet, Graham is still a pretty ruthless type, and she's a headstrong piece who likes her own way. Get yourself caught between the two of them, kid, and you might be in the middle of something you can't finish.' He holds up his hand, palm towards me, in a Hollywood redskin gesture. 'Friend.'

I take a deep breath. 'It is finished.'

'Does she know that?'

'Yes.'

'Will she stand for it?'

'She'll have to.' I consider. 'It's a long story, Ben, but I've re-met somebody I used to know years back. I'd like to marry her, in fact.'

'Well! Congratulations!'

'Oh, no, it's much too early for that. I don't even know if she'll have me. In fact, it looks bloody unlikely, the way things stand at present. But I'm not saying anything more about that, if you don't mind, because I've got enough egg on my face.'

I turn to the door. Ben strikes another match.

'Keep me posted,' he says as I go out.

The M62 Trans-Pennine motorway is a beautiful road, curving, lifting and swooping, thrusting through cuttings and launching itself across valleys. The early motorway architecture round London tends to be twentieth-century brutal; here the technique of later years shows itself in the grace of light bridges springing out of cutting-walls. On the Yorkshire side, the yielding of the moorland tops to deep green valleys, the scattering of buildings on the high spurs, and the towns lower down, open in me an unexpected ache for a life and a place I know I can never return to find till I'm able to bring my own peace of mind with me.

Yesterday was a bad day, with all that happened in the morning and then me dithering through the afternoon, on the point of ringing Donna but not able to bring myself to do so and give her a chance to send me packing with a few disembodied words. I've re-run in my mind a hundred times the scene in the pub and afterwards, trying to remember precisely her movements, the look on her face, just exactly what she said; trying to fathom what it all meant.

I've come to the conclusion that telling Ben as much as I did was both foolish and cowardly, as if I were redeeming a sordid lapse by a show of respectable aspiration. Wouldn't Miriam have sneered if she'd seen me! And today, at the mill in Bolton, I've let an elderly works engineer patronize me, because I was selling and he was buying, and cutting him down to size will have to wait till later, if I ever get a chance at all.

So I'm not exactly lost in admiration for myself as I take the exit road off the motorway and head down the valley towards home.

216

I find my mother sitting in the living-room, stitching together the parts of a heavy, rust-coloured cableknit sweater.

'Just the man I want to see,' she says. 'Take your jacket off and come over here.'

'What's all this in aid of?' I ask, as I do as I'm told and she holds the pieces up against me and tugs them into shape.

'I thought it was your birthday on Thursday?'

'It is.'

'Well, then. When are you going back?'

'Tomorrow morning.'

'If I get this sewn up today you can take it with you. Save me the postage. I took the measurements from an old jumper I found in your drawers upstairs. I'm glad to see you don't vary much.'

'I'd ask you how you're feeling, if I could get a word in edgeways.'

'Oh, I'm nicely on the mend. I shall make old bones yet.'

'You will if you don't go thinking you can carry on like you did before,' Chris says from the scullery doorway.

'Eh, Christine, stop cossetting me, will you! I've had a nice rest these last few days and I shall soon be as right as rain.'

Chris and I raise eyebrows at each other before she goes to make some tea. My mother, sat with her knitting at this time of day, and wearing the kind of frock she would normally change into only for the evening, has the curious air of not belonging to the household, like some elderly aunt on a visit.

'Where's me dad?'

'Gone for a walk in the park.'

'And how is he?'

'Oh, he comes and goes.'

'You're not climbing all those stairs, are you?'

'No. They've brought me a bed down into the front room. Our Christine has even borrowed a hip-bath 'at I can use in front of the fire.'

217

'A bungalow,' I say to her. 'I've told you before I'll tell you again: you want to get this place sold and buy a bungalow.'

'And where will you lot sleep when you come home if we move into a bungalow?'

'There'll be nobody to come home and see if you and me dad don't start taking more care and listening to good advice. This place is too big for you to look after. If it comes to that, you ought to qualify for an old people's flat.'

'I'm going into no old people's flat. When you live in old people's flats there's nowt but other old folk round you, and all you see is the hearse coming to take 'em away. Talk about making sure you know your days are numbered . . .' She stitches for a minute. 'I had Ingrid call to see me at the week-end.'

'Oh, yes? What did she want?'

'She'd heard tell 'at I'd been poorly an' our Christine was here, so she said she'd thought she'd call in. She had her little lass with her. A bonny bairn, she is.'

'How old is she now?'

'Going on five. She started school this time. We've never lost touch altogether, you know, though it's a year or two since I saw her last. I allus got on well enough with Ingrid.'

Yes, I think; after practically calling her a little whore when I first came home and told you I'd made her pregnant.

'Does she seem happy?'

'Yes. She seems to have made a nice life for herself.'

'I always thought she would.'

'Aye . . . They live in a bungalow, and her mother lives in one next door. Seems they bought two together.'

'I hope he's happy with it.'

'Who.'

'Ingrid's husband.'

'Happen he's a better knack of handling her than you had.'

'Who?'

'Ingrid's mother.'

'Aye. He'll need it.'

'Different folk are happy with different things.'

'And different folk are unhappy with different things. I tried to make you understand that years ago.'

'You've gone your own way, so I don't see as it much matters what I understand.'

'But it does, you see, it does. I should have thought after all this time we could let it rest. Ingrid's happy, and I'm happy –'

'Are you?'

'I've just told you I am, haven't I? Why shouldn't I be?'

'I just wish I thought you were, lad.'

'Oh, come on! You'll be saying next "a mother can tell".'

'She can tell a lot more things than you think she can.'

'Mother, the be-all and end-all of everything for you is pairing off and multiplying.'

'It's the way of the world.'

'Not for everybody.'

'It is for most people.'

'Not for me.'

'I don't believe you.'

Try justifying yourself by telling *her* that you've met an old flame whom you want to marry, I think; but don't forget to mention that she's got a lad, born out of wedlock, and she's the woman who brought matters to a head between Ingrid and you.

Chris comes in with a tray. 'Now, who's ready for a cup of tea?'

As she pours, we hear the front door. The Old Feller comes through into the living-room, still wearing his cap and raincoat.

'Hello, lad. Have you been here long?'

'No, not long. How are you, Dad?'

'Fair to middling. Have you been changing your motor car?'

'Mine's off the road. That's one of the firm's.'

'Aye . . . Looking after you, are they?'

'Who?'

'The firm.'

'Oh, yes.'

219

'They must think well of him if they can send him all that way to Australia, Dad,' my mother says.

'Oh, I'm one of their blue-eyed boys,' I say.

'As long as you don't take too much for granted,' my mother adds. 'The higher you fly the farther you have to fall.'

Chris gives me a little twinkle. This building you up with one hand and putting you down with the other, all in the name of sensible caution is something she knows from days of old. And my mother has never forgotten having her advice ignored when I left a good job at Whittakers' to work for Mr. Van Huyten, and the notion he'd put into my head that the business would one day be mine came to nothing when he died.

I jump up and help the Old Feller off with his coat. The coat, long, old-fashioned, with a thick detachable lining, seems heavier than he is, as though its weight must bow his shoulders. If the Old Lady is promising to live long enough to make old bones, the Old Feller is already there. They're going to be a worry from now on. No hopping into the car and driving off, confident they can take care of themselves. With my mother's heart attack they've moved all at once into a new phase of life, and I, for one, don't know what's the best way of dealing with it. I have a chat with Chris in the kitchen, under the pretence of peeling potatoes for her while she prepares the evening meal.

'What's to be done, Chris?' I ask her. 'You can't stay here for ever.'

'I've only been here a fortnight. Another fortnight won't harm, till we see how she bears up.'

'I don't feel much use. All I can do is tell them to get rid of this house.'

'I still think they ought to have somebody near them. We all live too far away.'

'Do they know you and David are thinking of emigrating?'

'No, and I don't want you to tell them. It's out of the question now.'

'What will David say?'

'What can he say? He's got no parents. I have, and they need me here.'

'It's a rotten decision to have to make, Chris.'

'Some decisions in this life you don't make. They're make for you.'

I scrape at the spuds. 'Have I done enough?'

She looks over my shoulder. 'Perhaps a couple more. They'll always fry up for breakfast if we don't eat them all tonight.'

'You know,' I say in a minute, 'the bloody irony of it is that even if me dad pops off Mother could quite easily soldier on for another ten years. Then it'll be a bit late for you to go anywhere, won't it? I don't want to sound brutal, but that's what it amounts to.'

'Oh, don't think I haven't thought it all out,' she says, 'because I have. But I've got no choice. And what's more, I can't promise myself or David that it's something we might do later on, because that's like waiting for them to die, and hoping they'll do it in time. What I've got to do now is make up my mind that we're not going, ever. If we were going we should have done it years ago. Now it's all too late.'

A picture of Donna, distressed and in tears, flashes into my mind as Chris says those words. Too late . . . Too late for Chris and David? Too late for Donna? Too late for Donna and me?

The early evening television news tells of peace hopes in the latest Middle East war and more bombings and shootings in Belfast. Is Spiro Agnew for the chop? Will Richard Nixon hand over the Watergate tapes? We watch and listen in that glassy-eyed semi-stupor which most people seem to have adopted as protection against the media's daily avalanche of the world's troubles. I brood my way through the meal. My mother remarks on my quietness and I fob her off with an excuse about work. We finish in time for her to settle down and watch *Crossroads*, while Chris and I clear away and wash up.

'Do you fancy a glass of beer, Dad?' I ask him when we've finished.

'Your dad can't do with cold night air and smoky pubs,' my mother says.

'No, but I thought I'd pop out and fetch a bottle. What d'you say, Dad? Could you fancy a drink?'

'Aye, aye,' he says, as though it doesn't matter one way or the other.

'Any preference?'

'They sell a very good bottle of light ale at the Bunch of Grapes,' he says. 'Or they used to.'

'I'll tell you what,' my mothers says, 'bring me a milk stout, if you're going. It might just help me sleep. You'll find me purse in the sideboard drawer.'

'Nay, I shan't need that. Chris,' I say on a thought, 'why don't you walk up with me for half an hour? Make a change for you.'

'Well . . .'

'Go on,' my mother says, 'get off, if you want to.'

'All right . . .'

Chris is not a woman to whom an invitation like that calls for half an hour of changing clothes and titivating; she touches up her lipstick, runs a comb through her hair, slips on a coat, and two minutes later we're on our way up the hill.

'I wish there was some way I could help more,' I tell her, 'instead of leaving it all to you.'

'Don't worry about it. We shall work something out. You might try to get home a bit more often. They do like to see you, you know.'

'I know.'

'Do you find it a bit stifling, coming back to the old ways?' she asks after a minute.

'She does tend to harp on about the way I live.'

Chris smiles. 'I know. I heard something of what she was saying to you while I was in the kitchen.'

'Times change. We live in a different world, though she doesn't seem to realize it.'

'You'll never change her now.'

'Don't I know it. I only wish I could satisfy her a bit more. I'll be damned if I'm going to change my life-style

222

to suit her, though. I finished with all that years ago.'

The pub is quiet. The only other customers in the lounge are two men in raincoats and trilby hats standing at the bar counter. Away from the town centre, it's one of those houses that get their best trade later in the evening. Chris asks for a dry Cinzano and I carry that and a pint for myself across to a table near the fire.

'Do you know,' I tell her,' I think this must be the first time you and I have ever been in a pub together.'

'Well, cheers!' she says.

'Cheers, love! And the last time I was in this place myself, well, that must have been Christmas, 1962, nearly eleven years ago. I came up with me dad, Jim and David. Boxing Day lunchtime.'

'That was the last time we were all together.'

'We've had Christmases at home since.'

'Well, David and I moved to Leicester not long after that.'

'Yes. And Ingrid and I split up the following spring . . . Mother tells me she was up at the week-end.'

'Yes. It was nice of her to call like that.'

'Yes. She said she seemed happy.'

'I thought she seemed so.'

'Well, that's all right, then.'

'Yes, it seems to have turned out well enough in the end.'

'She wouldn't have been happy if I'd stayed with her, you know, Chris.'

'No. You always seemed sure of that.'

'I was dead certain. Oh, I'm not trying to make out I left her for her own good. But it made it that much easier, knowing she'd be better off in the long run.'

There's a silence. Chris looks pensive. 'Did you ever see anything of the other girl again?' she asks finally.

'Which one?' I have to say, faking stupid to give myself time.

'The one you left Ingrid for.'

'Chris, I didn't leave Ingrid for that girl.'

'It was because of her, though, wasn't it? I mean, she

put it into your mind that there was something better, didn't she?'

'I'd always known there was something better for me. I left Ingrid because I wanted the freedom to find it for myself.'

'And have you found it?'

'I don't follow.'

'You've had ten years of freedom.'

'So I have.'

'I just wondered if you'd found it all it's cracked up to be.'

'You're beginning to sound like the Old Lady, Chris.'

'Sorry. I'm just interested in your welfare, as she is, and we haven't really talked for such a long time.'

'I haven't gone short of anything, you know, Chris. I couldn't start to tell my mother, but I've had my moments.'

'I don't doubt it. After all, you're a well favoured young man.'

I have to laugh at her choice of words. 'Thanks.'

She smiles in return. 'And don't kid yourself that she doesn't know.'

'How can she know?'

'Because she knows a bit about human nature. Give her credit, Vic. Anyway, a few moments don't make a lifetime, do they?'

'Look,' I say, keeping it light, 'if I'd known you were going to quiz me I'd never have asked you to come.'

'Well, as I said before, we haven't talked for a long time, and I just wanted to know how you really are. If you're happy, that's all.'

'Who's happy, Chris?' I say, letting my guard down.

'Oh, lots of people. More people than you might think. I'm happy, and so is David. We have our troubles and worries and discontents, but we put them right by building on the basis of what we've got.'

'You're lucky. I always did envy you.'

'How can you make somebody else happy if you're not happy yourself?'

224

'That was the trouble between me and Ingrid. All I did was make her miserable.'

'Not all the time. Not by any means.'

'Well, basically, and in the long run. And anyway, this is all ancient history. God almighty, all I get every time I come home is ancient history.'

'I'm sorry,' she says again. 'Your life's your own. That's the privilege you fought for, and that's what you've got.'

'You see,' I tell her, 'everybody seems to think I'm not living a real life at all, but just sort of . . . sort of marking time.'

'I suppose we can't help wondering what happened to that something better you went off to look for.'

'Well, let's say if I've not found it at least I've avoided a lot worse.'

And somehow or other, I think, I've managed to avoid Chris's question about whether I ever saw Donna again.

'Isn't it Vic?' a voice asks. 'Vic Brown?'

I look up and see that one of the two men has gone and the other one is standing over me.

'Yes, that's right.' I do know him. It comes. 'Rufus Widdop.'

His face breaks into a smile. I get up as he offers his hand, and we shake.

'No, sit down. I don't want to interrupt but I thought I recognized you when you came in.'

'This is my sister, Christine.'

He nods. 'I can see the resemblance.'

'Can you?' I turn to look at Chris. It's something I've never really thought about; not since we were kids, anyway. 'Rufus and I were in the same form at grammar school,' I tell her. 'I was going to say you'd changed, Rufus, but I think it was the hat that fooled me.'

'I get out and about in all weathers,' Rufus says.

'Can I get you another drink?'

'No, thanks all the same. I was just going.'

'You know, I was only looking at a form photograph of us all just last week.'

'What are you up to these days?'

'I'm in engineering.'

'Still living round here?'

'No, no. I live in The Smoke.'

'Married and a family, I expect?'

'No. I was once. It didn't take.'

'Ah!'

'What about you?'

'Twelve years coming up. Three kids.'

'And what are you doing for a living? Wait a minute, don't tell me.' A picture of the two of them standing at the bar comes back to mind. 'You're a copper, aren't you?'

A cool little smile touches his lips. 'C.I.D. Detective-sergeant.'

'I shall have to watch out.'

'I'm sure you've no cause to.' He glances at his watch. 'Anyway, I must run. I just thought I wouldn't leave without having a word.'

'I'm glad you did.'

He lifts his hand. 'I'll see you around.'

'In another eighteen years or so, perhaps.'

He laughs. 'Yes, maybe.' He nods at Chris. 'Good-bye.'

'So long, Rufus,' I say.

I watch him cross the room to the door with the purposeful stride of a man who knows exactly where he's going.

'Well, well,' I say. 'He was on that photo we had out last week. Standing next to me. Old Rufus a copper. He was a real blue-eyed buggeroo at school. He'd look any master in the eye and swear blind he was innocent. "Who, me, sir? Not me, sir." '

'It probably stands him in good stead now.'

'Yes, he can probably pick out the villains. Now there was a family with a real resemblance. There were four brothers and there was no mistaking who they were. Very striking, the similarity. But I knew Rufus first and I kind of took the pattern from him, if you see what I mean, even though he wasn't the eldest. The others were all slightly misformed variations on him, as though a sculptor had set out to shape a head and done several with noses and ears and mouths just a bit wrong, and then satisfied himself with Rufus. I suppose people who knew the others first felt the same about him, that he was one of the variations.'

I look at her glass. 'Manage another?'

'If you're having one.'

'Let's be little devils.'

I fetch her a refill and get a Scotch for myself.

'Don't you care for the beer?'

'Can't take much on a full stomach.'

I've relaxed a bit. Nothing's solved, but the combination of Chris's company, seeing Rufus – though he might well have turned into a real hard case – the quiet room, and the drink has eased the tension in me.

'Right, then, what are we going to talk about now?'

'You'd better tell me about Australia,' Chris says with a wry smile, 'since it looks as if that's the nearest I'll get to it.'

The Old Feller's built the fire up when we get in and the two of them are sitting cocooned in an almost overpowering warmth, still watching television. Whatever did we do with our time before we had the box? Stuck our noses into other people's business, I suppose.

'Are you going to get us all drunk?' my mother asks me over the waves of studio audience laughter as I put the four pint bottles of light ale and the two small milk stouts on the table.

'That'll be the day,' I tell her.

'Was it quiet up there?' the Old Feller asks.

'Like the tomb.'

'It's early doors yet, I suppose.'

'Yes. I ran into an old school mate. Rufus Widdop.'

'Widdop?' my mother says.

'They lived in – where was it? – Archer Street. There were four brothers.'

'I can't place 'em.'

'No, probably not. He's a copper now. C.I.D.' Chris has

got glasses and a bottle-opener. 'Shall I pour you a drink now. Dad?'

'Aye, please.'

'Our Christine was telling me you were looking at some old school photographs when you were here last,' my mother says. 'I got her to seek some more in the tin trunk, upstairs. Where did you put 'em, Christine?'

'In the sideboard cupboard.'

'Get 'em out, will you, and show 'em our Victor. There might be something he fancies keeping.'

Chris gets a bundle of albums and envelopes out of the sideboard and puts them on the table. She sits across from me, half watching the television screen, as I turn them over. I never knew we owned so many photographs. They're nearly a complete family history. The older ones are posed and professional-looking. Not so many amateurs around taking quick snaps in those days. There's one of Uncle William, the Old Feller's older brother, in his First World War uniform, at attention, a little stick under one arm. How young young men looked in those days! All innocently going off to the slaughter. They joined up together in gangs in that war – Pals – and in a big push they sometimes died together. Whole streets of young lads wiped out. Imagine all those faces on that school photograph of mine obliterated in one afternoon. It doesn't bear thinking about. But things like that happened.

There's a picture of an outing between the wars, with my mother as a fresh-faced young lass in a party, the women in cloche hats, the men in enormous flat caps, gathered beside an open-topped charabanc. One of my father in his band uniform, trombone at rest. Wedding pictures of Chris and David, Jim and Claudine, Ingrid and me. Chris and David with Bobby, at his christening. Baby pictures of all three of us kids. Holiday snaps; my mother in white shoes, the Old Feller in baggy flannels and open-neck shirt.

'I took this one myself,' Chris says, 'with that box camera we used to have. You could never take them at that

228

age because you used to laugh till your hands shook.'

She pushes across the picture she means, a shot of me standing on a stone pier beside a whelk-stall, holding a huge crab by one claw. It must have been dead, lent to me as a prop by some kindly stall-holder, but my face is half grinning, half frozen with trepidation, as though I don't really believe that the crab can't come back to life and give me a savage, revengeful nip. How old was I? About eight or nine.

Something draws me to contemplate the picture, to dwell on the face that's my face, yet also strangely reminiscent of someone who might not be me, like a lost twin, someone closer to me than, for instance, Jim. A lock of hair, the slant of an eyebrow, the twist of a mouth. As with a place you think you've been to before or a name on the tip of the tongue, my mind gropes for something, some focus. And then, as I tilt the picture to the light, in a suspicion that's hardly dawned before it's wiped out by a complete and staggering certainty.

I don't think I make a sound, but the shock of it makes me tremble from head to foot in a sudden convulsion of knowledge. I have to get out of their way till I can control myself: my mother is just too sharp sometimes at divining the change in a person's aura. She turns her head as I get up, clattering the chair against the table. I go out and up the stairs to the bathroom, where I lock myself in. I find myself standing in front of the mirror, studying my face as the thoughts tumble about behind my eyes. Why, oh, why, I'm thinking, did what's now so blazingly obvious never occur to me before? I'm consumed with an overwhelming urge to spring into rapid action; but I hold myself in. I must have time to think. Time, time, time . . . There will, I know, be plenty of that in the coming night.

15

When she comes through the stage-door it's with the young chap and the girl with all the teeth. 'Hi!' they give me. 'Hi!' I give them back. They move on discreetly, the chap calling over his shoulder.

'See you up there, Donna.'

'Yes, in a minute, perhaps.' She looks at me. 'Hello.'

'Hello.'

'Have you been out front tonight?'

'No. Did you leave the ticket?'

'No. When I didn't hear from you I didn't know whether to expect you or not.'

'Did you expect to hear from me after that performance on Sunday night?'

'It wasn't a performance.'

'All right. Did you want to hear from me, that's more to the point.' Talk like that, I think, is like inviting her to turn and walk away from me. But I know something she doesn't know I know and she's going nowhere, for a while anyway, without me, because I can stop her in her tracks here in the street. When she doesn't answer I take her by the arm to lead her in the other direction from the pub. 'Let's go.'

'Where to?' she asks, coming with me but lagging behind my stride.

'To where we can talk.'

If she has half-expected me to turn up and take her to that supper I suggested, she's made no concessions in the way of dress: under her topcoat are the same sweater and jeans she wore on Sunday. So I expect that would have ruled out the Savoy Grill in any case. I let go of her when we reach the car and go round to unlock the passenger door.

'What happened to the MG?'

'It's off the road.'

'Do we need to drive?'

'Yes. Get in.'

She looks for a moment as if she'll refuse. I wait. I don't feel that I'm carrying this off very well. Two days of mental rehearsal have robbed me of towering righteous anger and brought me to the demeanour of somebody sulky with minor grievance. I want an explanation, but I want it to be good, because I still want her. She comes round and slides in.

'Don't you ever wear a skirt nowadays?' I ask her as I start the engine.

'Trousers are convenient.'

'So are frozen chips and keg beer.'

'Which I gather you don't approve of.'

'There's one thing to be said for them: their quality's always the same.'

Frozen chips? How did frigging frozen chips get into this?

'You're in a very domineering mood tonight.'

'Don't you think it's about time I was?'

'I don't know what you mean by that.' I say nothing to enlighten her and after a moment she says, 'Will you tell me where we're going, please,' in a tone of voice that a couple of days ago would have killed stone dead all the hope in me. But we're involved now, and nothing she can say or do will alter that. Whether it's to be the kind of involvement I've prayed for, or something more tormentingly frustrating than ever, remains to be seen.

'We're going to my place,' I tell her.

'Oh, are we?'

'I've got a couple of steaks ready to shove under the grill, a bottle of wine, a bottle of Scotch, several bottles of Canada Dry, and if you think I'm planning to try to

231

get some hold on you by getting you drunk and then making a pass, you're wrong.'

'I see. Actually, you seem more in the mood to kill somebody.'

'Oh, I don't think it'll come to that.'

She knows by now; or she thinks she does. She's never seen me like this before and there can – to her, I guess – be only one reason for it. It slumps her into uneasy silence and I feel her giving me little sidelong looks as I drive. We say nothing else during the journey. I have to park some way from the house and though she acquiesces enough to walk with me along the street, at the gate she lingers while I open the front door. Her pride and hard-won independence rile at being taken in charge like this, but not enough, I'm betting, to stop her from seeing it through.

'Are you coming?' I say to her, standing in the open doorway.

She walks towards me, still with an air of sufferance, and I close the door behind her and lead the way upstairs.

There are tumblers and a bottle of Scotch waiting on the low table. I leave her standing in the middle of the floor while I fetch ice and the Canada Dry she likes with her whisky from the fridge in the kitchen. When I come back she's contemplating the three birthday cards standing on the mantelpiece: one from my mother and father, another from Chris and signed for her and David and Bobby, the third from Jim and Claudine and the twins.

'I haven't wished you a happy birthday.'

'It's got about an hour and a quarter to redeem itself,' I tell her, 'Sit down. Let me take your coat.'

I mix her a drink. She takes a sip, sitting forward on the edge of the chair, elbows on knees.

'How long have you lived here?'

'Three years.'

'Is the furniture yours?'

'Yes. I picked it up piece by piece from junk shops and auctions and the like.'

She makes no comment. I want to ask her if she

approves, but I've left the role of the damp-eyed suppli-
cant behind, I'd like to think for good. I offer her a cigarette. She prefers one of her Gauloise. She exhales
smoke on an audible sigh and seems to shiver a little.

'Are you warm enough?'

'Yes.'

I switch on another bar of the electric fire all the
same. As I straighten up again she says:

'Well . . . You'd better get it off your chest. Whatever
it is.'

'You know what it is.'

'Do I?'

'I want to show you something.' I hand her the photograph of the boy that was me, with the crab. She looks at
it for some time before she speaks. Then she nods.

'Yes . . . There's no mistaking that.'

'Isn't there?' I ask her.

'No. Is this the first thing that made you realize?'

'Yes. Your mother knew, though, didn't she?'

'She guessed when she saw you. She challenged me
with it. She said I had to say something to you. I told her
it wasn't the right time.'

'The right time was years ago, wasn't it? How the hell
could you do it to us, to him and to me? All those years,
all that time, slipping by, gone, wasted. You didn't want
me so you kept Tom from me.'

'It wasn't like that.'

'Wasn't it? You'd better tell me what it was like,
then.'

'Don't shout at me, please.'

'I didn't know I was. Go on, tell me.'

'I don't know where to start.'

'Try at the beginning, when you went to bed with
Carter after leaving me.'

'I did write to you when I'd decided to stay on in
London and you never replied.'

'It would never work for us, you said. I don't want you
to leave your wife for me, you said.'

'But I told you I still wanted to see you. I just didn't

233

want you to thrash around and do something irrevocable. I didn't want to be responsible for that. Then I met Clive again. You knew there'd been something between us before and that it hadn't worked out.'

'But you couldn't resist having another go.'

'I hadn't heard from you.'

'So you went to bed with Carter and it happened to be in the same month as that last time with me. It won't wash, you know, Donna. You were still warm from being in bed with me when you slept with Carter. You went to bed with him before you wrote to me.'

'All right. So I still couldn't resist him in one way. Even though it hadn't worked before I still had to have another try.'

'And why wasn't it any good?'

'It just wasn't. It was over. There was nothing left.'

'Nothing left for him, or nothing for you?'

'For neither of us. Only bright false smiles and "see you around, then". It happens, you know. It happens every day.'

'So I've heard.'

Her chin comes up. 'Have you been so damned pure and lilywhite all these years?'

'Anyway, you found you were pregnant. And by the way, what happened to precautions? I thought you were a liberated young woman who knew how to take care of herself.'

'I took precautions with you and, well, I didn't with Clive. It happened that . . . Well, let's say I thought it would be all right.' At my derisive grunt she shoots me a look, still with defiance in it. 'I seem to remember you taking a chance once.'

'You'd had experience, love.' I tell her. 'You should have known better.'

'Better than to trust the precautions I took with you, as well, I suppose?' I shrug, giving her the point, but reluctantly. 'I missed a period,' she says, 'then another. I told Fleur. She jumped to the conclusion that it was Clive. What else could I think myself, in the circumstances? But then it occurred to me that I couldn't be sure. Not positively. And Clive didn't want me, nor I him. So I told him nothing. I'd finished seeing him, anyway, by that time.'

'You didn't want me, either, did you?'

'Not enough. Not enough at first to want you to throw up everything for me and then find out I couldn't give you back as much as you wanted. And afterwards, what could I expect from you when I was carrying a baby that was probably another man's.'

'Didn't you ever get the letter, saying I'd left Ingrid anyway?'

'Yes. I thought you couldn't know the full facts. I didn't know what to think. It was a mess. There was only one thing I did know I wanted out of it and that was the baby. At least, I thought, I'd do one constructive thing. Fleur said the sensible thing was to get rid of it. I've no religious objections to abortion, I'm not even against it on personal moral grounds. A simple little operation and I could have had a clean start again. But I couldn't do it. I didn't want to do it. I wanted the child.'

'Because it was Carter's.'

'Because it was mine.' She finishes off her whisky at a gulp and holds out her glass. 'May I have another one, please?'

I pour for her, a good stiff one.

'So, I told my parents that it was just one of those things; ships that pass in the night and all that; nothing to try to build a lifetime on. They were upset, of course, and disappointed. But they adjusted to it and helped me all they could. When Tom was born he was more like my father than anyone else. I could see nothing of Clive in him at all, but it wasn't until his features began really to form that I could be absolutely sure. As time went by it seemed to me more and more evident. I don't know why you didn't see it the moment you laid eyes on him.'

'He's like you.'

'He's like you too. My mother knew.'

'I wasn't looking for it. I'd blamed Carter for ten

235

years. I still blamed him then, thought he was a callous sod for not wanting to see his own flesh and blood. Christ!'

'Well, it all seemed too late. What could I do, try to find you, wherever you were, and write to you and say you've got a son, come and see what you think of him?'

'I don't know. There must have been something you could do besides keep quiet about it.'

'How did I know what kind of life you were leading, what I could disrupt or perhaps destroy? How did I know what you felt after all that time?'

'So you let things slide.'

'It's easy enough to let things slide. You let them slide by not doing something it seems impossible to do. And the years pass by. I tried to build a good life for Tom and myself. He's had a good upbringing, you know.'

'I expect so. But he's also spent a lot of time wondering who his father is and why he's never wanted to see him.'

'I thought at one time of telling him his father was dead.'

'That I was dead?'

'That his father was dead.'

'I am his father, Donna.'

'He doesn't know that. He likes you, but he doesn't know.'

'He's going to have to know.'

'Is he?'

'Oh, yes. Somehow or other he's got to be told. Because he's going to wonder why he's seeing so much of me in future, if he doesn't know.'

She's silent again, her hand to her face. I wonder if she's going to start crying.

'Would you have told me, or sent me away without my knowing?'

'I thought . . . I thought you'd surely never forgive me.'

'Was that so important?'

She shakes her head quickly, her face still covered. It could mean no, or that she can't speak for the moment.

'How important was it, Donna?'

'I didn't want to send you away.'

'Didn't you?'

Another shake of the head. She gulps whisky.

'The oddest thing was, something had reminded me of you. I can't remember what, but I'd been thinking about you only a few minutes before I looked up in the pub and saw you standing there. I'd never forgotten you. How could I, with Tom around? I never held out any hope that I'd see you again.'

'Hope?'

She shakes her head. 'I'm not saying any of it very well.'

'Try. I want to know.'

'I thought perhaps the worst thing could be that we *should* meet and that it would all get stirred up again without there being anything at all in it for us. That you'd wonder what you'd ever seen in me, that I'd feel, depending on the circumstances, that I had to tell you about Tom all the same.'

'And?'

'I saw you. I didn't know where to put myself for a minute. Then I took hold of myself and spoke to you, and you looked fit and well and happy, and you were cool with me. I couldn't blame you, even on the basis of what you did know, let alone all you didn't.'

'It's what I wanted you to think.'

'Yes. Then it was as though you couldn't carry it off. You let me see that you still wanted me, or wanted me all over again, and I didn't know what to do, because I thought, I was so afraid, that when you found about Tom you'd never be able to forgive me, and that would be the end of it.'

'And you didn't want that?'

'No.'

'What do you want now?'

'I don't know.'

Perhaps it's enough to be going on with. I can't push her any more at present.

'Can you eat something?'

'I think so.'

I go into the kitchen, put the steaks under the grill

and open the bottle of Burgundy. I hear water gurgle in
the pipes as she runs a tap in the bathroom. When she
appears in the doorway she's washed for face and re-
done her make-up.

'Can I help?'

'You can mix the salad, if you like. It's all there. I
thought we'd dispense with potatoes, unless you want
some.'

'No, the salad will be fine.'

'Oil and vinegar in the cupboard above you; knives in
the drawer by your right hand.'

'You're well organized.'

'I've learned to be.'

'Have you always looked after yourself?'

'Except for the occasional brief interlude.'

'Nothing at all permanent?'

'No. What about you?'

'What?'

'Interludes?'

'One or two.'

'Any you regret?'

'No.'

'I suppose I really meant "miss".'

'Same answer.'

We're not very far apart. I could almost reach out
and touch her without leaving the spot. As it is, a turn
and a step take me to her side and one movement brings
her round to face me. I hold her for several moments,
very still, savouring the scent of her, enfolding her
body's warmth, my hand on the back of her head pressing her face into my neck.

'I asked you what you wanted. You said you don't
know. What is it you don't know?'

'How much. How soon. For how long. You come at me
head-on, Vic. You take my breath away the speed at
which you make up your mind what you want and go for
it. It's been less than a week. I can't commit myself so
quickly.'

'I'm dogged as well, you know.' I warn her. 'I shan't

lose you this time. I shall just hang on and wear you down.'

'Yes . . .'

'Do you want me to try?'

'Yes.'

I tilt her face up to me and slowly, very deliberately kiss her for the first time in ten and a half years. I feel with a surge of hope what I take to be longing in the responsive tremble of her mouth and the movement of her hand along my shoulder to my neck.

'I was mad with jealousy when Fleur told me you were pregnant. I wanted it to be mine. I wanted to watch you grow bigger every month, big with what we'd been to each other. Or what you'd been and still were to me. That's what I missed, you see. What I can never get back again. Unless . . . You must have been so bloody lonely. Weren't you lonely?'

'For a time. Until he came.'

'Did he give you a bad time?'

'No.'

I have to leave her to see to the food.

'Tom Brown,' I say, as it occurs to me. 'My brother has twin girls called Delphine and Cordelia, and I've got a son called Tom. Tom Brown.'

'It's not very original, is it?' Donna says.

'No.' Then I have to laugh out loud. 'I was in Rugby only yesterday. Oh, bloody hell!'

'Vic,' she says in a moment, 'you won't barge in head-long and tell him, will you?'

'No, love. We'll find a way. Pick the right time. I can wait, now I know.'

She sighs, glances at her watch. 'Oh lord! Look how late it is already.' I take a deep breath.

'Why dun't tha gi' thi' mother a ring an' tell her tha're stoppin' aht terneet?'

'What was that?'

'Why don't you telephone your mother and say you're with some friends at a party and you're staying up town tonight?'

239

'And . . .?'

'Stay here.'

I want to add, so there's no mistake, 'with me'. I baste the steaks with melted butter and slip them back under the grill to finish, not daring to look round at her, waiting for her response. When I do turn, to get out wine glasses and cutlery, she's gone from the room. I hear the low murmur of her voice. I'm putting the food on to a tray when she appears again, silently, and leans for a moment, arms folded, in the doorway.

'All ready.'

'Where shall we eat? At the low table?'

'I thought so. It's cosier in there.'

She moves forward to help me carry. 'My mother says she hopes the spare bed is clean and aired.'

I look at her, mouth agape. 'You're a liar.'

'Her very words.' A pause, timed to a professional split second. 'There is a spare bed, of course?'

A grin cracks my face apart. 'There's a perfectly adequate sofa.'

'That's all right, then,' she says, her own face beginning to slip as she turns her back and leaves me.

I stand looking vaguely round the kitchen, totally at a loss for a moment to think what wants doing next, as I'm buoyed up by a happiness too powerful now for that tiny seed of anxiety which in the small hours will bloom into terror at what the morning might bring. She's a woman of her time; staying with me tonight does not pledge her all; and loving her as I do, more than at present she loves me, there could, I think, be many such mornings before we come through. To what? A lasting peace? Hardly that. But to something that will serve in its place. Even now, I know that some kind of end is a part of whatever beginning we're about to make. So then we must live as though it will never happen, until the day it does. And for what we might be given between may the Lord make us truly thankful. Amen.

I follow her into the living-room. She is sitting on the edge of her chair, stretching across to lay a place for me. As I stand over her for a moment, she looks up, straight into my eyes, and gives me a shy little smile of recognition and assent. I sit down and join her.

'There,' I say, 'that looks all right, doesn't it?'

THE END

A Raging Calm
Stan Barstow

Set in a thriving, recognisable urban city, *A Raging Calm* is a story of conflicting passions, of loyalty and betrayal, and of the agony of an illicit love affair.

'Stan Barstow is one of the very best of our regional novelists and *A Raging Calm* is a fine example of his work. It is humane and it is perceptive. It never fakes feeling in the interests of drama, yet it remains dramatically alive. Deeply felt and skilfully told, the novel will certainly enhance Mr Barstow's already high reputation'
EVENING STANDARD

'A major novelist'
PUNCH

0 552 99193 7

BLACK SWAN